THE BURNING OF ROME

ALFRED J. CHURCH

EONN PUBLISHING

CONTENTS

1

THE EMPEROR'S PLAN

THE reigning successor of the great Augustus, the master of
some forty legions, the ruler of the Roman world, was in
council. But his council was unlike as possible to the
assembly which one might have thought he would have gathered
together to deliberate on matters that concerned the happiness, it
might almost be said, of mankind. Here were no veteran generals
who had guarded the frontiers of the Empire, and seen the barbarians of the East and of the West recoil before the victorious eagles of
Rome; no Governor of provinces, skilled in the arts of peace; no
financiers, practised in increasing the amount of the revenue without
aggravating the burdens that the tax-payers consciously felt; no
philosophers to contribute their theoretical wisdom; no men of business to give their master the benefit of their practical advice. Nero
had such men at his call, but he preferred, and not perhaps without
reason, to confide his schemes to very different advisers. There were
three persons in the Imperial Chamber; or four, if we are to reckon
the page, a lad of singular beauty of form and feature, but a deaf
mute, who stood by the Emperor's couch, clad in a gold-edged scarlet
tunic, and holding an ivory-handled fan of peacock's feathers, which
he waved with a gentle motion.

Let me begin my description of the Imperial Cabinet, for such it really was, with a portrait of Nero himself.

The Emperor showed to considerable advantage in the position which he happened to be occupying at the time. The chief defects of his figure, the corpulence which his excessive indulgence in the pleasures of the table had already, in spite of his youth, increased to serious proportions, and the unsightly thinness of his lower limbs, were not brought into prominence. His face, as far as beauty was concerned, was not unworthy of an Emperor, but as the biographer of the Cæsars says, it was "handsome rather than attractive." The features were regular and even beautiful in their outlines, but they wanted, as indeed it could not be but that they should want, the grace and charm in which the beauty of the man's nature shines forth. The complexion, originally fair, was flushed with intemperance. There were signs here and there of what would soon become disfiguring blotches. The large eyes that in childhood and boyhood had been singularly clear and limpid were now somewhat dull and dim. The hair was of the yellow hue that was particularly pleasing to an Italian eye, accustomed, for the most part, to black and the darker shades of brown. Nero was particularly proud of its color, so much so indeed, that, greatly to the disgust of more old- fashioned Romans, he wore it in braids. On the whole his appearance, though not without a certain comeliness and even dignity, was forbidding and sinister. No one that saw him could give him credit for any kindness of heart or even good nature. His cheeks were heavy, his chin square, his lips curiously thin. Not less repulsive was the short bull neck. At the moment of which I am writing his face wore as pleasing an expression as it was capable of assuming. He was in high spirits and full of a pleased excitement. We shall soon see the cause that had so exhilarated him.

Next to the Emperor, by right of precedence, must naturally come the Empress, for it was to this rank that the adventuress Poppæa had now succeeded in raising herself. Her first husband had been one of the two commanders of the Prætorian Guard; her second, Consul and afterwards Governor of a great province, destined indeed himself to occupy for a few months the Imperial throne; her third was the heir of Augustus and Tiberius, the last of the Julian Cæsars. Older than the Emperor, for she had borne a child to her first husband more than twelve years before, she still preserved the freshness of early youth. Something of this, perhaps, was due to the extreme care which she devoted to her appearance, but more to the expression of innocence and modesty which some strange freak of nature—for never surely did a woman's look more utterly belie her disposition—had given to her countenance. To look at her certainly at that moment, with her golden hair falling in artless ringlets over a forehead smooth as a child's, her delicately arched lips, parted in a smile that just showed a glimpse of pearly teeth, her cheeks just tinged with a faint wild-rose blush, her large, limpid eyes, with just a touch of wonder in their depths, eyes that did not seem to harbour an evil thought, any one might have thought her as good as she was beautiful. Yet she was profligate, unscrupulous, and cruel. Her vices had always been calculating, and when a career had been opened to her ambition she let nothing stand in her way. Nero's mother had perished because she barred the adventuress' road to a throne, and Nero's wife soon shared the fate of his mother.

The third member of the Council was, if it is possible to imagine it, worse than the other two. Nero began his reign amidst the high hopes of his subjects, and for a few weeks, at least, did not disappoint them, and Josephus speaks of Poppæa as a "pious" woman; but we hear nothing about Tigellinus that is not absolutely vile. Born in poverty and obscurity, he had made his way to the bad eminence in which we find him by the worst of arts. A man of mature age, for by this time he must have numbered at least fifty years, he used his greater experience to make the young Emperor even worse than his natural tendencies, and all the evil influences of despotic power, would have made him. And he was what Nero, to do him justice, never was, fiercely resentful of sarcasm and ridicule. Nero suffered the most savage lampoons on his character to be published with impunity, but no one satirized Tigellinus without suffering for his audacity.

The scene of the Council was a pleasant room in the Emperor's seaside villa at Antium. This villa was a favourite residence with him. He had himself been born in it. Here he had welcomed with delight, extravagant, indeed, but yet not wholly beyond our sympathies, the birth of the daughter whom Poppæa had borne to him in the preceding year; here he had mourned, extravagantly again, but not without some real feeling, for the little one's death. It was at Antium, far from the wild excitement of Rome, that he had what may be called the lucid intervals in his career of frantic crime.

The subject which now engaged his attention, and the attention of his advisers, was one that seemed of a harmless and even a laudable kind. It was nothing less than a magnificent plan for the rebuilding of Rome. All the ill- ventilated, ill-smelling passages; all the narrow, winding streets; all the ill- built and half-ruinous houses; all, in short, that was unsanitary, inconvenient, and unsightly was to be swept away; a new city with broad, regular streets and spacious promenades was to rise in its place. At last the Empire of the world would have a capital worthy of itself. The plan was substantially of Nero's own devising. He had had, indeed, some professional assistance from builders, architects, and others, in drawing out its details, but in its main lines, certainly in its magnificent contempt for the expedient, one might almost say of the possible, it came from his own brain. And he had managed to keep it a secret from both Poppæa and Tigellinus. To them it was a real surprise, and, as they both possessed competent intelligence, however deficient in moral sense, they were able to appreciate its cleverness. Their genuine admiration, which so practised an ear as Nero's easily distinguished from flattery, was exceedingly pleasing to the Emperor.

"Augustus," he said, after enjoying for a time his companions' unfeigned surprise, "said that he found a city of brick and left a city of marble. I mean to be able to boast that I left a new city altogether. Indeed, I feel that nothing short of this is worthy of me, and I thank the gods that have left for me so magnificent an opportunity."

"And this vacant space," asked Tigellinus, after various details had been explained by the Emperor: "What do you mean, Sire, to do with this?"

A huge blank had been left in the middle of the map, covering nearly the whole of the Palatine and Esquiline Hills.

"That is meant to be occupied by my palace and park," said the Emperor.

The Prime Minister, if one may so describe him, could not restrain an involuntary gesture of surprise.

Nero's face darkened with the scowl that never failed to show itself at even the slightest opposition to his will.

"Think you, then," he cried in an angry tone, "that it is too large? The Master of Rome cannot be lodged too well."

Tigellinus felt that it would be safer not to criticise any further. Poppæa, who, to do her justice, was never wanting in courage, now took up the discussion. The objection that she had to make was in keeping with a curious trait in her character. "Pious" she certainly was not, though Josephus saw fit so to describe her, but she was unquestionably superstitious. The terrors of an unseen world, though they did not keep her back from vice and crime, were still real to her. She did not stick at murder; but nothing would have induced her to pass by a temple without a proper reverence. This feeling quickened her insight into an aspect of the matter which her companion had failed to observe.

"You will buy the houses which you will have to pull down?" she said.

"Certainly," the Emperor replied; "that will be an easy matter."

"But there are buildings which it will not be easy to buy."

The scowl showed itself again on Nero's face.

"Who will refuse to sell when I want to buy?" he cried. "And besides, you may be sure that I shall not stint the price."

"True, Sire, but there are the temples, the chapels; they cannot be bought and sold as if they were private houses."

Nero started up from his couch, and paced the room several times. He could not refuse to see the difficulty. Holy places were not to be bought and pulled down as if they were nothing but so many bricks and stones.

"What say you, Tigellinus?" he cried after a few minutes of silence.

"Cannot the Emperor do what he will? Cannot the priests or the augurs, or some one smooth the way? Speak, man!" he went on impatiently, as the minister did not answer at once.

"The gods forbid that I should presume to limit your power!" said Tigellinus. "But yet—may I speak freely?"

"Freely!" cried Nero; "of course. When did I ever resent the truth?"

Tigellinus repressed a smile. His own rise was certainly not due to speaking the truth. He went on:—

"One sacred building, or two, or even three, might be dealt with when some great improvement was in question. That has been done before, and might be done again, but when it comes to a matter of fifty or sixty, or even a hundred,—very likely there are more, for they stand very thick in the old city,—the affair becomes serious. I don't say it would be impossible, but there would be delay, possibly a very long delay. The people feel very strongly on these things. Some of these temples are held in extraordinary reverence, places that you, Sire, may very likely have never heard of, but which are visited by hundreds daily. To sweep them away in any peremptory fashion would be dangerous. There would have to be ceremonies, expiations, and all the thousand things which the priests invent."

"Well," exclaimed the Emperor after a pause, "what is to be done?"

"Sire," replied Tigellinus, "cannot you modify your plan? Much might be done without this wholesale destruction."

"Modify it!" thundered the Emperor. "Certainly not. It shall be all or nothing. Do you think that I am going to take all this trouble, and accomplish, after all, nothing more than what any aedile could have done?"

He threw himself down on the couch and buried his face in the cushions. The Empress and the Minister watched and waited in serious disquiet. There was no knowing what wild resolve he might take. That he had set his heart to no common degree on this new scheme was evident. In all his life he had never given so much serious thought to any subject as he had to this, and disappointment would probably result in some dangerous outburst. After about half an hour had passed, he started up.

"I have it," he cried; "it shall be done,—the plan, the whole plan."

"Sire, will you deign to tell us what inspiration the gods have given you?" said Tigellinus.

"All in good time," said the Emperor. "When I want your help I will tell you what it is needful for you to know. But now it is time for my harp practice. You will dine with us, Tigellinus, and for pity's sake bring some one who can give us some amusement. Antium is delightful in the daytime, but the evenings! . . ."

"Madam," said Tigellinus, when the Emperor had left the room, "have you any idea what he is thinking of?"

"I have absolutely none," replied Poppæa; "but I fear it may be something very strange. I noticed a dangerous light in his eyes. It has been there often lately. Do you think," she went on in a low voice, "there is any danger of his going mad? You know about his uncle Caius."

"Don't trouble yourself with such fears," replied Tigellinus. "It is not likely. His mother had the coolest head of any woman that I have ever seen; and his father, whatever he was, was certainly not mad. And now, if you will excuse me, I have some business to attend to."

He saluted the Empress and withdrew. Poppæa, little reassured by his words, remained buried in thought,—thought that was full of disquietude and alarm. She had gained all, and even more than all, that she had aimed at. She shared Nero's throne, not in name only, but in fact. But how dangerous was the height to which she had climbed! A single false step might precipitate her into an abyss which she shuddered to think of. He had spared no one, however near and dear to him. If his mood should change, would he spare her? And his mood might change. At present he loved her as ardently, she thought, as ever. But—for she watched him closely, as a keeper watches a wild beast—she could not help seeing that he was growing more and more restless and irritable. Once he had even lifted his hand against her. It was only a gesture, and checked almost in its beginning, but she could not forget it. "Oh!" she moaned to herself,—for, wicked as she was, she was a woman after all,—"Oh, if only my little darling had lived! Nero loved her so, and she would have softened him. But it was not to be! Why did I allow them to do all these foolish idolatries? And yet, how could I stop it? Still, I am sure that God was angry with me about them, and took the child away from me. And now there are these new troubles. I will send another offering to Jerusalem. This time it shall be a whole bunch of grapes for the golden vine."

Poor creature! the thought of a sacrifice of justice and mercy never entered into her soul.

2

THE HATCHING OF A PLOT

ON the very day of the meeting described in my last chapter, a party of six friends was gathered together in the dining-room—I should rather say one of the dining-rooms—of a country house at Tibur. The view commanded by the window of the apartment was singularly lovely. Immediately below, the hillside, richly wooded with elm and chestnut, and here and there a towering pine, sloped down to the lower course of the river Anio. Beyond the river were meadow-lands, green with the unfailing moisture of the soil, and orchards in which the rich fruit was already gathering a golden hue. The magnificent falls of the river were in full view, but not so near as to make the roar of the descending water inconveniently loud. At the moment, the almost level rays of the setting sun illumined with a golden light that was indescribably beautiful the cloud of spray that rose from the pool in which the falling waters were received. It was an effect that was commonly watched with intense interest by visitors to the villa, for, indeed, it was just one of the beauties of nature which a Roman knew how to appreciate. Landscape, especially of the wilder sort, he did not care about; but the loveliness of a foreground, the greenery of a rich meadow, the deep shade of a wood, the clear water bubbling from a spring or leaping from a rock, these he could admire to the utmost. But on the present occasion the attention of the guests had been otherwise occupied. They had been listening to a recitation from their host. To listen to a recitation was often a price which guests paid for their entertainment, and paid somewhat unwillingly and even ungraciously. Rich dishes and costly wines, the rarest of flowers, and the most precious of perfumes were not very cheaply purchased by two hours of boredom from some dull oration or yet duller poem. There was no such feeling among the guests who were now assembled in this Tibur villa. The entertainment, indeed, had been simple and frugal, such as it befitted a young disciple of the Stoic school to give to a party of like-minded friends. But the intellectual entertainment that followed when the tables were removed had been a treat of the most delightful kind. This may be readily understood when I say that the host of the evening was Lucan, and that he had been reciting from his great poem of the Pharsalia the description of the battle from which it took its name. To modern readers of Latin literature who find their standard of excellence in Virgil and Horace, the Pharsalia sounds artificial and turgid. But it suited the taste of that age, all the more from the very qualities which make it less acceptable to us. And, beyond all doubt, it lent itself admirably to recitation. A modern reader often thinks it rhetoric rather than poetry. But the rhetoric was undeniably effective, especially when set off by the author's fiery declamation, and when the recitation came to an end with the well-known lines:—

"Italian fields of death, the blood-stained wave
That swept Sicilian shores, and that dark day
That reddened Actium's rocks, have wrought such woe,
Philippi's self seems guiltless by compare."

It was followed by a round of genuine, even enthusiastic applause. When the applause had subsided there was an interval of silence that was scarcely less complimentary to the poet. This was broken at last by a remark from Licinius, a young soldier who had lately been serving against the Parthians under the great Corbulo, for many years the indefatigable and invincible guardian of the Eastern frontier of the Empire.

"Lucan," he said, "would you object to repeat a few lines which occurred in your description of the sacrifices on either side before the beginning of the battle? We heard how all the omens were manifestly unfavourable to Pompey, and then there followed something that struck me very much about the prayers and vows of Cæsar."

"I know what you mean," replied the poet; "I will repeat them with pleasure. They run thus:—

" 'But what dark thrones, what Furies of the pit,
Cæsar, didst thou invoke? The wicked hand
That waged with pitiless sword such impious war
Not to the heavens was lifted, but to Gods
That rule the nether world and Powers that veil
Their maddening presence in Eternal night.' "

"Exactly so," said Licinius. "Those were the lines I meant. But will you recite this in public? How will Nero, who, after all, is the heir of Cæsar, and enjoys the harvests reaped at Mutina, and Actium, and Philippi, how will Nero relish such language?"

"He is not likely to hear it. In fact, he has forbidden me to recite. He does not like rivals," he added with an air of indescribable scorn.

"Indeed," said the young soldier; "then you have seen reason to change your opinions. I remember having the great pleasure of hearing you read your first book. I was just about to start to join my legion. It must have been about two years ago. I can't exactly recollect the lines, but you mentioned, I remember, Munda, and Mutina, and Actium, and then went on:—

" 'Yet great the debt our Roman fortunes owe
To civil strife, if this its end, to make
Great Nero lord of men....' "

The other guests grew hot and cold at the more than military frankness with which their companion taxed their host with inconsistency. The inconsistency was notorious enough; but now that the poet had abandoned his flatteries and definitely ranged himself with the opposition, what need to recall it?

Lucan could not restrain the blush that rose to his cheek, but he was ready with his answer.

"The Nero of to-day is not the Nero of three years ago, for it was then that I wrote those lines."

"Yet even then," whispered another of the guests to his neighbour, "he had murdered his brother and his mother."

A somewhat awkward silence followed. Subrius, a tribune of the Prætorians, broke it by addressing himself to Licinius.

"Licinius," he cried, "tell our friends what you were describing to me the other day."

"You mean," said Licinius, "the ceremony of Tiridates' submission?"

"Exactly," replied Subrius.

"Well," resumed the other, "it was certainly a sight that was well worth seeing. A more magnificent army than the Parthian's never was. How the King could have given in without fighting I cannot imagine, except that Corbulo fairly frightened him. I could hardly have believed that there were so many horse-soldiers in the world. But there they were, squadron after squadron, lancers, and archers, and swordsmen, each tribe with its own device, a serpent, or an eagle, or a star, or the crescent moon, till the eye could hardly reach to the last of them. The legions were ranged on the three sides of a hollow square, with a platform in the centre, and on the platform an image of the Emperor, seated on a throne of gold."

"A truly Egyptian deity!" muttered the poet to himself.

"King Tiridates," the soldier went on, "after sacrificing, came up, and kneeling on one knee, laid his crown at the feet of the statue."

"Noble sight again!" whispered Lucan to his neighbour. "A man bowing down before a beast."

"And Corbulo?" asked one of the guests, Lateranus by name, who had not hitherto spoken. "How did he bear himself on this occasion?"

"As modestly as the humblest centurion in the army," replied Licinius.

"Yes, it was a glorious triumph for Rome," said Subrius the Prætorian; "but—"

He paused, and looked with a meaning glance at Lateranus.

Lateranus, who was sitting by the side of Lucan (indeed, it was to him that the poet had whispered his irreverent comments on the ceremony by the Euphrates), rose from his seat. The new speaker was a striking figure, if only on account of his huge stature and strength. But he had other claims to distinction; after a foolish and profligate youth, he had begun to take life seriously.

"Will you excuse me?" he said to the host, and walking to the door opened it, examined the passage hat led to it, locked another door at the further end, and then returned to his place.

"Walls have ears," he said, "but these, as far as I can judge, are deaf. We can all keep a secret, my friends?" he went on, looking round at the company.

"To the death, if need be," cried Lucan.

The four other guests murmured assent.

"We may very likely be called upon to make good our words. If any one is of a doubtful mind, let him draw back in time."

"Go on; we are all resolved," was the unanimous answer of the company.

Did there seem nothing strange to you when our friend Licinius told us of the Parthian king laying his crown at the feet of Nero's statue? What has Nero done that he should receive such gifts? Our armies defend with their bodies the frontiers of Euphrates and the Rhine? They toil through Scythian snows and African sands. And for what? Who reaps the rewards of their valour and their toil? Why, this harp-player, this buffoon, who sets the trivial crowns which reward the victories of the stage above all the glories of Rome. And why? Because, forsooth, he is the grandson of Julia the adulteress! I acknowledge the greatness of Julius, of Augustus, even of Tiberius. It was not unworthy of Romans, if the gods denied them liberty, to be ruled by such men. But Caius the madman, and Claudius the pedant,—did some doubtful drops of Imperial blood entitle them to be masters of the human race? And Nero, murderer of his brother, his mother, his wife, how much longer is he going to pollute with riot and bloodshed the holy places of Rome? If a

Brutus could be found to strike down the great dictator, will no one dare to inflict the vengeance of gods and men on this profligate boy?"

"The man and the sword will not be wanting when the proper time shall come," said Subrius the Prætorian in a tone of grim resolve. "But Rome must have a ruler. When we shall have rid her of this tyrant, who is to succeed?"

"Why not restore the Republic?" cried Lucan. "We have a Senate, we have Consuls, and all the old machinery of the Government of freedom. The great Augustus left these things, it would seem, of set purpose, against the day when they might be wanted again."

"The Republic is impossible," cried Subrius; "even more impossible than it was a hundred years ago. What is the Senate but an assembly of worn-out nobles and cowardly and time-serving capitalists? I know there are exceptions; one of them is here to-night," he went on with a bow to Lateranus; "and there is Thrasea, who, I know, will make one of us, as soon as he knows what we are meditating. But the Senate as a whole is incapable. And the people, where is that to be found? Certainly not in this mob that cares for nothing but its dole of bread, its gladiators, and its chariot-races. No; the Republic is a dream. Rome must have a master. The gods send her one who is righteous as well as strong."

"What say you of Corbulo, Licinius?" asked Sulpicius Asper, a captain of the Prætorians, who had hitherto taken no part in the conversation. "His record is not altogether spotless. But he is a great soldier, and one might conjure with his name. And then his presence is magnificent, and the people love a stately figure. Do you think that the thought has ever crossed his mind?"

"Corbulo," replied Licinius, "is a soldier, and nothing but a soldier. And he is absolutely devoted to the Emperor. I remember how ill he took it when some one at his table said something that sounded like censure. 'Silence!' he thundered. 'Emperors and gods are above praise and dispraise.' I verily believe that if Nero bade him kill himself he would plunge his sword into his breast without a murmur. No, it is idle to think of Corbulo. In fact he is one of the great difficulties that we should have to reckon with. Happily he is far off, and the business will be done before he hears of it."

"There is Verginius on the Rhine," said Subrius. "What of him?"

"An able man, none abler, if he will only consent."

"And Sulpicius Galba in Spain. What of him?"

"He is half worn-out," said Lateranus; "but he has the advantage of being one of the best born men in Rome. And the old names have not yet lost their power."

"Why not a philosopher?" asked Lucan after a pause. "Plato thought that philosophers were the fittest men to rule the world."

"Are you thinking of your uncle Seneca?" asked Lateranus. "For my part I think that it would be a pity to take him away from his books; and to speak the truth, if I may do so without offence, Seneca, though he is beyond doubt one of the greatest ornaments of Rome, has not played the part of an Emperor's teacher with such success that we could hope very much from him, were he Emperor himself."

"There are, and indeed must be, objections to every name," said Licinius after a pause. "The soldiers will take it ill if the dignity should go to a civilian; and if the choice falls on a soldier, then all the other soldiers will be jealous. Tell me, Subrius, would you Prætorians be content if the legions were to choose an Emperor?"

Subrius shrugged his shoulders.

"As for the armies of the East," Licinius went on, "I know how fiercely they would resent dictation from the West! Our friend Asper here, who, if I remember right, has been aide-de-camp to Verginius, knows whether the German legions would be more disposed to submit to a mandate from the Euphrates. What say you, Asper?"

Asper could do nothing better than imitate the action of his superior officer.

Licinius went on: "I am a soldier myself, and can therefore speak more freely on this subject. We have to choose between evils. Jealousy between one great army and another can scarcely fail to end in war. The general discontent of all the armies, if a civilian succeeds to the throne, will be less acute, and therefore less dangerous. What say you to Calpurnius Piso?"

"At least," cried Lucan, "he has the merit of not being a philosopher."

There was a general laugh at this sally. Piso was a noted bon vivant and man of fashion, and generally as unlike a philosopher in his habits and ways of life as could be conceived.

"Exactly so," said Licinius, undisturbed by the remark; "and this, strange as it may seem, is one of the qualities which commend him to those who look at things as they are, and not as they ought to be. This is not the time for Consuls who leave their ploughs to put on the robes of office. The age is not equal to such simple virtues. It wants magnificence; it demands that its heroes should be well-dressed and drive fine horses and keep up a splendid establishment. It is not averse to a reputation for luxury. Piso has such a reputation, and I must own that it does not do him injustice. But he is a man of honour, and he has some solid and many showy qualities. He has noble birth; a pedigree that shows an ancestor who fought at Cannæ is more than respectable. He is eloquent, he is wealthy, but can give with a liberal hand as well as spend, and he has the gift of winning hearts. And then he is bold. We may look long, my friends, before we find a better man than Piso."

"There is a great deal of truth in what you say; more truth than it is pleasant to acknowledge," said Lateranus. "But we must weigh this matter seriously. Meanwhile, will Piso join us?"

"I feel as certain of it as I could be of any matter not absolutely within my knowledge," replied Licinius. "Will you authorize me to sound him? Whether he agree or not, I can guarantee his silence."

Many other matters and men were discussed; and before the party separated it was arranged that each of the six friends should choose one person to be enrolled in the undertaking.

3

IN THE CIRCUS

TWO days after the conversation related in my last chapter Subrius and Lateranus were deep in consultation in the library of the latter's mansion on the Esquiline Hill. The subject that occupied them was, of course, the same that had been started on that occasion.

"Licinius tells me," said the Prætorian, "that he has spoken to Piso, and that he caught eagerly at the notion. I must confess that at first I was averse to the man. It seemed a pity to throw away so magnificent an opportunity. What good might not an honest, capable man do, if he were put in this place? It is no flattery, but simple truth, that the Emperor is a Jupiter on earth. But it seems hopeless to look for the ideal man. That certainly Piso is not. But he is resolute, and he means well, and he will be popular. He is not the absolute best, the four-square and faultless man that the philosophers talk about; very far from it. But then the faultless man would not please the Romans, if I know them; and to do the Romans, or, for the matter of that, any men, good, you must please them first."

"And how does the recruiting go on?" asked Lateranus.

"Excellently well," said Subrius, "within the limits that are set, that every man should choose one associate. Asper and Sulpicius have both chosen comrades, and can answer for their loyalty as for themselves. Lucan has taken Scævinus. I should hardly have thought that the lazy creature had so much energy in him; but these sleepy looking fellows sometimes wake up with amazing energy. Proculus has chosen Senecio, who is one of the Emperor's inner circle of friends."

"Ah!" interrupted Lateranus, "that sounds dangerous."

"There is no cause for fear; Senecio, I happen to know, has very good reasons for being with us, and, of course, he is a most valuable acquisition. When the hour comes to strike, we shall know how and where to deal the blow. Then there is Proculus, whom you have chosen. And finally I, I flatter myself, have done well. Whom think you I have secured?"

"Well, it would be difficult to guess. Your fellow tribune Statius, perhaps. I should guess that he is an honest man, who would like to serve a better master than he has got at present."

"Statius is well enough, and we shall have him with us sure enough when the time shall come. But meanwhile I have been doing better things than that. What should you say," he went on, dropping his voice to a whisper, "if I were to tell you that it is Fænius Rufus?"

"What, the Prefect?" asked Lateranus in tones of the liveliest surprise.

"Yes" replied Subrius; "the Prefect himself."

"That is admirable!" cried the other. "We not have hoped for anything so good. But how did you approach him?"

"Oh! that was not so difficult. To tell you the truth, he met me at least half- way. These things are always in the air. Depend upon it, there are hundreds of people thinking much the same things that you and I are thinking, though not, perhaps, in quite so definite a way. And why not? The same causes have been at work in them as in us, and brought about much the same result."

"True! but we must be first in the field. So we must make haste."

"There I agree heartily with you. Delay in such matters is fatal. The secret is sure to leak out. And with every new man we take into our confidence—and we must add a good many more to our number

—the danger becomes greater. Will you come with me on a little visit that I am going to pay? I have an acquaintance whom I should like you to see. He may be useful to us in this matter. I will tell you about him. In the first place, I would have you know that my friend is a gladiator."

Lateranus raised his eyebrows. "A gladiator!" he exclaimed in a doubtful tone. "He might be useful in certain contingencies. But he would hardly suit our purpose just now."

"Listen to his story," said Subrius. "I assure you that it is well worth hearing; and I shall be much surprised, if, when you have heard it, you don't agree with me that Fannius, for that is my friend's name, is a very fine fellow. Well, to begin with, he is a Roman citizen."

"Great Jupiter!" interrupted Lateranus, "you astonish me more and more. A citizen gladiator, and yet a fine fellow! I never knew one that was not a thorough-paced scoundrel."

"Very likely," replied the Prætorian calmly. "Yet Fannius you will find to be an exception to your rule. But to my story. The elder Fannius rented a farm of mine three or four miles this side of Alba. He might have made a good living out of it. There was some capital meadow land, a fair vineyard, and as good a piece of arable as is to be found in the country. His father had had it before him. In fact, the family were old tenants, and the rent had never been raised for at least a hundred years. Then there was only one son, and he was a hard- working young fellow who more than earned his own keep. The father ought, I am sure, to have laid by money; but he was one of those weak, good-natured fellows, who seem incapable of keeping a single denarius in their pockets. It is only fair to say that he was always ready to share his purse with a friend. In fact, his practice of foolishly lending helped him to his ruin as much as anything else. That, and the wine-cup, and the dice-box were too much for him. About five years ago, a brother-in-law—his dead wife's brother, you must understand—died suddenly, leaving an only daughter, with some fifty thousand sesterces for her fortune, not a bad sum for a girl in her rank of life. He had been living, if I remember right, at Taren-tum, and, knowing nothing about his brother-in-law's embarrassments, he had naturally made him his daughter's guardian and trustee. Fannius, who was at his wit's end to know where to find money, his farm being already mortgaged up to the hilt, accepted the trust only too willingly. The son, disgusted at seeing extravagance and waste which he could not stop, had gone away from home, and was serving under Corbulo. Perhaps if he had been here, he might have been able to put a stop to the business. Well, to make a long story short, the elder Fannius appropriated the money little by little. Of course he was always intending to make it good. There was to be a good harvest, or a good vintage, or, what, I believe, he really trusted in more than anything else, a great run of luck at the gaming- table. Equally of course he never got anything of the kind. Then came the crash. The younger Fannius came back with his discharge from the East, and found his father lying dead in the house. There can be no doubt he had killed himself. The son discovered in the old man's desk a letter addressed to himself in which he told the whole story. The girl was living with an aunt. He had always continued, somehow or other, to pay the interest on her money. She was going to be married, and the capital would have to be forthcoming. This, I take it, was the final blow, and the old man saw no other way of getting out of his trouble but suicide. Suicide, by the way, is pretty often a way of shoving one's own trouble on to somebody else's shoulders. Well, the poor fellow came to me. He had brought home a little pay and prize-money. I forgave him what rent was due, and bought whatever there was to sell on the farm—not that there was much of this, I assure you. So he got a little sum of money together, enough to pay the old man's debts. But then there was the niece's fortune. How was that to be raised? It was absolutely gone; not a denarius of it left. I would have helped if I could, but I was positively at the end of my means. Still I could have raised the money, if I had known what young Fannius was going to do. But he said nothing to me or to any one else. He went straight to the master of the gladiators' school and enlisted. You see his strength and skill in arms were all he had to dispose of, and so, to save his father's honour and his cousin's happiness, he sold them, and, of course, himself with them. It was indeed selling himself. You know, I dare say, how the oath runs which a free man takes when he enlists as a gladiator?"

"No; I do not remember to have heard it."

"Well, it runs thus:—

" *'I, Caius Fannius, do take hereby the oath of obedience to Marius, that I will consent to be burnt, bound, beaten, slain with the sword, or whatever else the said Marius shall command, and I do most solemnly devote both soul and body to my said master, as being legally his gladiator.'*

"The young man had no difficulty in making good terms for himself. He was the most famous swordsman of his tribe. Indeed, I don't know that he had his match in the whole Field of Mars. He got his fifty thousand sesterces, paid the money over just in time to prevent the truth coming out, and thus cheerfully put his neck under this yoke. What do you say to that? Have I made good my words?"

"To the full," cried Lateranus enthusiastically. "He is a hero; nothing less."

The two friends had by this time arrived at their destination, "the gladiators' school," as it was called, kept by a certain Thraso. Subrius inquired at one of the doors whether he could see Fannius, the Samnite—for it was in this particular corps of gladiators, distinguished by their high-crested helmet and oblong shield, that the young man was enrolled.

"He has just sat down to the midday meal," said the doorkeeper.

"Then we will not disturb him, but will wait till he has finished," replied Subrius.

"Would you like to see the boys at their exercises, sir?" asked the man, an old Prætorian, who had served under Subrius when the latter was a centurion. "They have their meal earlier, and are at work now."

"Certainly," said Subrius, and the doorkeeper called an attendant, who conducted the two friends to the training-room of the boys.

It was a curious spectacle that met their eyes. The room into which they were ushered was of considerable size and was occupied at this time by some sixty lads, ranging in age from ten to sixteen, who were practising various games or exercises under the eyes of some half-a-dozen instructors. Some were leaping over the bar, either unaided or with the help of a pole; others were lunging with blunt swords at lay figures; others, again, were practising with javelins at a mark. With every group there stood a trainer who explained how the thing was to be done, and either praised or blamed the performance. Every unfavourable comment, it might have been noticed, was always emphasized by the application of a whip. Did the competitor fail to clear the bar at a certain height, fixed according to his age and stature, did he strike the lay figure outside a certain line which was supposed to mark the vital parts, did his javelin miss the mark by a certain distance, the whip descended with an unfailing certainty on the unlucky competitor's shoulders. Even the vanquished of two wrestlers, whose obstinate struggle excited a keen interest in the visitors, met with the common lot, though he had shown very considerable skill, and had indeed been vanquished only by the superior weight and strength of his adversary.

From the boys' apartment the friends went in to see the wild beasts. The show of these creatures was indeed magnificent, and, in fact, unheard of sums had been expended on obtaining them. The Emperor was determined to outdo all his predecessors in the variety and splendour of his exhibitions. Nor were his extravagances wholly unreasonable. A ruler who was not a soldier, who could not, therefore, entertain the Roman populace with the gorgeous display of a triumph, had now to fall back upon other ways of at once keeping them in good humour and impressing them with a sense of his greatness. The whole world, so to speak, had been ransacked to make the collection complete. Twenty lions, magnificent specimens most of them, had been brought from Northern Africa. To secure these monarchs of the desert, the most famous hunters of Mauretania had been engaged for pay commensurate with the perils and hardships which they had to undergo.

"I am told, sir," said the doorkeeper, "that they cost, one with another, fifty thousand sesterces apiece. It is the taking them alive, you see, that makes it so expensive. And the pits, too, which are one way of doing this, often break their bones. So they are mostly netted;

and netting a lion is nasty work. That fellow there"—he pointed as he spoke to a particularly powerful male—"killed, they tell me, four men before they got him into the cage."

Next to the lions were the tigers. They, it seemed, had been even more costly than their neighbours, for they had come considerably further. Secured among the Hyrcanian Mountains, they had been brought down to the Babylonian plains, embarked on board rafts on the Euphrates, and so carried down to the sea. The long and tedious journey had killed half of them before they could be landed at Brindisium, and their average cost had been at least half as much again as that of the lions. Panthers from Cilicia, bears from the Atlas Mountains, and from the Pyrenees, elks from the forests of Gaul and Germany, were also to be seen, and with them multitudes of apes and monkeys, and whole flocks of ostriches, flamingoes, and other birds conspicuous either for size or plumage.

The man was particularly communicative about the elephants. An Indian, he said, had been hired to bring over a troop of performing animals of this kind, and their cleverness and docility were almost beyond belief.

"One of them," he told Subrius and his companion," can write his name with his trunk in Greek characters on the sand. Another has got, the keeper tells me, as far as writing a whole verse. A third can add and subtract. This last, having failed one day in his task, and being docked of part of his food, was found studying his lesson by himself in his house. You smile, sir," he said, seeing that Lateranus could not keep his countenance. "I only tell you what the keeper told me, but I can almost believe anything after what I have seen myself. And then their agility, sir, is something marvellous, even incredible. Who would think that these big creatures, which look so clumsy, can walk on a tight-rope. Yet that I have seen with my own eyes. And the man promises a more wonderful display than that. We are to have four elephants walking on the tight-rope and carrying between them a litter with a sick companion in it." At this the friends laughed outright.

"Clemens," said Subrius, "what traveller's tales are these?"

"I can only say," returned the man, "that my head is all in a whirl from what I have seen with my own eyes and heard during the last few days."

"Fannius will have finished by this time," said Subrius, when they had completed the round of the cages. "Lead the way, Clemens."

It was a singular sight that presented itself to the two friends as they stood surveying the scene at the door of the room in which the gladiators had been taking their meal. It was a large chamber, not less than a hundred feet in length by about half as many in breadth. The number of gladiators was about eighty, but as this was one of the afternoons on which the men were accustomed to receive their relatives and friends, there must have been present nearly four times as many persons. Some of the better known men were surrounded by little circles of admirers, who listened to everything that they had to say with a devotion at least equal to that with which the students of philosophy or literature were accustomed to hang upon the lips of their teachers. The gladiators bragged of what they had done or were about to do, or, putting themselves into attitudes, rehearsed a favourite stroke, or explained one of those infallible ways to victory which seem so often, somehow or other, to end in defeat. Others sat in sullen and stupid silence, others were already asleep, somnolence being, as Aristotle had long before remarked, a special characteristic of the athletic habit of body. The men were of various types and races, but the faces were, almost without exception, marked by strong passions and low intelligence.

"On the whole," said Lateranus, after watching the scene for a few minutes, "I prefer the brutes that do not pretend to be men. Lions and tigers are far nobler animals than these wretches; and as for elephants, whether or no we believe our friend Clemens' marvellous stories about them, it would be an insult even to compare them, so gentle, so teachable, so sagacious as they are, with these savages."

"True in a general way," said the Prætorian, "yet even here Terence's dictum could be applied. Even here there is something of human interest. Look at that stout fellow there."

Lateranus turned his eyes in the direction to which his companion pointed. The "stout fellow" was a gigantic negro.

"Good Heavens!" cried Lateranus in astonishment, for a pure-blood negro was still a somewhat uncommon sight in Rome. "Did you ever see the like? Or have they trained some gigantic ape to bear himself like a man?"

"No," replied the Prætorian, who had a soldier's appreciation of an athletic frame. "If so, they have trained it very well. I warrant he will be an awkward adversary for any one whom the lot may match with him when the day shall come."

"May be," said the other; "but what a face! what lips! what a nose! what hair! To think that nature should ever have created anything so hideous!"

"But see," cried Subrius, "there is one person at least who seems not to have found our black friend so very unsightly."

And, indeed, at the moment there came up to the negro a pretty little woman whose fair complexion and diminutive stature exhibited a curious contrast to his ebony hue and gigantic proportions. To judge from the blue colour of her eyes and the reddish gold of her hair, she was a Gaul, possibly belonging to one of the tribes which had been settled for many generations in the Lombard plains, possibly from beyond the Alps. Further Gaul had now been thoroughly latinized, and its people were no longer strangers in Italy. She carried in her arms a little whitey brown baby, whose complexion, features, and half woolly hair indicated clearly enough his mixed parentage. The negro took the child from her arms, his mouth opening with a grin of delight which showed a dazzlingly white array of teeth.

"See," cried Lateranus, "Hector, Andromache, and Astyanax over again! Only Hector seems to have borrowed for the time the complexion of Memnon!"

"But we are forgetting our friend Fannius," said Subrius. "Where is he? Ah! there I see him," he exclaimed, after scanning for a minute or so the motley crowd which so thronged the room as to make it difficult to distinguish any one person. "And he, too, seems to have an

Andromache. I thought he was an obstinate bachelor. But in that matter there are no surprises for a wise man."

Fannius was just at that moment bidding farewell to two women. About the elder of the two there was nothing remarkable. She was a stout, elderly, commonplace person, respectably dressed in a style that seemed to indicate the wife of a small tradesman or well-to-do mechanic. The younger woman was a handsome, even distinguished looking girl of one and twenty or thereabouts. Her features were Greek, though not, perhaps, of the finest type. A deep brunette in complexion, she had soft, velvety brown eyes that seemed to speak of a mixture of Syrian blood. This, too, had given an arch to her finely chiselled nose, and a certain fulness, which was yet remote from the suspicion of anything coarse, to her crimson lips. Perhaps her mouth was her most remarkable feature. Any one who could read physiognomies would have noticed at once the firmness of its lines. The chin, just a little squarer than an Apelles, seeking absolutely ideal features for his Aphrodite, would perhaps have approved, but still delicately moulded, harmonized with the mouth. So did the resolute pose of her figure, and the erect, vigorous carriage of the head. She was dressed in much the same manner as the elder woman, naturally with a little more style, but with no pretension to rank. Yet at the moment when the two friends observed the group she was reaching her hand to Fannius with the air of a princess, and the gladiator was kissing it with all the devotion of a subject. The next moment she dropped a heavy veil over her face and turned away.

The gladiator stood looking at her as she moved away, so lost in thought that he did not notice the approach of Subrius and his companion.

"Well, Fannius," cried the Prætorian, slapping him heartily on the shoulder, "shall we find you, too, keeping festival on the Kalends of March?"

Fannius turned round and saluted. The Prætorian, after formally returning the salute, warmly clasped his odd acquaintance by the hand, a token of friendship which made the gladiator, who remembered only too acutely the degradation of his position, blush with pleasure.

"You are pleased to jest, noble Subrius, about the worshipful goddess. What has a poor gladiator, who cannot call his life his own for more than a few hours to do with marriage? And Epicharis, though Venus knows I love her as my own soul, has her thought on very different matters."

"Well, well, never despair!" returned the Tribune. "Venus will touch the haughty fair some day with her whip. But, Fannius, when are you coming to see me? It seems an age since we had a talk together. My friend here, too, who is to be Consul next year, wishes to make your acquaintance."

"I am not my own master, you know; but if I can get leave, I will come to- night."

"So be it; at the eleventh hour I shall expect you."

4

A NEW ALLY

"LATERANUS," said the Prætorian to his friend, as they sat together after dinner, "did you notice the face of the girl who was taking leave of our friend Fannius when we first espied him this afternoon?"

"Yes, indeed, I did," said the Consul elect; "it was a face that no one could help noticing, and having once seen, could hardly forget."

"That is exactly as it struck me; and I am sure that I have seen it before; and not so very long ago. But where? That puzzles me. Now and then I seem to have it, but then it slips away again. Depend upon it, she is no ordinary woman. Very beautiful she is, but somehow it is not the beauty, but the resolute strength of her face that impresses one. And what did the man mean when he said that she 'thought about other things.' I have a sort of presentiment that she will help us."

"You surprise me," said Lateranus. "And yet—"

At this point he was interrupted by the appearance of a slave who announced the arrival of the expected guest.

For some time the conversation was general, Fannius taking his part in it with an ease and readiness that surprised Lateranus, and even exceeded the expectations of his old friend and landlord. It naturally turned, before very long, on the details of life in the "gladiators' school." Fannius explained that he had only a few more weeks to serve. After the next show, which was to take place in September, he would be entitled to his discharge. He had been extraordinarily successful in his profession, and the "golden youth" of Rome, who had backed him against competitors, and won not a little by his victories, had made him liberal presents. "You have always taken a kind interest in my fortunes," he said to Subrius, "and I am not afraid of worrying you with these matters. If I live to receive the wooden sword, I shall have a comfortable independence. But who knows what may happen? a gladiator, least of all. You know, sir, the proverb about the pitcher and the fountain. And that reminds me of a little service that I have been thinking of asking you to do for me. I should even have ventured to call, if you had not been kind enough to come. I want you to take charge of what I have been able to save. I should have made a will, and asked you to do me the service of seeing its provisions carried out in case of need, but I feel doubtful whether, situated as I am, I can make a will that would be valid. What I will ask you to do, then, will be this, to take charge of my property now, and if anything should happen to me, to distribute it according to the directions contained in this paper."

"Very good," replied Subrius. "The gods forbid that there should arise any need for my services, but, if there should, you may be sure that I will not fail in my duty as your friend."

"Many thanks, sir," said Fannius, producing some papers from his pocket. "These are acknowledgments from Cassius, the banker, of deposits which I have made with him. Thras has charge of what I possess in coin, and will have instructions to hand it over to you. And here is the paper of directions. Will you please to read it? Is it quite plain?"

"Perfectly so," answered the Tribune. "But there is one question which I must take the liberty of asking. You mention a certain Epicharis. Who is she? Where am I to look for her?"

"She lives with her aunt by marriage. Galla is the aunt's name, and she cultivates a little farm on this side of Gabii. Any one there will direct you to it. She is the young woman whom you saw speaking to me this afternoon."

"I guessed as much," said Subrius, "and I have been puzzling myself ever since trying to make sure whether I had seen her before."

"That you might very easily have done," replied the gladiator. "She was much with the Empress Octavia. Indeed, she was her foster-sister."

"Ah!" cried Subrius; "that accounts for it. Now I remember all about it. I was on guard in the Palace with my cohort on the day when the Empress Octavia was sent away to Campania. My men were lining the stairs as the Empress came down. The poor Empress was almost fainting. Two of her women were supporting her, one on each side. I remember how much struck I was with the look of one of them, far more Imperial, I thought, than that of the unhappy creature she was holding up. 'That is a woman,' I said to myself, 'whom no man will wrong with impunity!' It was not a face to be forgotten. I remembered it at once when I saw it this afternoon; but I could not fix the time and place. Now you have enlightened me."

"Yes, yes," said Fannius, "you are right; she was with the Empress then; indeed, she remained with her till her death. Oh! sir, it is a piteous story that she tells. But perhaps I had better not speak about those things."

"Speak on without fear," replied the Prætorian. "I am one of the Emperor's soldiers, and my friend here has received the honour of the Consulship from him; but we have not therefore ceased to be Romans and men. Whatever you may tell us will be safely kept—"

The speaker paused, and then added in a deliberate and meaning tone, "As long as it may be necessary to keep it."

The gladiator cast a quick glance at him, and resumed. "Well, Epicharis was with her mistress from the unlucky day when she was carried across the threshold of her husband's house, down to the very end. They were both children then, only twelve years of age, and the poor Empress was really never anything else. But Epicharis soon learnt to be a woman. From almost the first she had to protect her mistress. Nero never loved his wife. Epicharis says she was too good for him, or, indeed, for almost any man; that she ought to have had a philosopher or a priest for her husband."

"I don't know that philosophers or priests are better than other men," interrupted Subrius; "but go on."

"Well, as I said, Nero never loved her, but, for a time, he was decently civil to her. Then her brother died, was—"

"Was poisoned, you were going to say," said Subrius. "That is no secret. Everybody in Rome knows it."

"Epicharis tells me that the Empress never shed a tear. She had learnt to hide her feelings, as children do when they are afraid of their elders. Then the Empress-mother came by her end. As long as she was alive the wife's lot was tolerable. But after that—oh! gentlemen, I could not bring myself to say a tenth of the things that I have heard. They are too dreadful. The poorest, unhappiest woman had not so much to bear. I used to think when I was a boy that the fine ladies who lived in great houses, and were dressed in gay silks, and rode about in soft cushioned carriages, must be happy; but now that I have had a look at what goes on behind palace walls, I don't think so any more. Then came what you saw, sir, on the palace stairs. It is no wonder that the poor Empress should look miserable after what she had gone through in those days, seeing, for instance, her slave-girls tortured in the hope that something might be wrung out of them against her. Epicharis herself they did not touch; she was free, you see; but they threatened her. I warrant they got nothing by that. She has a tongue, and knows how to use it. She let that monster Tigellinus know what she thought of him, and his master too. She has told me that she saw the Emperor wince once and again at the answers she made. Then Octavia was sent away. It was a great relief to go; to be away from the dreadful palace. She ran about the gardens and grounds of the villa,—it was to Burrus' house near Misenum, you will remember, she was sent,—and made friends with the little children; in fact, she was happier than she had ever been in her life before. 'Now that I am out of their way, and do not interfere with their plans, they will let me alone, and, perhaps, forget me.' This is what she would say to Epicharis. 'I am sure that I don't want to marry again, and you had better follow my example, dear sister,'—she would often call Epicharis 'sister.' 'Husbands seem very strange creatures, so difficult to please, and always imagining such strange things about one. You and I will live together for the rest of our lives, and take care of the poor people. It really is much nicer than Rome, which, you know, I never really liked.' So she would go on. She did not seem to have any fears, the relief of being free after eight years' slavery—for really her life was nothing else—was so great. But Epicharis never deceived herself, though she had not the heart to undeceive her mistress. Indeed, what would have been the good? The poor woman was fast in the toils, and the hunters were sure to come. But it was of no use to tell her so, and make her miserable before the time. But, as I said, Epicharis was clever enough to know what the end must be. She was sure that Nero would never let Octavia alone."

"No," said Subrius; "he had wronged her far too deeply ever to be able to forgive."

"Just so," observed Lateranus; "and if he could have done it there was Poppæa, and a woman never spares a rival, especially a rival who is better than herself. Besides he dared not let his divorced wife live. You see she was the daughter of Claudius, and her husband, supposing that she had married again, would have been dangerously near the throne. And then the people loved her; that was even more against her than anything else."

"That is exactly what Epicharis thought, so she has often told me. After a few days came news that there had been great disturbances in Rome; that the people had stood up like one man in the Circus, and shouted out to the Emperor, 'Give us back Octavia!' and that Nero had annulled the divorce. Some of the poor woman's attendants were in high spirits. You see they did not like Campania and a quiet country house as much as their mistress did. 'Now,' they said, 'we shall get back to Rome; after all, a palace is better than a villa.' Next day the news was more exciting than ever. There had been a great demonstration all over Rome as soon as it was known that the divorce had been cancelled, and that Octavia was Empress again. The people had crowded into the capital and returned thanks in the temples. Poppæa's image had been thrown down, and Octavia's covered with flowers and set up in the public places. The Empress' women, foolish creatures that they were, were more delighted than ever. 'Now,' they said, 'we shall be going back to Rome in triumph.' But Epicharis knew better; she was quite sure that this was only the beginning of the end. And, as you know, gentlemen, she was right; before the end of another week the soldiers had come from Rome."

"Ah!" said Subrius, "a lucky fever-fit saved me from being sent on that errand. My cohort had been detailed for the duty; the sealed orders, which I was not to open till I reached the villa, had been handed to me; and then at the last moment, when I was racking my brain, thinking how I could possibly get off, there fortunately came this attack. I never had thought before that I should be positively glad to have the ague."

"Well, sir, from what Epicharis has told me, you were spared one of the most pitiable sights that human eyes ever saw. Octavia was sitting in the garden when the Tribune came up and saluted her. She gave him her hand to kiss. 'I suppose you have come to take me back to Rome,' she said. 'Well, I am sorry to leave this beautiful place; but if my husband and the people really want me, I am willing to come. Can you give me till to-morrow to get ready?' The Tribune turned away. Epicharis says that she saw him brush his hand over his eyes."

"Well," interrupted the Prætorian, "it must have been something to make that brute Severus—for he was on duty in my place, I remember—shed a tear."

" ' Madam,' said the Tribune, 'you mistake. We have come on another business. You are not to return to Rome. We are to take you to Pandataria.' 'Pandataria!' cried the poor child, roused to anger, as even the gentlest will sometimes be; 'but that is a place for wicked people. I have done nothing wrong; else why should the Emperor have made me his wife again!' 'Madam,' said the Tribune, 'I have to obey my orders.' After that she said nothing more. After all, she was a little relieved that she was not to return to Rome, and she did not know what going to Pandataria really meant. Well, that very night she was hurried off; only one attendant was allowed her. Tigellinus, I fancy, had forgotten that Epicharis, whom he had plenty of reason to distrust and hate, was with her. Anyhow he had given no directions to the Tribune, and the Tribune was not disposed to go beyond his orders in making the poor banished woman unhappy. So Epicharis went. The island, she told me, was a wretched place; as to the house, it was almost in ruins. The shepherd who looks after the few sheep, which are almost the only creatures on the island, said that scarcely anything had been done to it since the Princess Julia left it, and that must have been nearly sixty years before. However, she seemed to reconcile herself to the place easily enough. It was her delight to wander about on the shore, picking up shells and seaweeds. Such things pleased her as they please a child, Poor creature! she had not time to get tired of it. In the course of about fourteen or fifteen days a ship came with some soldiers on board—"

"They told us in Rome," said Subrius, "that she was killed by falling from a cliff, and possibly had thrown herself off."

"Epicharis tells a very different story. When the Empress saw the soldiers, she said in a very cheerful voice—you see she had not the least idea that her life was in danger, and Epicharis had never had the heart to tell her,—'Well, gentlemen, what is you business this time? Where are you going to take me now? I must confess that I liked Misenum better than this.' 'Madam,' said the Centurion in command 'with your permission I will explain my business when I get to the house, if you will be pleased to return thither.' He said this, you see, to gain time. On the way back he contrived to whisper into Epicharis' ear what his errand really was. She knew it already well enough, you may be sure. 'You must break it to her,' he said. That was an awful thing for the poor girl to do. She is not of the tearful sort,—you know; but she sobbed and wept as if her heart would break, when she told me the story. The Empress went up to her bed-chamber to make some little change in her dress. As she was sitting before the glass, Epicharis came and put her arms round her neck. The Empress turned round a little surprised. You see she would often kiss and embrace her foster- sister, but it was always she that began the caress and the other that returned it. 'What ails you, darling?' she said, for Epicharis' eyes were full of tears. 'O dearest lady, I cannot help crying when I think that we shall have to part!' 'Surely,' said the Empress, 'they are not going to be so cruel as to take you away from me. I will write to the Emperor about it; he can't refuse me this little favour.' 'O lady,' said Epicharis, who was in despair what to say,—how could one break a thing of this sort?—he will grant you nothing, not even another day.' 'What do you mean?' said Octavia, for she did not yet understand. 'O lady,' she cried, 'these soldiers are come—' and she put into her look the meaning that she could not put into words. 'What!' cried the poor woman, her voice rising into a shrill scream, 'do you mean that they are come to kill me?' and she started up from her chair. Epicharis has told me that the sight of her face, ghastly pale, with the eyes wide open with fear, haunts her night and day. 'Oh, I cannot die! I cannot die!' she cried out. 'I am so young. Can't you hide me somewhere?' 'O dearest lady!' said Epicharis, 'I would die to save you. But there is no way. Only we can die together.' Then she took out of her robe two poniards, which she always carried about in case they should be wanted in this way. 'Let me show you. Strike just as you see me strike. After all it hurts very little, and it will all be over in a moment.' 'No, no, no!' screamed the unhappy lady, 'take the dreadful things away. I cannot bear to look at them. I will go and beg the soldiers to have mercy.' And she flew out of the room to where the Centurion was standing with his men in the hall. She threw herself at the man's feet—it was a most pitiable thing to see, Epicharis said when she told me the story—and begged for mercy. Poor thing, she clung to life, though the gods know she had had very little to make her love it. The Centurion was unmoved,—as for some of the common soldiers, they were half disposed to rebel,—and said nothing but, 'Madam, I have my orders.' 'But the Emperor must have forgotten,' she cried out; 'I am not Empress now, I am only a poor widow, and almost his sister.' Then again, 'Oh, why does Agrippina let him do it?' seeming to forget in her terror that Agrippina was dead. After this had gone on for some time, the officer said to one of his

men, 'Bind her, and put a gag in her mouth.' Epicharis saw one or two
of the men put their hands to their swords when they heard the order
given. But it was useless to think of resisting or disobeying. They
bound her hand and foot, and gagged her, and then carried her into
the house. They had brought a slave with them who knew some thing
about surgery. This man opened the great artery in each arm, but
somehow the blood did not flow. 'It is fairly frozen with fear,'
Epicharis heard him say to the Centurion. Then the two whispered
together, and after a while the men carried the poor woman into the
bath-room. Epicharis was not allowed to go with her; but she heard
that she was suffocated with the hot steam, and that, as far as any one
knew, she never came to herself again. That, anyhow, is something to
be thankful for."

"They told a story in Rome," said Lateranus, "that the head was
brought to Poppæa. Do you think that it is true? Did Epicharis ever
say anything about it to you ?"

"No," replied Fannius; "she never knew what became of the body.
She was never allowed to see it; it was burnt that night, she
was told."

"And so this is the true story of Octavia," said Subrius after a
pause. "You remember, Lateranus, there was a great thanksgiving for
the Emperor's deliverance from dangerous enemies, and the enemy
was this poor girl. Why don't the gods, if they indeed exist (which I
sometimes doubt), rain down their thunderbolts upon those who
mock them with these blasphemous pretences?"

"Verily," cried Lateranus, "if they had been so minded Rome would
have been burnt up long ago. Have you not observed that we are
particularly earnest in thanking heaven when some more than
usually atrocious villainy has been perpetrated?"

The gladiator looked with a continually increasing astonishment
on the two men who used language of such unaccustomed freedom.
Subrius thought it time to make another step in advance.

"As you have taken us into your confidence," he said, "about the
contents of your will, you will not mind my asking you a question
about these matters."

"Certainly not," answered the man. "You need not be afraid of offending me."

"If things go well with you, as there is every hope of their doing, and you get your discharge all right, what do you look forward to?"

The gladiator shifted his position two or three times uneasily, and made what seemed an attempt to speak, but did not succeed in uttering a word.

"If Epicharis does not become your legatee, as I sincerely hope she may not, is she to have no interest in your money?"

"Ah, sir, she will make no promises, or rather, she talks so wildly that she might as well say nothing all."

"What do you mean?"

"I may trust you, gentlemen, for I am putting her life as well as my own in your hands?"

"Speak on boldly. Surely we have both of us said enough this evening to bring our necks into danger, if you chose to inform against us. We are all sailing in the same ship."

"It is true. I ought not to have doubted. Well, what she says to me is this, 'Avenge my dear mistress on those who murdered her, and then ask me what you please.' She won't hear of anything else. I have asked her what I could do, a simple gladiator, who has not even the power to go hither or thither as he pleases. She has only one answer, 'Avenge Octavia!' "

"It is not so hopeless as you think. There many who hold that Octavia should be avenged, aye, and others besides Octavia. We are biding our time, and there are many things that seem to show that it is not far off. You will be with us then, Fannius?"

"Certainly," said the gladiator. "I want to hear nothing more; the fewer names I know, the better, for then I cannot possibly betray them. Only give me the word, and I follow. But how about Epicharis?" he went on; "is she to hear anything?"

"I don't like letting women into a secret," said Lateranus.

"Nor I," said Subrius, "as a rule; but if there is any truth in faces, this particular woman will keep a secret and hold to a purpose better than most of us. Shall we leave it to Fannius' discretion?"

To this Lateranus agreed.

After some more conversation the gladiator rose to take his leave. A minute or so afterwards he returned to the room. "Gentlemen," he said, "there is a great fire to be seen from a window in the passage, and from what I can see it must be in the Circus, or, anyhow, very near it."

5

A GREAT FIRE

THE two friends hurried to the window. At the very moment of their reaching it a great flame shot up into the air. It was easy to distinguish by its light the outline of the Circus, the white polished marble of which shone like gold with the reflection of the blaze.

"It can scarcely be the Circus itself that is on fire," cried Subrius; "the light seems to fall upon it from without. But the place must be dangerously near to it. Hurry back, Fannius, as quick as you can. We shall come after you as soon as possible, and shall look out for you at the Southeastern Gate."

The gladiator ran off at the top of his speed, and the two friends lost no time in making themselves ready to follow him. Discarding the dress of ceremony in which they had sat down to dinner, for indeed, the folds of the toga were not a little encumbering, they both equipped themselves in something like the costume which they would have assumed for a hunting expedition, an outer and an inner tunic, drawers reaching to the knee, leggings and boots. Lateranus was by far the larger man of the two; but one of his freedmen was able to furnish the Prætorian with what he wanted.

"Don't let us forget the hunting-knives," said Lateranus; "we may easily want something wherewith to defend ourselves, for a big fire draws to it all the villains in the city."

By this time all Rome knew what was going on, and the friends, when they descended into the street, found themselves in the midst of a crowd that was eagerly hurrying towards the scene of action. A fire exercised the same fascination on the Roman public that it exercises to-day in London or Paris. No one allowed his dignity to stand in the way of his enjoying it; no one was so weak but that he made shift to be a spectator. Senators and Knights struggled for places with artisans and slaves; and of course, women brought their babies, as they have brought them from time immemorial on the most inconvenient and incongruous occasions.

Arrived at the spot, the friends found that the conflagration was even more extensive and formidable than they had anticipated. The Circus was still untouched, but it was in imminent danger. A shop where oil for the Circus lamps had been sold was burning fiercely, and it was separated from the walls of the great building only by a narrow passage. As for the shop itself, there was no hope of saving it; the. flames had got such a mastery over it that had the Roman appliances for extinguishing fire been ten times more effective than they were, they could hardly have made any impression upon them. To keep the adjoining buildings wet with deluges of water was all that could be done. A more effective expedient would have been, of course, to pull them down. Subrius, who was a man of unusual energy and resource, actually proposed this plan of action to the officer in command of the Watch, a body of men who performed the functions of a fire-brigade. The suggestion was coldly received. The officer had received, he said, no orders, and could not take upon himself so much responsibility. And who was to compensate the owners, he asked. And indeed, the time had hardly come for the application of so extreme a remedy. As a matter of fact, it is always employed too late. Again and again enormous loss might be prevented if the vigorous measures which have to be employed at the last had been taken at the first. No one, indeed, could blame the Prefect of the Watch for his unwillingness to take upon himself so serious a responsibility, but the conduct of his subordinates was less excusable. They did nothing, or next to nothing, in checking the fire. More than this, they refused, and even repulsed with rudeness, the offers of assistance made by the bystanders. A cordon was formed to keep the spectators at a distance from the burning houses; for by this time the buildings on either side had caught fire. This would have been well enough, if it had been desired that the firemen should work unimpeded by the pressure of a curious mob; but, as far as could be seen, they did nothing themselves, and suffered nothing to be done by others.

Subrius and Lateranus, though they were persons of too much distinction to be exposed to insult, found themselves unable to do any good. They were chafing under their forced inaction, when they were accosted by the gladiator.

"Come, gentlemen," he said; "let us see what can be done. The fire has broken out in two fresh places, and this time inside the Circus."

"In two places!" cried Subrius in astonishment. "That is an extraordinary piece of bad luck. Has the wind carried the flames there?"

"Hardly, sir," replied the man, "for the night, you see, is fairly still, and both places, too, are at the other end of the building."

"It seems that there is foul play somewhere," said Lateranus. "But come, we seem to be of no use here."

The three started at full speed for the scene of the new disaster, Fannius leading the way. One of the fires, which had broken out in the quarters of the gladiators, had been extinguished by the united exertions of the corps. The other was spreading in an alarming way, all the more alarming because it threatened that quarter of the building in which the wild beasts were kept. The keeper of the Circus, who had, within the building, an authority independent of the Prefect of the Watch, exerted himself to the utmost in checking the progress of the flames, and was zealously seconded by his subordinates; but the buildings to be saved were unluckily of wood. The chambers and storehouses underneath the tiers of seats were of this material, and were besides, in many cases, filled with combustible substances. In a few minutes it became evident that the quarters of the beasts could not be saved. The creatures seemed themselves to have become conscious of the danger that threatened them, and the general confusion and alarm were heightened by the uproar which they made. The shrill trumpeting of the elephants and the deep roaring of the tigers and lions, with the various cries of the mixed multitude of smaller creatures, every sound being accentuated by an unmistakable note of fear, combined to make a din that was absolutely appalling. The situation, it will be readily understood, was perplexing in the extreme. The collection was of immense value, and how could it be removed? For a few of the animals that had recently arrived the movable cages in which they had been brought to the Circus were still available, for, as it happened, they had not yet been taken away. Others had of necessity to be killed; this seemed better than leaving them to perish in the flames, for they could not be removed, and it was out of the question to let them loose. This was done, to the immense grief of their keepers, for each beast had its own special attendant, a man who had been with it from its capture, and who was commonly able to control its movements. The poor fellows loudly protested that they would be responsible for the good behaviour of their charges, if they could be permitted to take them from their cages; but the Circus authorities could not venture to run the risk. An exception was made in the case of the elephants. These were released, for they could be trusted with their keepers. A part of the stock was saved—saved at least from the fire—by a happy thought that struck one of the officials of the Circus. A part of the arena had been made available for an exhibition of a kind that was always highly popular at Rome—a naval battle. This portion was on a lower level than the rest, and could be flooded at pleasure by turning on the water from a branch of one of the great aqueducts. This was now done, and a good many of the creatures were turned into the place to take their chance. They would at least suffer less from being drowned than from being burnt alive.

Throughout the night Subrius and Lateranus exerted themselves to the utmost, and their efforts were ably seconded by the gladiator.

The day was beginning to break when, utterly worn out by their labours, they returned to the house. Fannius was permitted by his master to accompany them. The man had contrived to collect his slave gladiators, with the exception of two who had perished in a drunken sleep. These he had removed to a house which he possessed in the suburbs, and which was commonly used as a sanatorium for the sick and wounded. Fannius, who, as a freeman, bound by his own voluntary act, and serving for purposes of his own, was not likely to run away, he allowed to accompany Lateranus to his home.

They were not permitted to enjoy for long their well-earned repose. It was barely the second hour when a loud knocking at the outer gate roused the porter, who, having himself watched late on the preceding night, was fast asleep. Looking through the little opening which permitted him to take a preliminary survey of all applicants for admission, he saw an elderly slave, who, to judge from his breathless and dishevelled condition, had been engaged in a personal struggle.

The slave was really an old acquaintance, but the porter was still stupid with sleep, and the newcomer was greatly changed in appearance from the neat and well-dressed figure with which the guardian of the door was familiar.

"Who are you, and what do you want?" he asked in a surly tone. "The master can see no callers this morning; he was up late and is fast asleep,—though, indeed," he added in an undertone, "you do not look much like a caller."

"Waste no time," cried the man; "I must see him, whether he be awake or asleep. It is a matter of life and death."

"Good Heavens!" cried the porter, recognizing the voice; "is it you, Dromio? What in the world brings you here in such a plight?"

"The furies seize you!" cried Dromio, shaking the gate in a fury of impatience; "why don't you open?"

Thus adjured the porter undid the bar, calling at the same time to a slave in the inner part of the house, who was to take the visitor to Lateranus' apartment.

"You must see the master, you say?" said the porter. "I don't like to wake him without necessity. He did not come back last night till past the middle of the fourth watch."

"Must see him? Yes, indeed," cried Dromio. "The gods grant that I may not be too late."

The other slave appeared at this moment. "Lead me to your master," said Dromio; "quick, quick!"

Lateranus, roused from the deep sleep into which he had fallen, was at first almost as much perplexed as the porter had been.

"Who is this?" he cried to the slave; "did you not understand that I would have no—"

"Pardon me, my lord," cried Dromio, as he took one of Lateranus' hands and kissed it. "I come from the Lady Pomponia."

"There is nothing wrong, I hope?"

"Dreadfully wrong, I fear. The gods grant that she may be still alive!"

"What has happened?"

"Her house is attacked, and she begs your help. I will tell you the story afterwards, but I implore you, by all the gods, do not lose a moment!"

Lateranus touched three times a hand-bell that stood by his side, at the same time springing from his couch on to the floor and beginning to dress. The summons of the bell, signifying as it did that the presence of the steward was required, soon brought that official to the chamber.

"Arm the cohort at once," said Lateranus, "and send a runner to tell the Tribune Subrius that he is wanted."

The "cohort" was not of course the regular military division known by that name, but a retinue of young freedmen and slaves who were regularly drilled in arms.

"It shall be done, my lord," said the steward, saluting.

"And now," said Lateranus, "while I am dressing tell me what it is all about."

Dromio then told his story.

"Rather more than an hour ago a man knocked at the door, and said that he wished to see the Lady Pomponia. You know my mistress' ways—what a number of strange pensioners she has. In her house it is impossible to be surprised at any visitor. Still there was something about this man that made the porter suspicious. One thing was that the fellow spoke with a strong Jewish accent, and many of the Jews have a very great hatred against the mistress. Anyhow the porter kept the door shut, and said that he must have the stranger's name and business. 'Lucian is my name,' said the man, 'and I bring a message from Clemens the Elder.' That, you know, is one of the priests whom my lady makes so much of. That seemed satisfactory, and the porter opened the gate. Then what does this fellow do but put his foot on the threshold so that the door should not be shut again, and whistles a signal to his companions, who, it seems, were in waiting round the next corner. Anyhow some five and twenty as ill-looking ruffians as you ever set eyes on came running up. By good luck the porter had his youngest son Geta sitting in the lodge, 'Help!' he cries, and Geta who is a regular Hercules, comes running out, seizes the first fellow by the throat and throws him out, deals just in the same fashion with a second, who was half over the threshold, and bangs to the gate. At that a regular howl of rage came from the party outside. 'Open, or we will burn the house down,' shouted their leader. Pomponia, by this time, had been roused by the uproar. She understood what was to be done in a moment; she always does; we sometimes say that she must have learned something of this art from the old General. 'Haste, Dromio,' she said to me, 'by the back way, before they surround the house, and tell Lateranus that I want his help.'"

"That she shall have as quick as I can give it," said Lateranus; "but where are the Watch? Are houses to be besieged in Rome as if it were a city taken by storm?"

"My lord," answered Dromio, "that is just what Rome seems to be. The Watch are fairly dazed, I think, by this dreadful fire, which is growing worse every hour, and if we waited for them to help us we should certainly all have our throats cut in the meanwhile."

At this moment the steward entered the room. "The cohort is ready," he said.

6

BAFFLED

THE company which Lateranus called his "cohort" consisted of about thirty men, divided into three guards, as we may call them, of ten. They were armed after the fashion of the "gowned" or civilian cohort of the Prætorians, which was accustomed to keep guard in the Emperor's palace; that is, they had neither helmet or shield or pike, but carried swords and lances. Even these arms they never wore except within the precincts of the house, and then only when they were being drilled and practised in sword play and other military exercises. Lateranus always spoke of the cohort as a plaything of his own which had no serious purpose, and it may readily be understood that he was careful not to make any display of it. Any master was at liberty to put weapons into the hands of his dependents in an emergency. The only difference was that these dependents had been trained to use these weapons skilfully and in concert. And now the emergency was come which was to put their utility to a practical test. One of the guards of ten was left to protect the house. Lateranus, who was apparently unarmed, but carried a short sword underneath his outer tunic, proceeded with the other two at the "double" to the scene of action.

The relieving force was not a moment too soon in arriving. The outer gates of the mansion had been forced open, and the assailants were applying crowbars to the door which led to the private apartments of Pomponia. This, indeed, had given way; naturally it had not been made strong enough to resist a violent assault; but the domestics within had piled up a quantity of heavy furniture which had to be removed before the besiegers could make good their entrance. This obstacle saved the house. Before it could be got rid of, the relieving party arrived, and took the assailants in the rear. The leader of the latter at once recognized that his purpose had been defeated, and desisted from his attempt without challenging a struggle with the new arrivals. His bearing, however, was curiously unlike what might have been expected from the ringleader of a lawless gang surprised by a superior force. So far from displaying any embarrassment, he appeared to be perfectly at his ease, and accosted Lateranus with all the air of an equal.

"You have been beforehand with me this time, sir," he said in a quiet tone, which nevertheless was full of suppressed fury. "I shall not forget it."

Lateranus smiled.

"Neither will they for whom I act," went on the other, "and that you will find no laughing matter."

"I shall always be ready to answer for myself," said Lateranus firmly. "Since when has your mistress taken it upon herself to send storming parties against the houses of innocent citizens?"

To this the man made no reply. "You will not hinder our departure," he went on after a pause. "You will find it better not to do so."

Lateranus shrugged his shoulders. "You can go," he said; "it is not my business to do the duty of the guards, but if there is any justice in Rome, you shall hear of this again."

"Justice!" cried the fellow with an insolent laugh; "we know something much better than that."

Meanwhile the cohort had been waiting with eagerness for the end of the colloquy. All had their hands on the hilt of their swords, and all were ready to use them. Profound was their disappointment when, instead of the expected order to draw, came the command to stand at ease. One by one the assailants filed out of the court, their leader being the last to leave the place.

"What ails the master?" said one of the younger men, in an angry whisper to his neighbour.

"Hush!" replied the man addressed. "Don't you see that it is Theodectes?"

"Theodectes!" said the other; "who is Theodectes?"

"The favourite freedman of Poppæa. Is not that enough for you?"

Meanwhile Lateranus, leaving instructions that the cohort should remain for the present in the court, made his way to the apartment where Pomponia was awaiting him.

"Welcome!" she said, coming forward and taking his hand with a peculiarly gracious smile; "the Lord has sent you in good time."

Pomponia Græcina, to give the lady her full name, was a woman of singularly dignified presence. She was now not far from her seventieth year, and her abundant hair, which, contrary to the fashion of the ladies of her time, she wore with a severe plainness, was of a silvery whiteness. But her figure was erect; her complexion retained no little of the bloom of youth,—a bloom which, again in opposition to contemporary custom, owed nothing to the resources of art; and her eyes could flash, on occasion, with a fire which years had done nothing to quench. Her history was one of singular interest. She came of a house not originally noble, but distinguished by having produced many eminent citizens and soldiers. Perhaps the most famous of these had been Pomponius Atticus, the friend and correspondent of Cicero. Atticus, to speak of him by the name by which he is commonly known, had played with extraordinary skill the part of an honest man who desires to be on good terms with all parties at once. He had been so loyal to the vanquished Republicans, that Cicero, till very near the time of his death, kept up an affectionate correspondence with him; and was yet so friendly with the victorious Imperialists that his daughter married the chief friend of Augustus, and his granddaughter became the wife of Tiberius. These great alliances did not result in happiness to his descendants, for one of the last of his race, Julia, the granddaughter of Tiberius, was put to death by the Emperor Claudius, prompted by his wicked wife Messalina. Julia's death was a lasting grief to her kinswoman, the Pomponia of my story. Never afterwards could she bear to mix in the brilliant society of the Imperial Court. But there was another reason why she held herself aloof from the fashionable world of Rome. She had come, how it is impossible to say, under the influence of some early preacher of the Christian faith; and a Christian woman, when the life of the court was such as we know it to have been in the days of Claudius and Nero, had no alternative but to live in retirement. So marked was her attitude that it excited suspicion; and she was actually accused—on what grounds we cannot say, possibly on the testimony of some member of her household—of being addicted to a superstition not recognized by Roman law. With a woman of ordinary rank it might have gone hard, but Pomponia had a powerful protector in her husband. He was one of the most distinguished soldiers of Rome, and was, happily for himself, too old to excite the jealous fears of the Emperor. When he made it a matter of personal favour that in the case of his wife an ancient practice should be revived, and that he as her husband should be constituted her judge, his request was granted. That he himself shared her faith we can hardly suppose, but he had seen its results in the blamelessness of her life, and the trial held by a family council, over which he himself presided, ended, as was doubtless his wish, in the acquittal of the accused. Since that time she had lived unmolested, though, as we have seen, she had enemies.

Pomponia went on: "Here is some one else who has to thank you for your timely aid. I will present you to her."

She drew aside as she spoke the curtains that hung over an arch leading into a smaller apartment. Into this she disappeared for a moment, and then returned leading by the hand a girl who may have numbered some eighteen summers.

"Claudia," she said, "this is Plautius Lateranus, my husband's nephew, whom we are to have for our Consul next year, and who meanwhile has delivered us from a very great danger. And this," she went on, turning to Lateranus, "is Claudia, whom I venture to call my daughter, as indeed she is, though not after the flesh."

The Roman, though he had known all the beauties of the Imperial Court for more than twenty years, was fairly surprised by the loveliness of the girl, a loveliness that was all the more startling because it was in some respect so different from that which he had been accustomed to admire in Italian maids and matrons. Her eyes, as far as he could see them, for they were bent downwards under their long lashes, were of a deep sapphire blue, the eyebrows exquisitely pencilled, the forehead somewhat broader and higher than agreed with the commonly accepted canons of taste, but of a noble outline, and full, it seemed, of intelligence. The nose was slightly retroussé, but this departure from the straight line of the Greek and the acquiline curve of the Roman feature seemed to give the face a peculiar piquancy; the lips were full and red; the complexion, while exquisitely clear, had none of the pallor which comes from the indoor habit of life. Claudia had never been afraid of the sun and the wind, and they had dealt kindly with her, neither freckling nor tanning her face, but giving it an exquisite hue of health. Her hair, of glossy chestnut hue, was not confined in the knot which Roman fashion had borrowed from the art of Greece, but fell in long curling locks on her shoulders. Lateranus bowed over the girl's hand, and carried it to his lips.

"I greet you, fair cousin," he said with an admiring glance, "for if my aunt, who always speaks the truth, calls you daughter, my cousin you must needs be."

Claudia muttered a few words that probably were meant for thanks. They did not catch the listener's ear, though he noticed that they were spoken with the hesitation of one who was using an unfamiliar language. Then the colour which had covered the girl's cheek, as she came forward, with a brilliant flush, faded as suddenly. She cast an imploring look, as if asking for help, on the elder lady.

"Ah! my child," cried Pomponia, "you suffer. I have lived so long alone that I have grown thoughtless and selfish, or I should have known that you wanted rest after all that you have gone through. Sit you here till I can call Chloris." And she made the girl sit in the chair from which she had herself risen, while she pressed a hand-bell that stood on a table close by.

A Greek waiting-maid speedily appeared in answer to the summons.

"Have the litter brought hither," said Pomponia, "and carry the Lady Claudia to her room."

"Nay, mother," said the girl, "I should be ashamed to give so much trouble, and indeed, I do not want the litter. I will go to my room indeed, but it will be enough if Chloris will give me her arm."

"You are sure?" said the elder lady. "I have seen so little of young people of late years that I am at a loss."

"Yes, indeed, mother, quite sure," and she withdrew, supporting herself by the attendant's arm, but more in show than in reality, for indeed the faintness, quite a new sensation to Claudia's vigorous health, had quite passed away,

"My dear aunt," said Lateranus, when the girl had left the room, "this is indeed a surprise. From what quarter of the world have you imported this marvellous beauty? That she is not Latin or Greek I saw at a glance, and I have been puzzling my brain ever since to find out to what nation she belongs. Is she Gaul, or perhaps German?"

"Nay," replied Pomponia; "you must go further than Gaul or even Germany."

"Ah!" said Lateranus after reflecting for a minute or two. "By all the gods!—pardon me, aunt," he went on, seeing a shadow pass over his aunt's gentle face,—"I had forgotten. Verily, I have it! She must be British!"

"Now you are right."

"And how long has she been with you? I heard nothing of her when I was last here."

"A month only. Her coming, indeed, was quite unexpected, and to be quite candid, at first unwelcome. You know my way of life. I had grown so accustomed to being alone that I almost dreaded the sight of a new face."

"Well," said Lateranus, "a face like that need hardly frighten you."

"Ah, you think her beautiful?" cried Pomponia, her face lighted up with one of her rare smiles. "And don't you see just a little likeness to my dearest Julia?"

"Yes; there is certainly a likeness, especially about the eyes."

"As soon as I saw that, I began to love her; and indeed I soon found that she is worth loving for her own sake. And there is another reason, too, which I fear, my dear nephew, you will not understand."

"Ah! I see; she is of the same sect, I suppose. It has reached to Britain itself then. Wonderful!"

"Wonderful indeed, and more than wonderful if it were what you call it, a sect. Oh, dear Aulus, if you would but listen!"

"All in good time, dear aunt, perhaps when my Consulship is over. It would certainly be awkward if you made a proselyte of me before."

"In good time, dear Aulus! Nay, there is no time so good as this. Who knows what may happen before your Consulship is over?"

"Nay, nay, dear aunt; good words, good words! But tell me, who is this lovely Claudia?"

"You have heard your uncle speak of King Cogidumnus?"

"Yes, I remember the name. He lived somewhere, if I remember right, on the edge of the great southern forest, of which my uncle used to tell such wonders."

"Just so; he was the King of the Regni. Indeed, he is living still. Well, the King took our side. Claudius made him a Roman citizen, and allowed him to assume his own names, so that he is a Tiberius Claudius; and also enlarged his kingdom with some of the country which your uncle conquered."

"Yes, I remember now hearing about it from my friend Pudens. He was wrecked on the coast in one of those terrible storms that they have out there, and made his way to the chief town of the Regni. He found it, he told me, quite a little Rome, with a Senate, and a Forum, and baths, and a library, and I know not what besides. The King himself was quite a polished gentleman, spoke Latin admirably and even could quote Virgil and Horace. No one, to look at him, would have thought, so my friend Pudens used to say, that ten years before he had been running wild in the woods with very little on besides a few stripes of blue paint."

"Well," resumed Pomponia, "Claudia is his daughter."

"You astonish me more and more," cried Lateranus. "And pray, what brings her to Rome?"

"A prince who pays tribute to Rome in Britain can hardly feel quite safe. His countrymen are sure to hate him, and I am afraid that we who are his allies do not always treat him as we should. Claudia's father had a terrible fright three years ago, when Boadicea and the Iceni rebelled. His city would have been the next to be attacked after London, if Paulinus had not come up in time to stop them. London, you must know, is scarcely more than seventy miles off, and the Britons don't take much time over seventy miles. The King had every-thing ready to embark,—you see he has the advantage of being near the sea,—his wife, who is since dead, and Claudia, who is his only child, were actually on board a galley with the best part of his trea-sure. If the news had been bad instead of good, they would have sailed at once. Lately, it seems, he has been getting anxious again, and though he loves his daughter dearly,—the poor girl cannot speak of him without tears,—he felt that he should be much happier if she were safe. Then the death of the mother, who was an admirable woman, decided him. His nearest kinswomen are not people into whose charge he would like to put his daughter. So he sent her here, appealing to me on the score of his old friendship with my husband. I could not refuse, though I must confess that the idea was very distasteful to me. What should I do, I thought, with a young barbarian in my house? It was a wicked idea, even if it had been true, which it certainly is not. Who am I," she added in a low voice which she did not mean to reach her nephew's ears, "Who am I, that I should call aught that He has made common or unclean? In Him there is 'neither barbarian, Scythian, bond, nor free.'"

"You interest me greatly in your Claudia. But, my dear aunt, we have to consider the future, both for you and her. You know, of course, who is at the bottom of this business."

"Yes, I know—Poppæa."

"But tell me, for I confess it puzzles me, why does Poppæa hate you? That she will spare no one who stands in the way of her pleasure or her ambition I understand; but you, how do you interfere with her?"

"Listen, Aulus. Poppæa has another thing that she cares for besides pleasure and power, and that is what she calls her religion."

"But I thought—pardon me for mentioning such a creature in the same breath with you—I thought that you and she were of somewhat the same way of thinking in this matter."

"It was natural that you should. Most people who know anything at all about such things have the same notion. But it is not so. Briefly, the truth is this. The religion to which Poppæa inclines is the religion of the Jews; the faith to which, by God's mercy, I have been brought, rose up among the same nation. A Jew first gave it to men; Jews have preached it since. But those who still walk in the old ways hate them that follow the new, hate them worse than they hate the heathen. Poppæa, poor creature, knows nothing about such matters, but the men to whom she goes for counsel, the men who she hopes will find a way for her to go on sinning and yet escape the punishment of sin, the men who take her gifts for themselves and their temple, and pay for them with smooth words, they know well enough the difference between themselves and us; it is they who stir her up; it is they who have told her to make a first victim of me."

"I understand, at least in part, but what you say only makes me feel more anxious. What will you do? She has been baffled this time; but she won't take her defeat. If I am not mistaken, there is going to be a dreadful time in Rome when the law will be powerless; and I may not be able to protect you."

As he finished speaking, a slave knocked at the door of the apartment. Bidden to enter, he ushered in Subrius the Prætorian and a friend.

7

FLIGHT

"LET me present to you my friend Subrius, a Tribune of the Prætorians," said Lateranus, addressing Pomponia. "I sent for him as soon as your message reached me."

"You are very good in coming so readily to help a stranger," said Pomponia with a gracious smile.

"I do not think of the Lady Pomponia as a stranger," replied the Tribune. "I had the honour of serving my first campaign under her husband. Allow me, in my turn, to present to you my friend and kinsman, Marcus Annius Pudens. He has just returned on furlough from the Euphrates, and is staying with me in camp."

"I thank you, too, sir," said Pomponia. "It is very pleasant to find that one has so many friends."

"Well," said Lateranus, "you are come in time. Just now we don't want your swords, but we certainly want your counsel. Have I your permission," he went on, addressing himself to Pomponia, "to put the whole state of the case before these gentlemen?"

Pomponia signified her assent.

"Matters then stand thus. For reasons which it is needless at present to explain, the Lady Pomponia has incurred the enmity of Poppæa. I recognized the Empress' most trusted freedman as the leader of the attack which I had the good fortune to be able to repulse. If I know anything of her and him they won't accept defeat. The question is, what is to be done? What say you, Subrius?"

The Tribune considered awhile. "It is quite clear that Poppæa and her agent are taking advantage of an exceptional time. Commonly, even she would not have ventured so far. Men have not forgotten what Aulus Plautius did for Rome, and his widow could not have been murdered with impunity. But the city is now in an extraordinary state. Law is absolutely suspended. The Watch seems to have received instructions to do nothing, or even worse than nothing. I am convinced that this fire is not an accident; or, if it was so in the beginning, it is not in the extent to which it has reached. I am positive that this morning, as I was making my way to the camp, I saw a scoundrel throw a lighted torch through the window of a house. I seized the fellow; but his companions rescued him, and when I called for help to a squad of the Watch that happened to be close by, they stood still and did nothing."

"A big fire," remarked Pudens, "gives a fine opportunity for thieves, and they naturally make the best of it."

"True," replied the Tribune; "but why do the Watch behave as if they were in league with them? Did not the same thing strike you last night, Lateranus?"

"Yes," said Lateranus. "At first I thought that they were simply dazed by the magnitude of the disaster; afterwards I could not help seeing that they were deliberately increasing it."

"Well, then," resumed Subrius, "to come to the point that immediately concerns us. We have to reckon with an exceptional state of things. For the present, as I said, law is suspended. We can't reckon on the guardians of the peace; nor, so occupied is every one with saving themselves or their property, on the help of the public. And supposing that this house catches fire, what then? Just now it is not in danger; but who can tell what may happen? The wind may change, and then the flames might be down upon it in an hour. Or it may be deliberately set on fire. That, if I can trust my own eyes, is being done elsewhere. What would happen then? Depend upon it, Poppæa and the villains that do her bidding will be watching their opportunity, and what a terrible chance they would have of working their will amidst all the confusion of a burning house. That is my view of the situation."

"What, then, would you advise?" asked Pomponia in a tone that betrayed no agitation or alarm.

"I should say—seek some safer place," replied Subrius.

"For myself," said Pomponia after a pause, "I should be disposed to stay where I am."

"But, dearest aunt," cried Lateranus, "if what Subrius says is true, and I do not doubt for an instant that it is, that means certain death."

"And if it does, dear Aulus," replied Pomponia, "that does not seem so dreadful to me."

"But there are others," said Lateranus.

"You are right," Pomponia answered after a few minutes' reflection; "there are others. I should like, if it will not offend you, gentlemen, to ask for the counsel of one whom I greatly trust."

She pressed her hand-bell, and when the attendant appeared, said to him, "I would speak with Phlegon, if he is at leisure."

In the course of a short time, Phlegon, a Greek freedman, who was the superintendent of Pomponia's household, made his appearance. He was a man of singularly venerable appearance, nearly eighty years of age, but hale and vigorous.

"Phlegon," said Pomponia, "these gentlemen are agreed that if we stay here our lives are not safe, and they counsel us to flee. What say you? My feeling is for staying. Are we not ready? Have we not been living for twenty years past as if this might come any day? And does not the holy Paul say in that letter of which Clemens of Philippi sent us a copy the other day, 'I have a desire to depart and be with Christ'?"

"True, lady," said Phlegon; "but he goes on, if I remember right, 'But to abide in the flesh is more needful for you.' And you have others to think of, as he had. And did not the Master Himself say, 'When they persecute you in one city, flee ye to another'?"

"You are right, as usual, Phlegon," said Pomponia. "I will go; but whither? As you know, nephew," she went on, turning to Aulus, "I have sold all my country houses, as my husband's will directed me, except, indeed, the one at Antium."

"Well," said Lateranus, "it would hardly do for you to have Poppæa for a neighbour. But all my villas are at your disposal. There is one at Tibur; indeed, two at Tibur; only the second is but a poor place; one at Baiæ, another at Misenum, three at the Lake of Comum, one on Benacus, and—"

"Ah," said Subrius, laughing, "you never are able to go through the list of your country houses without stumbling. But I have an idea of my own for which I venture to think something may be said. There is a place belonging to me near Gabii. It can hardly be called a country house, it is so small, but it has, for the present purpose, some advantages. In the first place, it is very much out of the way; and in the second, it is very strong. In fact, it is an old fortress, dating back, I have been told by people who are learned in these matters, from the time of the Kings. It has a deep moat all round it, crossed only by a single bridge which can be removed at pleasure, and the walls are high and strong. In short, it is a place that would stand a siege, if need be. Anyhow, it is safe against a surprise. If the Lady Pomponia can put up with a very poor place and mean accommodation, the house, such as it is, is entirely at her service."

"An admirable plan!" cried Lateranus. "What say you, my dear aunt? I know that you do not set much store on outward things."

"No, indeed, I do not," replied Pomponia. "The offer of the Tribune Subrius I most gladly accept, but how to thank him sufficiently I do not know."

"There is no need of thanks, lady," said Subrius. "I owe everything to Aulus Plautius, who made a soldier of me when I might have been —I am not ashamed to own it—a poltroon. Do what I may, I shall never repay the debt."

"And when shall we start?" asked Pomponia.

"At once, to-night, I would suggest," answered Subrius. "The moon is nearly full, and you will barely reach my house before it sets."

Arrangements were made accordingly for a start that evening. Subrius would not be able to accompany them, for he had to be on duty in the camp, and thought it as well not to ask for leave of absence. His place was to be taken by his friend Pudens, an arrangement which would have its advantages, as the person of Pudens would not be known. For the same reason Lateranus, one of the best known, as he was one of the most popular men in Rome, determined to absent himself. But he furnished the two litters with their bearers, which were to convey Pomponia and Claudia, each with a single female attendant, and he also sent, by way of guard, the same detachment of his cohort which he had brought to the relief of the house in the morning. Pomponia's establishment, it should be said, was on the smallest scale, not because she was either poor or parsimonious, but because her great wealth was devoted to the benevolence which her faith was already beginning to make a new factor in human life.

Punctually at sunset the party started. The route chosen was naturally that which took them by the shortest way out of the city. But, small as was the space which they traversed, the sights which they encountered were harrowing in the extreme. The fire itself, in its active force, had passed elsewhere, but it had left behind it a hideous scene of desolation. Some of the larger buildings were still burning, sending up huge volumes of smoke, out of which a tongue of flame would now and then shoot forth. In some places the blackened walls stood erect, with a ghastly semblance of the human habitation which they had once contained; in others everything had fallen prostrate in undistinguishable confusion on the ground. Here and there an arch or portico tottered to its fall in a way that threatened the passer-by with instant destruction. Sometimes the traveller could see the pathetic remnant of a ruined home which by some strange chance the flames had spared, a hearth with the chairs still standing about it, a table spread with the remnants of a meal, a picture on a wall, a draught- board left just as the players had started up from it in their alarm, a harp, a baby's cradle. Now and then they came across the corpse of some unhappy inmate who had been struck by a falling stone, or half buried under some huge beam. There had not been time to remove these ghastly remains, or the calamity was so overpowering that men had lost their respect for the remains of the dead,

—always one of the worst signs of a general despair. In many places poor creatures who had lost their all were groping among the yet smoking ruins for any possession of a more durable kind that might have survived or escaped the ravages of the flames. Elsewhere, sufferers too broken by their loss to make any effort, sat by the smouldering remains of what had once been a happy home, in a mute and tearless despair. Outside the walls, the scene, though deplorable enough, was yet diversified with a more cheerful element. Groups of people, surrounded many of them by a strange and incongruous medley of possessions which they had contrived to rescue from the flames, were camping out round fires which they had lighted. Many were cooking their evening meal; some were staring motionless into the flames; not a few, with the irrepressible gayety of a southern nature, were singing merry songs or joining in some uproarious chorus.

The sight of all this distress so affected the compassionate heart of Pomponia that she could scarcely be induced to pass on. It was not, indeed, till she had exhausted all the stock of money that she had brought with her, in relieving what seemed the most urgent cases of need, that she could be persuaded to continue her journey. It was, perhaps, well for her comfort that Phlegon, who was more prudent, though not less kindly than his mistress, made a point of keeping a secret store, which he produced when everything seemed exhausted. On this occasion, when banking, in common with all other business was suspended, this resource was found particularly useful.

The party had left Rome and its environs some way behind them, when a turn of the road brought them into a full view of the quarter where the conflagration was then raging most furiously. The twilight had now passed, and the moon was low in the heavens, so that the darkness brought the awful spectacle into more prominent relief.

"Oh, mother!" cried Claudia, who had begun to use this endearing name to the elder lady, "do you think that this is the end of the world that is come?"

"Nay, my daughter; there is much to happen before that can be."

"But is Rome, think you, to be destroyed? Did not the holy

Clement say something to this purpose the other day? Did he not speak—you know that I know very little of these things—of cities that had been destroyed for their wickedness? Is not Rome very wicked?"

"Truly, my daughter; yet the Lord hath much people there, and will have more before the end shall come."

Both felt it to be a relief when another turn of the road hid again the terrible spectacle. Both turned their eyes southward, where the stars were beginning to come out in the dark purple depths of the summer night. Another half-hour's journey brought them without further adventure to their journey's end.

8

PUDENS

THE young soldier whom Subrius had put in charge of the party had fulfilled his office with a punctilious observance of his military duty. There was probably little or no danger to be apprehended after the party had once got beyond the precincts of Rome, but Pudens did not on that account relax his watchful attention to his task. During one of the halts, when Pomponia appealed to his help in distributing her charities to the sufferers from the fire, he had caught a glimpse of one of the occupants of the other litter; but, though this glimpse had greatly excited his curiosity, he did not suffer himself to indulge it. Always in the front or the rear of the party, according as the nature of the route seemed to suggest, he conducted the little company with as much precaution as if it was traversing an enemy's country. But his thoughts were busy with Pomponia's unknown companion. He was tormented, one might almost say, with that tantalizing experience which is familiar to most of us, when the recollection of a face, name, or a word seems ever to be within our grasp, and yet ever eludes us. And, all the time, he was conscious of a strange feeling that the matter was one of supreme importance to him, one, in fact, which might change the whole tenour of his life. It is no wonder then that he looked forward with impatience to the termination of the journey when he would have, he hoped, a chance of satisfying his curiosity.

His hopes were not disappointed. The ladies indeed were helped out of the litters by their own attendants, and he felt that it would have been an intrusion for him to come forward; still it was natural that he should be near, and chance favoured him with a full view of the unknown traveller. Just as the younger woman stepped from her litter, the moon shone through the clouds that had obscured it during the latter part of the journey, and fell full upon her face, and on a lock of long, light-coloured hair that had escaped from its fastening, and fallen upon her shoulder. In an instant his mind was illuminated with a flash of recognition and recollection. If confirmation had been wanted, it would have been supplied by the tone of her voice, as she chanced to address to Pomponia a few words expressive of delight at the safe termination of their journey.

"Great Jupiter!" said Pudens to himself, "it is Claudia!"

In the surprise of the moment the words were spoken half aloud. The girl, catching the sound of her name, and equally taken by surprise, half turned, but recollected herself before the action was completed. But the gesture showed outlines of figure and a pose that were familiar to the young man, as he stood, himself almost invisible in the shadow, eagerly watching the scene.

It is now time for me to explain to my readers who Pudens was, and how he came to have made acquaintance with the Princess from Britain.

Annius Pudens was the son of a man who had the reputation of being the very richest member of the wealthiest class in Rome, the knights. The elder Pudens had made his immense fortune by farming the public revenue and by money- lending. It would not have been well to inquire too closely into the methods by which it was accumulated. Some of his rivals used to say—the remark may of course have been suggested by the jealousy of trade—that his contracts were often obtained on remarkably easy terms, and from officials who had themselves been treated with equal consideration by the contractor in other matters. But nothing was ever proved, or, indeed, attempted to be proved. The loans Pudens had the prudence to make a long way from Rome. The rate of interest was higher in the provinces than in the capital, and the recovery of a debt could be effected without making any unpleasant disturbance. The small tributary kings, who were permitted by the good pleasure of Rome to keep up a shadowy sovereignty in some of the regions of the East, were among Pudens' best clients. Thirty, forty, even fifty per cent was not too much for these potentates to pay when some caprice of the moment was to be gratified. Rulers who have lost the realities of power commonly think more of its indulgences, and they emptied their treasuries to secure a beautiful slave, a fine singer or musician, or a jewel of unusual size. Pudens had always the gift of knowing exactly how far he could go. This knowledge, and the fact that his claims would be backed up by Roman arms, insured him against loss. The general result of his operations, public and private, was, as has been said, the acquisition of an enormous fortune.

The elder Pudens had one great object always before him, and this was to give his son all that was desirable in life; one, I say, because this was really the motive of that devotion to money-making, which was commonly believed to be his ruling passion. For this son, an only child, left motherless in early infancy, nothing was too good, nothing too costly. Unfortunately, the father, who was a man of limited intelligence and feeble judgment, except in the one matter of money-making, set about securing his object in the very worst fashion imaginable. He knew that money can do much, and he imagined that it can do everything. He believed that he could furnish his child with all that he ought to have if he only paid enough for it. Himself a man of frugal and even parsimonious habits,—the common pleasures of life had no attractions for him,—he gave the child the very costliest establishment that could be purchased for money. For the nurses who attended to his wants when he was an infant, the slaves who waited on him in his boyhood, he gave the highest possible prices, and thought that in giving them he was necessarily securing the best of service. And he had, it must be owned, some ill luck in efforts that were really well meant. A friend had told him that slaves were not to be trusted, and he put a lady of respectable family over his son's establishment. Unfortunately, she was a selfish, unprincipled woman, whose only object was to make a purse for herself and to secure an easy life by indulging her young charge. A still more fatal mistake was the choice of a tutor. A smooth-tongued Greek, who concealed under a benign and even venerable exterior almost every vice of which humanity is capable, palmed himself off upon the credulous father, and was installed as the "guide, philosopher, and friend" of the unlucky son.

Happily for himself, the younger Pudens had a nature that refused to be entirely spoiled. He had an innate refinement that shrunk from the worst excesses, a kindly and unselfish temper that kept his heart from being utterly hardened by indulgences, a taste for sport and athletics that gave him plenty of harmless and healthy employment, and a love of letters which commonly secured for study some part of his days and nights.

Still he was on the high road to ruin, when, just as he was entering on his nineteenth year, he lost his father. Happily, the elder Pudens, in appointing a guardian for his son, had for once made a wise choice. He had asked Subrius, who was a distant kinsman, to accept the office, and the Prætorian had consented, little thinking that he should ever be called upon to act, for indeed the testator was little older than himself. When he found that his guardianship had become an actual responsibility, he acted with vigour. He seized the opportunity when the son was under the softening impression of his recent loss, and used it with the very best effect. He avoided anything like rebuke, but appealed to the young man's pride and to his adventurous spirit, as well as to the momentary disgust at his useless and discreditable existence which had come over him. Active service as a soldier was the remedy which Subrius prescribed, and, if the expression may be allowed, lost no time in administering. Almost before the young Pudens could reflect, he was on his way to join as a volunteer the army of Britain, then under the command of one of the most distinguished generals of the time, Suetonius Paulinus.

His career was very near being cut short before he reached his destination. The galley which was to convey him from Gaul to the port of Regnum encountered a violent gale from the southwest on its way, was driven on to the Needles, then, as now, one of the most dangerous spots on the southern coast, and dashed in pieces. The only survivors of the wreck were Pudens and two young sailors. He owed his life to his vigorous frame and to his power of swimming; powers well known on the Campus, where he had been accustomed to distance all competitors, sometimes crossing the Tiber as many as ten times. He struggled to one of the little bays of beach which were to be found at the foot of the cliffs of Vectis, contrived to climb the almost precipitous face of the rock, and after various adventures,—his perils were not ended with his escape from the waves,—contrived to reach Regnum in safety.

Cogidumnus, the native ruler, a far-sighted prince, who had discovered that the friendship of Rome, if not actually desirable, was at least better than its enmity, received the stranger in the most hospitable fashion. Pudens, after giving, not very willingly, a couple of days to rest, was on the point of setting out to join the army of Paulinus when news from Eastern Britain changed all his plans. The powerful tribe of the Iceni had broken out in open revolt. The colony of Camalodunum had been utterly destroyed, and Boadicea, the leader of the rebellion, had sworn that every town in Britain that had accepted the Roman supremacy should share its fate. Swift messengers were on their way to recall Paulinus from the Northwest, whither he had gone to attack the Druid stronghold of Mona. Whether he would get back in time, or, getting back in time, would be strong enough to save the friendly Britons of the South from the fate that threatened them, seemed only too doubtful.

These gloomy tidings reached Regnum in the early morning, just as Pudens was about to start. The King was intending to ride with his guest for the first stage of his journey, a stage which would take him across the Downs into the valley of the stream now known as the Western Rother. His daughter, an active and spirited girl of sixteen, who as an only and motherless child was her father's habitual companion, was going to form one of the party. Just as they were riding out of the court-yard of the palace, a messenger hurried up in breathless haste. He had been sent by the King's agent at Londinium, a trader to whom Cogidumnus was accustomed to consign such goods in the way of skins, agricultural produce, and the like as he had to dispose of. He had traversed in about twenty-four hours more than seventy miles, mostly of rough forest paths, and was in the last stage of exhaustion. The message, written, for safety's sake, on a small piece of paper which its bearer could have made away with in a moment, ran thus:—

"Camalodunum has been destroyed. Boadicea will enter Londinium in a few hours. I have heard nothing of Paulinus. Save yourself."

In the course of about half an hour the messenger, who was a well-trained and practised runner, had recovered sufficiently to be able to tell what he knew. Suetonius, he said, had returned, and had actually marched into Londinium, but had evacuated it again, feeling that he was not strong enough to hold it. He had about ten thousand men with him, less by nearly a half than what he had expected to put into the field, because,—so the messenger had heard,—the commanding officer of the Second Legion had refused to leave his quarters. Paulinus, accordingly, had occupied a strong position to the north of the city, and had left Londinium to its fate. Of what had happened since his departure the messenger could not speak with certainty, but looking back when he reached the highest point of the range now known as the Hog's Back, he had seen a great glare of light in the northeastern sky, and did not doubt that Londinium was in flames.

The King was perfectly aware of the gravity of the situation. Verulamium, situated as it was little more than twenty miles from Londinium, would probably be the next object of attack; after that his own turn would come. In the meantime, what was to be done? The King's natural impulse was to make the best preparations that he could for defending Regnum. He had begun to make a hasty calculation of what was wanted and of what he had at his command, when the Princess showed herself in a character that fairly astonished the young Roman.

"Father!" she cried, "it is idle to think of our defending ourselves here. If Paulinus cannot stand against Boadicea and her army, how shall we do it, when we shall be left alone with all Britain against us? Send every man we have to help the Romans now. Then they will be of some use. I wish to Heaven I were a man that I might go with them!"

Pudens was not unaccustomed to see precocity in his own country-women. Roman girls began to think and talk of love and lovers before they were well in their teens. But this clear and vigorous intelligence, this ready comprehension of affairs in one who seemed little more than a child, surprised him beyond measure. The advice itself seemed admirable, and he seconded it with all his might, offering at the same time his own services in any capacity in which they might be made useful. The upshot of the matter was that in the course of the day an advance force of some hundreds of men started to join the Roman army. The King himself was to follow as speedily as possible with the remainder of his available troops; Claudia, with her attendants, was put for safety on board a galley in the harbour, the captain having instructions to make for a port in Gaul in case any disaster should happen. She accepted the situation with a practical good sense which impressed Pudens almost as much as her spirit and promptitude had done before.

He did not see her again. He started that evening, and was able to reach the camp of Paulinus before the great battle which may be said to have settled the fate of Britain for the next three centuries. He was seriously wounded in the battle with the Iceni, and after his recovery did not care to prolong his service with the general, who, though a great soldier, was a harsh administrator. He had come to see war, and the task of hunting down the defeated rebels, in which Paulinus would have employed him, was not to his taste. Pleading a wish to enlarge his military experience, he obtained permission to transfer himself to the Army of the Upper Rhine, and from thence again to the Armenian frontier. Here his health had somewhat failed, and he had been sent home on leave. But wherever he had been he had carried with him the recollection of that bright, eager face, that clear, ringing voice. It was a strange sentiment, one which he scarcely acknowledged to himself and which he would certainly have found it impossible to define. She was but a child, and he had seen her once only, and then for but a few minutes. He had scarcely exchanged a word with her. But her image seemed to cling to his thoughts with a strange persistence. In the battle and in the bivouac "her face across his fancy came," till he began to fancy it a talisman of safety, and now, when he found himself again in Rome, it made the old evil associations into which opportunity and the want of employment might have thrown him again, seem utterly distasteful.

It is easy to believe that as he rode slowly back to the city that night, leaving some half-dozen trusty men to protect the house, the familiar image presented itself to his thoughts more vividly than ever.

9

AN IMPERIAL MUSICIAN

NERO, as my readers will have guessed, had not been able to keep his secret. The audacity of his plan—an Emperor setting his own capital on fire that he might rebuild it after his own designs—had inspired him with a delight that quite exceeded his powers of self-control. He could not help letting drop hints of his purpose in the presence of Poppæa, and these were further explained by words which she overheard him muttering in his sleep. Tigellinus, though no confidences were made to him, was equally well aware of what his master intended. No department in the public service but contained some of his creatures, and the secret instructions that the Emperor gave to the commanding officers of the watch, summoned, it should be said, to Antium for the purpose of receiving them, did not long escape him. The despot's two councillors were rendered, as may readily be supposed, not a little anxious by their master's frantic caprice. Both were ready enough to use it for their own purposes. Poppæa, as we have seen, found in it, as she hoped, an opportunity of destroying Pomponia; while Tigellinus had grudges of his own to pay off under cover of the general terror and confusion. But they could not help feeling great apprehensions of the effect on the popular feeling. An Emperor might murder and confiscate as much as he pleased, so long as it was only the noble and wealthy who suffered; but when his oppression began to touch common folk, the trader or the artisan, then danger was at hand. If the Romans began to suspect that they had been burnt out of their homes to gratify a caprice of their ruler, not all his legions would be able to save him.

The anxiety of Nero's advisers was greatly increased by his obstinacy in refusing to go to Rome. Relays of messengers came from the capital in rapid succession, bringing tidings of the progress of the fire, but the Emperor positively refused to leave Antium.

Tigellinus ventured on a strong remonstrance.

"Pardon me, Sire," he said, "if I say that the Roman people will take your absence at this time very ill. It has pleased the gods"—he was careful, it will be seen, not to hint that he knew the truth—"to visit them with a great calamity, and they will expect some sympathy and help from him whom they regard as a god upon earth. No ruler could endure to be away when the seat of Empire is in flames, much less one who is justly styled the Father of his Country."

The advice, sugared though it was with flattery, was decidedly unpalatable. Nero's brow darkened, as he listened, with the frown that always gathered upon it when any one ventured to hint that there were any limitations on his power, or that he could be called to account by any one for the way in which he exercised it.

"What do you say?" he cried, with an angry stamp of the foot. "A pretty thing, indeed, that a father should be called to account by his children! Who will venture to say whether I ought to go or to stay?"

In the course of the second day news arrived that the palace itself was in danger. If Tigellinus hoped that this intelligence would move the Emperor he was greatly disappointed. Nero received the tidings with what appeared to be complete indifference.

"A paltry place," he cried with a contemptuous shrug of his shoulders, "and not in the least worthy of an Emperor! Let it burn, and welcome! I shall be saved the trouble of pulling it down. And besides," he added with a laugh, "the people about whom you think so much, my Tigellinus, will surely be satisfied now. What can they want more than to see my house burning as well as their own?"

Tigellinus was in despair. So imperious was the necessity that he was meditating another remonstrance, which yet he felt would probably do nothing more than endanger his own head, when Poppæa's woman's wit suggested a way out of the difficulty.

"What a spectacle it must be!" she said to Tigellinus in a low tone that was yet carefully modulated to catch the Emperor's ear. "All Rome in flames! There never has been anything like it before; there never will be again. If we are to have the city burnt, let us at least have the consolation of seeing the blaze."

Nero fell promptly into the trap. "You are right, my soul," he cried. "It must be a splendid sight, and I am losing it. Why did you not think of it before? Tigellinus, we will start at once. There is not a moment to be lost."

The Emperor's impatience to be gone, now that the idea had been suggested to him, was as great as his indifference had been before. He would allow no time for the preparations for departure. The slaves would follow, he said, with what was wanted. Too much of the sight had been lost already. "Good Heavens!" he cried, "what a fool I have been! The finest spectacle of the age, and I am not there to see it!"

Within an hour's time he was on horseback, and was riding at full speed northward, accompanied by Tigellinus and by such an escort as could hastily be got ready. Poppæa followed in a carriage as rapidly as she could.

The distance between Antium and Rome, which was something like thirty miles, was covered by the horsemen in less than three hours. From the first a heavy cloud of smoke was visible in the northeastern sky; as the riders went on they encountered other signs of the disaster. There was a constant stream of carts and wagons loaded with furniture and other miscellaneous effects, that were travelling southward. The owners of the property accompanied them on foot, though now and then a child or an old man or woman might be seen perched on the top of the goods. These, of course, were people who had been burnt out by the fire, and who were now seeking a temporary home with relatives or friends whom they were fortunate enough to possess in the country. As they approached the walls, the fields on either side of the road were covered with tents and huts in which the homeless refugees had found shelter. The roads themselves were lined with people who, indeed, had no other occupation but to watch the passers- by. The beggars, always numerous along the great thoroughfares, were now in greater force than ever. Tigellinus, who, vicious as he was, was a man of intelligence and foresight, had brought with him all the money that he could collect. This Nero scattered with a liberal hand among the crowds as he rode along. This is a kind of bounty that has always an effective appearance, though the money commonly falls into the hands of those who need it least. The spectators cheered the Emperor, whose well-known features were recognized everywhere, with tumultuous shouts. But there were not a few who turned away in silent disgust or wrath. They did not, indeed, attribute directly to him the calamity which had overtaken them, as they might have done had they known the truth, but they laid it at his door all the same. He was a great criminal, a murderer, and a parricide; his offences were rank before heaven, and had brought down, as the offences of rulers are apt to bring down, the anger of the gods upon his people.

The palace was not, it was found, in immediate danger. All the efforts of the Watch and of two cohorts of Prætorians, which had been called in to help them, had been directed to saving it. How long it would escape was doubtful. If the wind, which had lulled a little, were to rise again, its destruction was certain.

The Emperor would have been disappointed if this destruction had been finally averted. We have seen that one of the great features of the new Rome that he had planned was an Imperial palace far larger and more splendid than anything that the world had ever seen before. Still he was glad of the respite, for it enabled him to put into execution a scheme, extravagantly strange, even for him, which he had conceived during his rapid journey from Antium to Rome.

"A spectacle," he thought to himself, "and if so, why not a performance? What a splendid opportunity! We always feel that there is something of a sham in the scenery of a theatre, but here it will be real. An actual city on fire! What could be more magnificent? I have it," he went on after a pause. "Of course it must be the Sack of Troy. What a pity it is that I did not think of it sooner, and I might have written something worthy of the occasion. The Lesser Iliad is but poor stuff, but we must make the best of it."

This grotesque intention was actually carried out.

The first care of the Emperor on reaching the palace was to have a rehearsal of his contemplated performance. If there were any cares of Empire pressing for attention,—and it may be supposed that the ruler of the civilized world returning to his capital had some business to attend to,—they were put aside. The rest of the day Nero spent in practising upon the harp some music of his own composition, while a Greek freedman recited from the Lesser Iliad a passage in which the sack and burning of Troy were related.

In the evening the performance took place. A large semicircular room in the upper story of the palace, commanding from its windows a wide prospect of the city, was hastily fitted up into the rude semblance of a theatre. An audience, which mainly consisted of the Emperor's freedmen and of officers of the Prætorian Guard, sat on chairs ranged round the curve of the chamber. In front of them was the extemporized stage, while the burning city, seen through the windows, formed, with huge masses of smoke and flame, such a background as the most skilful and audacious of scene-painters had never conceived. The performance had been purposely postponed till a late hour in the evening, and no lights were permitted in the room. On the stage were the two figures, the reciter and the Imperial musician, now thrown strongly into relief as some great sheet of flame burst out in the background, and then, as it died away again, becoming almost invisible. An undertone of confused sound accompanied the music throughout. Every now and then the voice of the reciter and the notes of the harp were lost in some shrill cry of agony or the thunderous crash of a falling house. Seldom in the history of the world has there been a stranger mixture of the ludicrous and the terrible than when "Nero fiddled while Rome was burning."

At one time it was not unlikely that this strange farce might have been turned into a genuine tragedy. Subrius was one of the Prætorian officers invited to witness the performance, and chance had placed him close to the stage. Again and again as the Emperor moved across it, intent upon his music, and certainly unsuspicious of danger, he came within easy reach of the Tribune's arm.

"Shall I strike?" he whispered into the ear of Lateranus, who sat by his side. "I can hardly hope for a better chance."

Probably a prompt assent from his companion would have decided him; but Lateranus felt unequal to giving it. He was staggered by the suddenness of the idea. The decision was too momentous, the responsibility too great. Was it right to act without the knowledge of the other conspirators? Then nothing had been prepared. Nero might be killed, but no arrangements had been made for presenting a successor to the soldiers and to the people. Finally, there was the immediate danger to themselves. It would indeed be a memorable deed to strike down this unworthy ruler in the very act of disgracing the people, to strike him down before the eyes of the creatures who flattered and fawned on him. But could they who did it hope to escape? "The desire of escape," says the historian who relates the incident, "is always the foe of great enterprises," and it checked that night a deed which might have changed the course of history.

"No!" whispered Lateranus in reply, "it is too soon; nothing, you know, is ready. We shall not fail to find another opportunity."

Half reluctant, half relieved, Subrius abandoned his half-formed purpose. But he could not rid himself of the feeling that he had missed a great chance.

"Do you believe in inspirations?" he asked his friend, as they were making their way to the camp, where Lateranus was his guest.

"I hardly know," replied the other. "Perhaps there are such things. But, on the whole, men find it safer to act after deliberation."

"Well," said Subrius, "if ever I felt an inspiration, it was to-night when I whispered to you. I fear much that we shall never have so fair a chance again."

"But nothing was ready," urged his companion.

"True," replied Subrius; "but then one does not prepare for such an enterprise as this as one prepares for a campaign."

"And the risk?"

"True, the risk. It is not that one is afraid to venture one's life; but one wants to see the fruit of one's deed. Yet I much misdoubt me whether this is not a fatal weakness. One ought to do the right thing at the time, and think of nothing else. If Cassius Chærea had taken any thought for his own safety, he would never have slain the monster Caius. I feel that hereafter we shall be sorry for what we have done, or, rather, not done, to-day."

10

A GREAT BRIBE

HE fire continued to devour its prey almost without let or hindrance. Even before the end of the performance described in my last chapter it had come so near that the heat could be distinctly felt by the spectators. Nero, whose ambition it was to imitate the imperturbable self-possession of a great actor, affected to be unconscious of what everybody else felt to be inconvenient, if not alarming. He gave the whole of the piece down to the very last flourish or roulade, and, when at last it was concluded, came forward again and again to receive the applause which a clique of duly practised flatterers did not fail time after time to renew.

In spite, however, of this seeming composure, the Emperor was seriously agitated. The fire was a monster which he had created, but which he could not control. It did not limit its ravages to what he wished to see swept away. Even the most reckless of rulers could not view with total indifference the destruction of relics of antiquity which he knew that his subjects regarded with universal reverence. The damage indeed was incredibly great. It may be said, in fact, that all ancient Rome disappeared. Among the losses was the very oldest structure in the city, one that dated from before its foundation, going back to the little Greek colony which had once existed on the Palatine, the altar which Evander the Arcadian consecrated to Hercules, and at which, it was said, the hero himself had feasted. Another was the temple vowed to Jupiter the Stayer by Romulus in the anxious moment when the fate of the infant Empire seemed to be hanging in the balance; a third was the palace of Numa, still roofed with the primitive thatch under which the earliest of the Roman law- givers had been content to find shelter. A fourth, the most disastrous loss of all, as appealing most strongly to the public sentiment, was what may be called the Hearth of the Roman People, the Temple of the Household Gods of Rome, which stood on the summit of the Palatine Hill. Not only was the building destroyed, but the images themselves, said to be the very same that Æneas had carried out of burning Troy, and, undoubtedly, of an immemorial antiquity, perished with it.

Active exertions were now taken to check the conflagration. On the sixth day a huge gap was made by the destruction of a great block of buildings at the foot of the Esquiline, the Emperor himself superintending the operation. For a time this energetic remedy promised to be effective; but, after nightfall, the fire broke out again, and raged for three days longer, this time consuming regions of the city which Nero himself in his wildest mood would never have dreamt of destroying. When at last the second outburst was checked, it was found that out of the fourteen districts into which Rome was divided, four only remained untouched. In three there was absolutely nothing left; in the other seven some buildings, most of them bare walls, still stood, but many more had perished, or were in such a state that they would have to be pulled down.

Eager as he was to commence the building of a new and more splendid Rome, Nero was obliged first to consider the pressing needs of the houseless multitude which crowded every open space in the neighbourhood of the city. Policy, for of sympathy he seems to have been hardly capable, made him spare neither trouble nor expense in relieving their wants. To house them he gave up the splendid structures which Agrippa, the son-in-law of Augustus, had erected in the Field of Mars. The noble colonnades, the baths, commonly reserved for the Imperial use, the vast enclosures where the people still met, not indeed to elect, but to register their master's choice of Consuls, Prætors, and Tribunes; even the temples were thrown open to shelter the houseless crowds. As these did not suffice, huts and tents were hastily erected in the Emperor's own gardens, slight structures, of course, but still sufficient for the purpose, for it was the height of summer, and it was the sun rather than the rain from which shelter was chiefly wanted.

The sufferers, of course, had to be fed as well as lodged. The gratuitous distributions of corn, which it was customary to make, were more frequent and more extensive, for there was a total suspension of business, and many who were not usually pensioners on the bounty of the State had to be relieved. To meet the case of those who were too independent to receive alms, and yet were scarcely above the need of them, the price of corn was lowered by a subvention to the merchants from the Emperor's purse. Wheat became cheap beyond all precedent, a bushel being sold for two shillings. The wealthy nobles, either from compassion for the sufferers, or, where this was wanting, at a peremptory suggestion from Nero, supplemented the Emperor's bounty by a copious distribution of gifts. These gifts were always common, even respectable people condescending to supplement their income by what they received from the great houses to which they were attached by the tie of clientship; now they became more frequent and more extensive, and were on a much more liberal scale.

The enormous operations of clearing away the ruins and building a new city furnished an immense amount of employment and stimulated trade; in fact, in one way or another, put a great deal of money in circulation. But, in addition to food, shelter, and employment, the people wanted another thing, if they were to be kept in good humour, and that was amusement. In furnishing this Nero consulted his own tastes as well as his interests. As soon as was possible, and even while much that would have been thought far more necessary yet remained to be done, Nero made preparations to give a grand entertainment, the splendour of which could not fail, he hoped, to put Rome into a good humour. It is quite possible that from his point of view he was right. The passion of the populace for these great shows was bound-less. Of the two things for which they were said to have bartered their freedom, gratuitous food and gratuitous spectacles, the latter was the more coveted. Rome would have preferred being hungry to being dull.

The solid structure of the great Circus had, as has been said, resisted the fire. What had perished was hastily renewed, and no pains or money, scarce as money was at a time of such vast expenditure, was spared in collecting ample materials for exhibition. Gladiators were, of course, abundant, and gladiators were always the staple of a popular show. Give the Roman spectator bloodshed enough and he could not fail to be satisfied. Of the curiosities of the Circus, as they may be called, the rare beasts, the performing animals, and the like, there was a less plentiful supply. Many had been destroyed in the fire, and substitutes could not be provided in a hurry; still a certain number were available. The menageries of the great provincial towns were swept bare to supply this sudden demand from the capital, and private owners were eager to do their best to supply an Imperial customer, who paid well for what he bought, and had a way of taking by force what he wanted, if the persuasion of a large price was not enough.

The day of exhibition was in the latter end of September, somewhat less than three months, i.e.; after the catastrophe of the fire. It had not been possible to make the arrangements sooner, and indeed the Romans preferred the spring and autumn weather for their great shows. The more temperate weather suited the spectators better than did either the cold of winter or the extreme heat of summer. Everything favoured the spectacle. The day was both cloudless and windless, both circumstances that contributed to its success. Nothing, indeed, could have been finer than the sight of the vast building filled from end to end with a crowd of spectators, the men wearing spotless white gowns and crowned with garlands of flowers, the women habited in a rich variety of colours. The effect of the sun shining through the red and purple awning that was stretched over the heads of the people was itself very striking.

The show began, as usual, with the exhibition of rare and beautiful animals. Bloodshed, as has been said, was the staple of the entertainment; but as the hors d'œuvres, the soup, the fish, and the various
dishes lead up to the pièces de résistance in a banquet, so the appetite
of the Roman public was whetted with various curiosities before it
was allowed to reach the great business of the day. Ostriches, whose
white plumage was dyed with vermilion, for the false taste of the
Romans was not satisfied with nature, lions with gilded manes, and
antelopes and gazelles, curiously adorned with light-colored scarves
and gold tinsel, trooped in succession across the arena, each under
the charge of its keeper. The tameness of some of these animals was
wonderful. If one could not praise the art with which it had been
sought to heighten their natural beauty of form and hue, yet the skill
with which their innate savagery and wildness had been subdued
was truly admirable. Lions yoked with tigers, and panthers harnessed
with bears, were seen drawing carriages with all the docility of the
horse. Wild bulls were seen, now permitting boys and girls to dance
upon their backs, and now, at the word of command, standing erect
on their hind legs. A still more wonderful sight was when a lion
hunted a hare, caught it, and carried it in its mouth, unhurt, to its
master. This performance, indeed, brought down a tremendous
round of applause. Nero summoned the trainer of the lion to his seat,
and praised him highly for his skill. The man answered him with a
compliment which may fairly be described as having been as neat as
it was false. "It is no skill of mine, my lord," he said, "that has worked
this marvel; the beast is gentle because he knows how gentle is the
Emperor whom he serves."

Gentleness, certainly, was not the prevailing characteristic of the
sports that followed. A Roman's curiosity and love of the marvellous
were easily satisfied. Of fighting he never could have enough. He
loved best to do it himself,—it is but justice to say so much for him,—
and next he loved to see others do it. The first kind of combat exhibited was of beast against beast. A dog of the Molossian breed, much
the same as our mastiff, a breed famous then, as now, for strength
and courage, was matched with a bull, and came off victorious. A lion

was pitted against a tiger, but proved to be far inferior not only in courage, but in strength. A combat between a bull and a rhinoceros was a great disappointment to the spectators, who expected a novel sensation from combatants which, as far as was known, had never contended together before. First, the rhinoceros was very reluctant to engage with his adversary. Amidst yells and shouts of derision from the crowd he retreated into his cage. It was only after hot iron had been applied to its hide, the extraordinary thickness of which resisted the application of the goad, and trumpets had been blown into its ears, that the creature was induced to advance. And then the conflict, when it did take place, was of the very briefest. The bull, a naturally savage animal, who had been goaded into madness by fluttering pennons of red and by the pricks of spears, rushed furiously forward to vent its rage, after the manner of its kind, on the first object that it saw. The rhinoceros lifted its head and sent the bull flying into the air as easily as if it had been a truss of straw. When the bull came to the ground, it was absolutely dead, its enemy's horn having pierced a vital part.

Another novel spectacle, a lion matched against a crocodile, was scarcely more successful. The lion approached its strange antagonist, and laid hold of it, but rather it seemed from curiosity than from anger. A short inspection seemed to satisfy the beast that the strange, scaly creature was not a desirable or even possible prey. Loosing his hold, he carelessly turned away, and cantered round the arena, glaring in a very alarming way through the grating which separated him from the lowest tier of spectators. As for the crocodile, whatever its intentions, it was helpless. Its movements on land were far too cumbrous to allow it to force a battle on its antagonist.

When the wild beast show had been finished there was an interval for refreshment. The Emperor, anxious to please the multitude, had provided for the gratuitous distribution of an immense quantity of food. Slaves carrying huge baskets of loaves were followed by others with baskets, equally huge, of sausages. Almost every one who cared to have his food supplied in this way was able to get it for nothing. Wine was not absolutely given away, but it was sold at a rate so cheap that the poorest spectator could purchase enough or even more than enough. The smallest coin, an as, equivalent to something less than a half-penny, could purchase half a sextarius—a sextarius may be taken as roughly equivalent to a pint—of very fair liquor, rough, of course, but well- bodied and sound, and far superior to the posca or diluted vinegar which formed the staple drink of the lowest class. When the exhibition recommenced, about two hours after noon, the spectators were in a state of uproarious good humour.

The first exhibition of the afternoon was a chariot-race. The competing chariots were kept in a set of chambers, technically called "prisons," which were furnished with folding doors that opened out on to the race-course. When the presiding officer gave the usual signal for starting by dropping a napkin, slaves who were told off to perform this office simultaneously opened the doors of the "prisons," and the chariots, which were standing ready for a start within, made the best of their way out. In theory this was as fair a method of proceeding as possible; but in practise difficulties arose. The slaves did not always work with absolute uniformity. It was whispered that they were sometimes bribed to bungle over their task; and as the business of racing, and especially horse-racing, has always given occasion to a great deal of rascality, the suspicion was probably well-founded. On the present occasion there was certainly a hitch which may or may not have been accidental, but which certainly caused a great amount of irritation among the spectators. The doors of one of the "prisons" stuck fast for a few moments, and the chariot inside had, in consequence, a most unfavourable start. As the driver was a special favourite with the people, wore the most popular colours, and had the reputation of never having been beaten in a fair race, this contretemps was received with a perfect howl of execration. Man and horses did their best as soon as they were able to get away; chariot after chariot was passed, till of the six that had started, only one was left to vanquish. But this competitor could not be overtaken. He had got a start of nearly half a lap out of the seven which made up the course; and as he was a skilful driver, with an excellent team of horses, this advantage gave him the victory. For a moment, indeed, the race seemed undecided. Just as the two remaining competitors, all other rivals having by this time been distanced, were nearing the turning-point in the last lap, the charioteer who had been so unluckily delayed made a supreme effort to secure the advantage of the nearer curve. In his excitement he used the lash too freely. The spirited animal which he struck resented the blow, and swerved so violently as to throw the charioteer. The man burst into tears of vexation and rage, due at least as much to the feeling of self- reproach as to vexation at his ill-fortune. Not even the purse of gold which Nero threw to him, nor the sympathizing cries from his friends among the crowd, consoled him.

After this everything seemed to go wrong. When the gladiators came on the scene, which they did immediately after the decision of the chariot-race, the popular favourite was almost uniformly unlucky. A veteran net-fighter, who had been victorious in a hundred battles, and who was accustomed to charm the spectators by the easy dexterity with which he would entangle his adversary, made an unlucky slip as he was throwing his net, and was stabbed to the heart by a mere tyro, who had never before appeared in the arena. Another old favourite, a mirmillo, from some unaccountable cause lost his nerve, when confronted with an active young Thracian, in whom he had not expected to find a formidable enemy, and having delivered to no purpose his favourite stroke, actually turned to fly. The populace, forgetting as usual the poor fellow's many successes, expressed its disapprobation by an angry howl, and when the fugitive was struck down, absolutely refused to spare his life.

When at last the show was over, when the dead, of whom some thirty lay on the sand, had been examined by an attendant habited as Charon, ferryman of the Styx, and removed under the superintendence of another official who bore the wand of Hermes the Conductor of Souls, the irritation of the populace broke forth in angry cries levelled against no less a personage than the Emperor himself. The Circus, it must be remembered, was the place where something of the old liberty of the Roman people still remained. There it was still permitted to them to express their wants and their dislikes. The Emperors, despotic as they were, were prudent enough to allow a safety-valve for a discontent which, if always suppressed, might have become really dangerous; nor were they averse to thus learning without the intervention of others what their humbler subjects really thought and felt. On this occasion there was a really formidable manifestation of feeling. Loud cries of "Incendiary!" "Paris the Firebrand!" and, with allusion to former misdeeds, of "Orestes the Matricide!" "Vengeance for Agrippina!" "Vengeance for Octavia!" "Vengeance for Britannicus!" "Give us back the children of Augustus!" rent the air. The Emperor at first affected indifference or disdain. Coming to the front of the magnificent box from which he had witnessed the spectacle, he threw the contents of bags of coin among the crowd. Many of the malcontents were not proof against this bribe, and scrambled for the coins with the usual eagerness, but some were seen to spit upon what they had picked up, and throw them away again with a gesture of disgust. Nero then hastily left the Circus, closely guarded by a cohort of Prætorians. He had at last learnt that there was a formidable amount of discontent which he must find some means of allaying.

11

A SCAPEGOAT

O N the evening of the day of the great show just described, Nero was again deep in consultation with his two advisers. He had been profoundly impressed by the manifestations of popular feeling that he had that day witnessed in the Circus. Hitherto he had been, on the whole, in spite of his follies and excesses, a popular Emperor. The nobility hated him, not without cause, for the most illustrious among them could not feel that property or life were safe under his rule. The small party of independent patriots, which a hundred and twenty years of despotic rule had left, loathed and despised the young mountebank who was squandering away all the resources, and tarnishing all the glories of Rome. But the multitude had a strange indulgence for their young ruler. His presence, stately enough when the defects of his figure were concealed, his handsome face, his open hand,—for he could give away as well as spend,—his very vices, so magnificent was the scale on which they were practised, attracted a certain interest and even favour. As long as this popular favour lasted, and the soldiers were kept in good humour, a point on which his vigilance never relaxed, Nero felt himself safe, in spite of the hatred of the nobles and the philosophers. Accordingly the seditious cries that he had heard during the day, heard too at the close of an entertainment in which the amusement of the multitude had been provided for with lavish care, alarmed him greatly, and he lost no time in seeking advice.

No direct reference was made to the immediate occasion of the consultation either by the Emperor or by his advisers. It was not etiquette to suppose that any one would venture to utter injurious words against the Augustus, the Master of Rome, the equal of gods. The same silence was observed as to the real truth about the fire. Nero, as we have seen, had not been able to keep his own secret; he had even gone the length, in moments of abandonment, of boasting of his deed, and that to both of the persons present; but nevertheless both he and they agreed in speaking of it as a disastrous event of which the cause was yet to be discovered.

The Emperor opened the discussion:—

"Tigellinus," he said, "the gods have visited Rome with a great calamity. Such things do not happen without a cause. There must have been some great wickedness, some monstrous impiety at work. The people demand, and are right in demanding, the punishment of the guilty. Tell me, how are they to be found? And when they are found, how are they to be punished?"

"Sire," said Tigellinus, "I have inquired of the Triumvirs, and they tell me that they have in custody twenty or thirty wretches who were caught, red- handed, spreading the fire. Some of them were also convicted of robbery, and some of murder. What say you, Sire, to having a public execution of these malefactors? They might suffer together, and the spectacle might be made sufficiently imposing to satisfy the just indignation of the people."

The proposition was made and received with a perfect gravity which did credit to the power of acting possessed by the speaker and his hearers.

Nero affected to meditate. The real thought in his mind was that some of the victims might make awkward revelations. What he said was this:—

"The punishment, however exemplary, of some score of incendiaries, will not suffice. If it had been the case of some provincial municipality destroyed, it might have been otherwise. Is it not possible that the enemies of the Roman people, the Parthians or the Germans, have plotted the destruction of the seat of Empire?"

"The Parthians, Sire," returned Tigellinus with an air of profound humility, "are just now our very good friends, and whether they are guilty or not, it would be inconvenient to accuse them. We must begin by seizing the young Princes whom we have as hostages, and this would most certainly be followed by war."

"But Corbulo and my legions would be more than a match for these barbarians," replied the Emperor haughtily.

"True, Sire, most true," said the vizier with a sarcasm not wholly concealed by the deference with which it was veiled. "But Corbulo thinks that another campaign would not now be for the advantage of the Empire."

The speaker's real meaning was that the military successes of Corbulo made him at least as formidable to his master as to the enemy, and that it would not be politic to give him another opportunity of increasing them.

Nero, who was quick enough to know where his real danger lay, nodded his acquiescence.

"And the Germans?" he said after a pause.

Tigellinus slightly shrugged his shoulders. "That hardly seems probable. Those thick-witted barbarians can scarcely have devised such a plot."

A period of uneasy silence followed. Tigellinus was even more impressed than was Nero with the gravity of the situation, for he knew more of the very deep and widespread feelings to which the cries in the Circus had given expression, and he was absolutely at a loss for a policy. The people suspected Nero of having caused the late disaster, and suspected him with very good reason; what reasonable chance was there of turning these suspicions in some other direction?

Suddenly a great scheme crossed his mind. Himself of the

meanest origin, Tigellinus felt a jealous hatred for the old nobility. Not a few of the foremost members had already fallen victims to his craft, and now he seemed to perceive a chance of dealing the order a damaging blow.

"Sire," he began, "it is an enemy from within, rather than an enemy from without, that has to be dreaded. You remember the story of Catiline?"

"Surely," replied the Emperor.

"In those days," went on the favourite, "a set of needy and unscrupulous nobles, beggared by their own extravagance and luxury, plotted to overthrow the Republic, and one of their methods was conflagration. There are the same causes still at work,—pride, poverty, and extravagance. Where these are to be found there will always be a Catiline. Then the play was stopped before the prologue was spoken; now it may well be that we have had the first act."

"Is this a mere suspicion of yours, or do you speak from knowledge?" asked the Emperor.

Before the Minister could answer Poppæa interposed. She had a shrewd idea of what Tigellinus was aiming at—a huge proscription of the nobles, to be brought about by working on the suspicions of Nero, and to result in his own aggrandizement in wealth and power, on a scale equally huge. Such a scheme was not to her taste. Her own sympathies were largely aristocratic; she prided herself on a high descent, at least, on the mother's side. She was willing enough to join in the overthrow of this or that noble, and to share in his spoils, but a general ruin of the order did not suit her wishes or her plans. Among other reasons was her fear lest her associate should become too great. At present he was willing to be her ally, but she knew that he would like far better to be the only power behind the throne. And she had, besides, a scheme of her own to further, and animosities of her own to gratify.

"Sire," she began, "there are men in Rome who are enemies not only of the Roman people, but of the whole human race, and these may very well have begun their impious work by attempting to destroy the most glorious of the habitations of mankind. You have heard of Christus, and the people who call themselves after his name?"

"Surely," replied Nero. "Was not that Paulus, a Jew of Tarsus, if I remember right, a chief man among them?"

"Yes, indeed," cried Poppæa; "and a most pernicious fellow, a ringleader in all their mischievous doings! "

Poppæa, in fact, regarded the Apostle with feelings of the strongest aversion. Not long after his arrival at Rome, rather more than two years before, some rumour about him had reached her, and had greatly excited her curiosity. A famous Jewish teacher, she heard, had come to Rome. He was a prophet, it was said, and what was still more interesting, a worker of wonders. Accordingly she had sent for him. The interview had been a disappointment, and worse than a disappointment. She was then intriguing for a share in the Imperial throne, and wanted this wonderful seer to predict the future for her. She heard from his lips no prophecy in her sense of the word, but certain plain words about purity, justice, mercy, such as it is the highest function of the prophet to utter. She concealed her vexation, and even pretended to be impressed by what she had heard. "Would he," she said, "confirm his authority, as a teacher, by performing one of the wonders which he had the power, she was told, to work?" The Apostle peremptorily refused. He was permitted, he said, sometimes thus to relieve the sick and suffering, but he would not gratify an idle curiosity. With this the interview had ended, and she had never sought to repeat it. In process of time to this personal offence had been added another cause of dislike. Poppæa's Jewish friends in Rome had received communications from Jerusalem, which made them actively hostile to the Apostle, and she, though of course understanding little or nothing about the difference between Jew and Christian, had taken their side. When the Apostle was brought to answer for his life before the Emperor, all her influence had been used to bring about his condemnation, and his acquittal and subsequent release had caused her the greatest annoyance.

"Ah!" said Nero, "I always thought, my sweetest Poppæa, that you were somewhat too hard on the poor man. You would have had me condemn him, but I really could see no harm in him. I will allow that he did not appear to be quite in his right senses. He talked some quite unintelligible nonsense about his Master, as he called him. At one time he said that he was a man, and at another that he was a god. He maintained that he had died. That seemed a great point with him, though why any one should make so much of his Master having been crucified, it is hard to see. And then again he insisted that he was alive. Altogether he made the strangest jumble that I have ever heard from human lips. And he spoke Greek, I remember, but poorly, and with a very strong accent. Still, he had the air of a learned man, and he talked as if he really believed what he said. And certainly, whether he was in his senses or not, I could find no harm in him. No, my Poppæa, you were always a little unreasonable about this Paulus. If his followers are no worse than he, there can be nothing very wrong about them."

"Sire," replied Poppæa, "the kindness of your heart makes you unwilling to believe the truth. I cannot tell you a tenth part of the horrible things that are said, and I believe truly said, about these followers of Christus—Christiani they call them."

"Surely, my dearest," said Nero with a smile, "they are nothing worse than a new kind of Jew, and for the Jews, you have, I know, a liking."

"Sire," said Poppæa with no little heat, "they are as different from Jews as darkness is different from light. They are atheists, though they worship, I believe, some strange demons; they have no love for their country; they will not serve in the legions; in fact, as I said, they are the enemies of mankind. And as to the dreadful things which they do at their feasts, they are beyond belief. That they sacrifice children, and banquet on their flesh, is among the least of the horrors which they commit."

"Tigellinus," said Nero, "do you know anything about these Christians whom the Empress seems to dislike so much?"

"They are a strange people," replied the Minister, "who cling to their gloomy superstition with a most invincible obstinacy. That they never sacrifice to the gods, or even eat of the sacrifices of others, that they will not enter the Circus or the theatre, and lead altogether a joyless life—this I know. That they never serve in the legions can hardly be true. I heard that when you last gave a donation to the Prætorians, and the men came to receive it, wearing garlands on their heads, one man alone came carrying his garland in his hand. "The law of Christus, his Master," he said, "forbade him to crown himself." And to this he adhered most inflexibly, though he not only lost his gold pieces, but was almost beaten to death by the Centurions for disobeying orders."

"And what about these crimes that are laid to their charge?" asked the Emperor. "Are they really guilty of them, think you?"

"That I cannot say," Tigellinus answered; "but that the people believe them to be guilty I know for certain."

"And are they guilty, think you," Nero went on, "of this wickedness concerning the city?"

"That the people will believe them to be guilty, I do not doubt," said Tigellinus.

Nero caught eagerly at the idea. An obscure sect, for whom no one would feel any sympathy or compassion, who, on the contrary, were hated by all who had heard of them,—just the victims that he wanted.

"Doubtless," cried Nero, "we have found, thanks to the prudence and wisdom of the Empress, and to my own good fortune, the real criminals. I charge you, Tigellinus, with the care of seeing that these miscreants are properly punished."

"It shall be done, Sire, without delay; and that so completely that no one will have reason to complain of slackness of justice."

It was one of the arts by which this unscrupulous politician retained the Emperor's favour that he knew how to yield. His own scheme he was content for the present to postpone. It would be difficult and even dangerous to execute it. It might be more safely carried on piecemeal. Meanwhile, there was an urgent need which had to be met, and Poppæa's scheme seemed to provide for it in the best possible manner. Better scapegoats than these obscure sectaries, of whom few professed to know anything, and those few nothing that was not bad, could not well be found. He bowed his acquiescence and left the Imperial presence to devise a plan for carrying out his orders.

12

THE EDICT

THE young soldier Pudens had been fully employed since we last heard of him. The work of clearing away the débris of the fire had proved to be so vast that the ordinary supply of labour had been insufficient to meet the demand, and the help of the soldiers had been called in. A force, half naval and half military, which was raised from the fleets of Ravenna and Misenum, and which indeed was accustomed to do the work of pioneers, was told off for the purpose, and Pudens, partly through the interest of his friend Subrius, was appointed to be second in command. Among the civilians employed in the same work was an elderly man with whom he happened to be brought into frequent contact, and whose manners and conversation interested him very much. From some chance remark, Pudens learnt that his new acquaintance was a freedman, who had been emancipated by Pomponia shortly after her husband's death, and indeed in obedience to a request made in his will. The man could not say too much in praise of his patroness, of her blameless life, her boundless charity. "They call her sad and gloomy, sir," he said, on one occasion; "and indeed she does not care for the gayeties and pleasures of Rome; but a happier woman does not live within the borders of the Empire, if to be always content, to have nothing to repent of in life, and to fear nothing in death, be happiness." He was apparently going to say more, but checked himself. More than once Pudens observed a similar pause, and as he was not a little interested in the lady herself, and still more in her young companion Claudia, his curiosity was greatly excited. It should be said that, acting on a hint from Subrius, he had not attempted to improve his acquaintance with the two ladies. Visitors would attract attention, and it was necessary, he had been given to understand, that they should live for the present in complete retirement.

Before long an accident enabled him to penetrate the secret of the freedman's reserve. Returning to his quarters one evening in the late summer, he found his friend—for such the freedman had by this time become—in the hands of some soldiers. The spot happened to be on the boundary of two townships, and a statue of the god Terminus—a pedestal with a roughly carved head—had been placed there. The men, who were half tipsy, were insisting that the freedman —whom we may hereafter call by his name Linus—should pay his homage to the statue; Linus was resolutely refusing to comply.

"Hold!" cried Pudens, as he appeared on the scene, knowing of course nothing of what had happened, and only seeing a civilian in the hands of some unruly soldiers. "Hold! what do you mean by assaulting a peaceable citizen?"

"He is an atheist, a Christian; he refuses to worship the gods," cried one of the men.

"Who made you a champion of the gods?" retorted Pudens. "You are behaving more like robbers than like god-fearing men."

"Lay hold of him, too, comrades," shouted one of the men.

Pudens recognized the voice of the last speaker. He was a Deputy-Centurion, who had been for a time one of his own subordinates.

"What, Stertinius!" he cried, "don't you know any better than to mix yourself up in a brawl, if indeed it is not a robbery?"

Stertinius, who, like his comrades, was not quite sober, and in his excitement had not recognized the newcomer, was taken aback at being thus addressed by his name. The next moment his memory returned to him.

"Hold, friends!" he shouted to his companions; "it is the second in command of the pioneers."

The men immediately released their victim, and falling into line, stood at attention, and saluted.

Stertinius took it upon himself to be their spokesman: "We are very sorry to have annoyed one of your honour's friends, and hope that you and he will overlook the offence."

"Begone!" cried Pudens, who had a feeling that it would be better for the freedman's sake not to take the affair too seriously. "Begone! and in future let your devotion to Bacchus, at least, be a little less fervent."

When the men had disappeared the freedman explained to his protector what had happened.

"But," asked Pudens, when he had heard the story, "what made the fellows behave in this fashion to you? I presume that they don't commonly go about compelling people to do reverence to wayside statues."

Linus hesitated for a while before he replied to this question. "Sir," he said at last, "I will be frank with you. I won't ask you to keep secret what I tell you. You are not, I know, the man to betray a confidence; and, besides, there can hardly be any question of secrecy in this matter hereafter. These men have got hold of the notion that I do not worship the gods whom they worship. An ill- conditioned fellow, whom I once employed, and had to discharge for his laziness and dishonesty, told them something about me, and since then I have been very much annoyed by them."

"I don't understand you," said Pudens, who was quite unused to hear it treated as a serious matter whether a man did or did not believe in the gods. He was conscious of not believing in them himself in any real sense of the words; but he went through the usual forms of respect to their images, would put, for instance, a portion of food before the household god, when he remembered it, and, equally when he remembered it, would salute a wayside Mercury or Termi-nus. "What do you believe in then? The Egyptian trio, or what?"

Linus sank his voice to a whisper: "I am a Christian," he said.

The word conveyed, it may be said, no meaning to the young soldier. He had heard it, and that was all. Subrius, he now remembered, had said, when he was about to introduce him to Pomponia, "A really good woman, though they do say that she is a Christian," but the remark had made no impression on him.

"A Christian," he repeated. "What is that?"

"No harm, certainly," Linus answered; "but, on the contrary, I hope much good. One thing I have learnt from it, that there is but one God in heaven and earth, and that all these gods, as they call them, are but vain things, or worse. But don't suppose," he went on, "that I go out of my way to insult what others hold in reverence. That I have not learnt to do. Only, when any one would compel me, as those drunken soldiers would have compelled me, to pay honour to the idols, as we call them, I cannot do it. 'Thou shalt not bow down to them nor worship them,' says my law, and I should be false and disobedient if I did. They say dreadful things about us, sir, I know, things that it would be a shame to repeat; but they are not true, believe me, sir, they are not true. I have done many wrong things in other days, but my dear Lord, who died for me, has delivered me from the curse of evil."

He uttered these last words with a fervent earnestness which greatly impressed his hearer, though he had scarcely even the dimmest notion of what was meant. The young man, whose heart was touched and purified by an honest emotion which made the follies of the past seem hateful to him, was deeply interested and eager to hear more.

In the course of the next few weeks many conversations on the subject followed. Linus at first expressed himself with much reserve. Already a bitter experience had taught the disciples the need of their Master's caution, that they were not to cast their pearls before swine. But the earnestness of the inquirer was so manifest, he was so unmistakably absorbed in what he heard, that the freedman soon told him all that he himself knew. He even permitted him to see what he held to be the choicest of all his possessions, a record of the Master's life. Pudens was half disposed to be disappointed when the treasure, kept, it was evident, with the most elaborate care,—for three caskets, each fastened with the most elaborate locks that the ingenuity of the age could devise, had to be opened before it could be seen,—proved to be a parchment volume of the very plainest kind. None of the customary ornaments of a book were there. The edges had been left in their native roughness; the knobs of the wooden pin, so to call it, round which the parchment had been rolled, were not painted, much less gilded. A bailiff's account-book or tradesman's ledger could not well have had a plainer exterior. But when Linus opened the volume and read some of its contents, there was no more disappointment. He made choice of what was most suitable to his listener with much care. If we had the book now in our hands we should not be able, it may be, actually to identify it with any one of the four Gospels which we now possess. Still, it is not impossible that it may have been an early draft of that which bears the name of St. Luke, the companion, it will be remembered, of the long imprisonment of St. Paul, and not unreasonably believed by many to have availed himself of this oppor- tunity of putting together his "narrative concerning those matters which were fully established among" the early believers. If so, what could have been more appropriate for the needs of the inquirer than the story of the Prodigal's Return to his Father, of the Rich Man and the Beggar, of the Good Samaritan? As the reader went on to other passages less easy of comprehension, Pudens began to ask questions to which the freedman was not able to give a satisfactory answer. "He was unlearned and ignorant," he hastened to explain, "knowing and understanding enough to satisfy his own wants, but not competent to explain difficulties."

"But you have teachers and wise men among you, I presume," said the young soldier." Why should I not go to them?"

Linus hesitated. Circumstances had compelled him to put his own life in the young man's hands, for though there had been as yet no persecution, a man who owned himself to be a Christian felt himself to be doing as much as that. But to bring the lives of others into the same danger, to trust the safety of the little community to one who, a few weeks before, had been an absolute stranger, was another matter. And then the interests of the young man himself were to be considered. It was no light thing to suggest that he should openly associate with people of whom Rome, as far as it had heard anything at all about them, had the very worst opinion. Hence he had never proposed to his friend a visit to the Christian places of assembly, and when the young man himself had suggested it, he was conscious of no little perplexity. However, he had now gone too far to be able to draw back. If the young soldier had been trusted so far, he would have to be trusted altogether. Without making any further difficulty, Linus agreed to take his friend to an assembly that was to be held on the following day.

The meeting-place was outside the city walls. It was the old clubhouse of a guild of artisans, disused partly because it had fallen into bad repair, partly because the burial-ground in which it stood, and which had much to do with its original purpose, had been filled up by interments. The guild had removed its quarters to larger and more commodious premises elsewhere, and had been glad to lease what was almost a valueless property to the representative of the Christian community, in this case no other than Linus himself. It was an oblong building with a semicircular end, something like that form of chancel which we know under the name of apse. The place was absolutely without ornament, though at the back of the seat which lined the apse were curtains of some very rough material. No religious symbol of any kind was visible. It was important that in case of any investigation nothing should be seen that could give the meeting the character of a secret society. Against secret societies the government of the Empire was then, as always, mercilessly severe.

Pudens was not destined on that occasion to hear any such exposition of mysteries as he had been expecting from the authorized teachers to whom Linus had referred him. The community were intensely agitated by an unexpected blow which had suddenly fallen upon them. It had always, indeed, a certain consciousness of danger, for it was aware that it was undisturbed only because it was unknown; but some years had passed without any interference from the authorities, and a general feeling of security had been the result.

This was now to be destroyed, and, indeed, till more than two centuries and a half had passed, was not to be known again by the Christian Church.

A whispered introduction from Linus to the door-keeper was sufficient to secure the admission of Pudens. The building was nearly full, rather more than half the congregation being composed of slaves. The majority of the remainder were artisans, farmers, or small tradesmen, most of them showing by their features a Jewish origin. The sprinkling of men of higher rank was very small. Two wore a toga fringed with the narrow purple stripe that was the sign of equestrian rank. There were a few women, numbering, perhaps, a sixth part of the whole, who sat together on the hindermost benches.

Just as Linus and Pudens entered, the presiding minister rose from the seat which he occupied by the wall of the apse with a paper in his hand. He came forward as far as the railing which separated the semicircle from the rest of the building, and after a brief salutation addressed the assembled congregation.

"Brethren and sisters," he said, "a great danger threatens us. To-morrow, possibly to-day, if sufficient copies can be made, the edict which I am about to read to you will be published throughout Rome. Listen and judge for yourselves.

" 'NERO CLAUDIUS CAESAR DRUSUS GERMANICUS AUGUSTUS IMPERATOR TO THE SENATE AND PEOPLE OF ROME, GREETING:—

" '*Whereas it has come to my knowledge as a certain fact that that most terrible disaster by which the city of Rome has lately been visited, to wit, the conflagration, which, raging continuously for many days and nights, destroyed not only the dwellings of men, but the most precious monuments of our ancestors and the very temples of the immortal gods, was brought about by the malice of certain abandoned persons, who have assumed to themselves the name of Christians, and who, inflamed with an insatiable hatred of the human race, conceived the idea of destroying this, its fairest and noblest seat, I hereby charge and command all men whatsoever, that they do forthwith give up to the magistrates, and to other persons whom I shall appoint for that purpose, the names of all, whether men, women, or children,—for this infection has not spared even the tenderest age,—whom they know or suspect to be poisoned with this detestable superstition. And I hereby declare that such as shall be found guilty of this wickedness shall forthwith be visited with the most condign punishment. Farewell.'"*

The dismay which followed the reading of this document defies description. Of petty social persecution the Christians knew something; they had suffered also from one or two outbreaks of mob violence; already their heathen neighbours had begun to connect them with dear food and unhealthy seasons, as cause and effect; but this formal arraignment of them as men who had inflicted on their fellow-citizens the most frightful of sufferings, was an unprecedented and wholly overwhelming experience.

After a short pause the minister spoke again. "Brethren and sisters," he said in a voice whose calm and measured accents contrasted strangely with the excitement of his audience: "We do not now for the first time learn the truth of the Master's words, 'They shall accuse you falsely for My name's sake.' Yet I must confess that this charge, so monstrous in itself, and so far reaching in its application, exceeds the very worst that we could have feared. And now what shall I say to you? Great, indeed, is this tribulation, but the grace of Him who loved you and gave Himself for you is more than sufficient. It may be that He will deliver you even now from the mouth of the lion, even as he delivered our holy brother Paul from it not many months ago; but if not"—the speaker paused awhile, and then raising his voice went on with the world-famous defiance of the dauntless three to the Chaldaean tyrant—"if not, be it known unto thee, O King, that we will not serve the golden image which thou hast set up."

The bold utterance met with an immediate response from the congregation. A subdued murmur of approval went round, and every head was lifted higher.

The speaker went on: "But it is not so much to courage as to caution that I would at this moment exhort you. If it may be, do the Master's bidding when he said, 'If they persecute you in one city, flee ye to another.' If you must needs stay in Rome, be not overbold. Confess your faith, if you are called, but do not flaunt it in the faces of the persecutors. The Lord will support you in trials to which He brings you, not in those that you find for yourselves. Let us pray for His grace that we may be found faithful even unto death."

The whole congregation fell upon their knees and prayed in a silence that was only broken by some deep sob that could not be controlled. At last the minister rose, and stretching out his hands over his people, committed them with words of blessing to the Divine protection.

"How is it that your chief became possessed of that document so soon?" asked Pudens of his companion.

Linus smiled. "We have always had friends in Cæsar's household. It will not avail much now, I fear, but it at least gives us time to think."

"You will flee, of course," resumed the young man.

"Impossible," replied his companion. "I have a bedridden sister, and my place is with her. But let us hope that no one saw you to-day among us, no one, at least, who should not have seen you."

"But have you traitors among you?"

"Who has not? Do you not remember that the Master Himself had one in His own small company of twelve? But anyhow we must part; you must not be seen with me."

Pudens saw the prudence of this advice, and could not refuse to follow it. He wrung his new friend's hand, and with a fervent prayer, "Your Master keep you!" turned away.

For his own safety he had little fear. He could truly say that he was not a Christian, though he was conscious of a strange feeling that there would be something shameful about such a denial. The next moment he had forgotten all about himself. A thought had shot across his mind that made his blood run cold. What would be the fate of Pomponia? And if she was arrested,—and that she had a deadly enemy in Poppæa he knew,—how would it fare with Claudia?

13

IN HIDING

THE situation with which the young soldier found himself compelled to deal was one of great difficulty. Subrius' country house had been a sufficient shelter for the two ladies as long as it was only illegal violence on the part of Poppæa that they had to fear. But the case would be different when a regular proscription, in which they would certainly be included, had been ordered. The little fort-like house might resist a coup de main such as had been attempted at Pomponia's mansion, but it would have to open its gates at a summons from the Imperial authority, and that the Imperial authority would be invoked, and invoked without delay, by the animosity of Poppæa, could not be doubted for a moment. If resistance was impossible, what remained? Nothing but flight, and flight from a power which embraced, or in the view of a Roman seemed to embrace, the whole of the habitable world, was notoriously impossible.

There was a third alternative—concealment. Could that be contrived? Possibly; but where? Obviously under ordinary circumstances in Rome itself, for there is no hiding-place so safe as a crowded city. But then Rome, of which a third lay still in ruins from the fire, and another third was in process of rebuilding, was certainly not as suitable for the purpose as usual.

Suddenly an idea struck him. There was a certain grotesqueness about it which made him laugh in spite of the gravity of the situation. A little consideration showed him that this very grotesqueness was no small recommendation. His foster- mother was the wife of a temple servant who had the charge of a temple dedicated to one of the minor deities with which the Roman Pantheon was crowded. The temple itself, which had stood near the Circus, had perished in the fire, but the residence, which was at a considerable distance, had escaped, and as it did not come within the area of the projected improvements of the city, was not likely to be disturbed. It was here, then, that Pudens fancied he could find a fairly safe hiding-place for the two ladies. In his foster- mother's fidelity and devotion to him he could implicitly trust. Childless herself,—for she had lost all her offspring in their infancy,—she lavished all her mother's love upon her foster- child. Nothing that he could do was wrong in her eyes. She would give, he was sure, an asylum to the worst of criminals, if only he came with a recommendation from him. Her husband was an easy, good- natured man, accustomed to follow without a question the guidance of his wife, and not more zealous for the honour of the deity whom he served, than those who were behind the scenes of any temple commonly were.

Pudens' idea was to tell the wife the truth about her inmates, and to leave it to her to decide how much she would communicate to her husband. There was no time to be lost. He had one day before him, but no more. The Christian assembly had been held as usual in the very early morning, and it still wanted several hours to noon. All arrangements would have to be made before sunset; as soon as it was dark the ladies must leave their present abode, and they would have to be in their new asylum before the next morning.

The first thing to be done was to provide the shelter. Pudens made the best of his way to his foster-mother's house, and was lucky enough to find her before she went out to make her daily purchases in the market.

The good woman's astonishment when she heard the errand on which he had come was great. She had just heard of the Christians, but had the very vaguest ideas as to what they were. These ideas naturally reflected the popular prejudices.

"Of course," she said, "we will do anything that we can." Like the wise woman that she was, she always associated her husband with herself as far as words went. "We will do anything that we can for friends of yours; but I have heard that these Christians are very wicked people."

"Wicked, mother!" cried the young man; "these are two of the best women that ever lived."

"But why does the Emperor want to harm them, then?"

"Need you ask, mother, when you have such a woman as Poppæa stirring him up to all kinds of wickedness?"

There was still such a prestige about the Emperor that it was still the custom, at least in speaking, whatever the real belief may have been, to attribute his misdoings to bad advisers.

Statia—this was the foster-mother's name—had all the dislike that a good woman would be likely to feel for Poppæa, while she had a certain weakness for the handsome young Emperor, of whom she was ready to believe as much good and as little evil as the utmost stretch of charity would allow.

"Ah!" she cried; "so it is one of that mischievous woman's doings."

"And how about your husband?"

"Oh, it will be all right with him. I shall tell him that the ladies are people whom Poppæa hates. That will be enough for him. He thinks as ill of her as I do. You see it was Otho, her first—no, I am wrong, her second husband, that got him his present place, and he thinks that she has treated him very badly."

This matter satisfactorily settled, the next thing was to provide for the safe conveyance of the fugitives from the one place to the other. Here Pudens found himself face to face with a huge difficulty. The litter in which they had journeyed from Rome was out of the question. A secret known to eight bearers would hardly be a secret long. The younger woman would certainly be able to ride, and possibly to walk, for the distance was not beyond the strength of an active girl. The elder would as certainly be incapable of either exertion.

"What is to be done, Statia?" he asked, after turning the matter over for some time in his own mind.

For a time the good woman was utterly perplexed. At last an idea occurred to her.

"The ladies will come as early as possible to-morrow," she said. "That is your plan, is it not?"

"Just so," replied the young man.

"When the market carts come in from the country."

"Exactly."

"Then they must come in a market cart."

"Admirably thought of, mother; but how about the cart?"

"My brother Marcus, who has a farm for vegetables in the suburbs, will lend me one. I shall tell him that I am borrowing it for a friend who is moving her goods into the city. You will have to act the wagoner."

"That I can manage easily enough. It is not the first time that I have done it."

It had been a favourite frolic with Pudens, in his somewhat turbulent youth, to seek adventures in the disguise of a countryman. He had still the rough smock frock and leggings laid up somewhere in his house.

"I shall go to my brother this afternoon, and make everything ready for you. You must come dressed as a wagoner; and mind, you must not have the dress only, but the speech also. Can you manage this? Let me hear you try."

Pudens gave so excellent an imitation of rustic speech that the woman burst out laughing. "That will do," she cried; "nothing could be better."

Shortly after noon Pudens might have been seen starting from his house. He was on horseback, and was apparently bound on a journey, for he carried behind him a travelling valise. It contained, besides his own disguise, two plain cloaks, such as the country women commonly wore when they came into Rome; these were intended for the use of the two ladies. When he had got about six miles from the city, he dismounted, concealed the valise in a little wood by the wayside, and then mounting again, rode on to a little inn, a haunt of his earlier days, where he was consequently well known, and where no questions would be asked, and scarcely any curiosity felt about his proceedings. Here he put up his horse; and then, retracing his steps to the wood, assumed the wagoner's dress. Pudens had a certain genius for acting, and no one would have recognized the elegant and fashionable young soldier in the middle-aged, slouching country-man, a rustic of the rustics, as any one would have thought him, who plodded along the road in the direction of the farm where he was to find the vehicle.

Everything went well. Statia had been better than her word. She had induced her brother to provide a covered wagon, as being far more convenient for the purpose than a common cart. It was drawn by a couple of horses, about whose welfare the farmer gave many cautions to the supposed wagoner. "My sister tells me," he said, "that you are a careful man, who knows how to treat a good beast as he deserves. Don't you overdrive the poor creatures; be gentle with them up the hills if you have much of a load; see with your own eyes that they get their food when you put them up at the tavern—you know the place, the Phœnix, just outside the gate; an honest place enough, but hostlers will have their little tricks everywhere."

Pudens, who had commended himself to the farmer by some judicious praise of his animals, promised to take all imaginable care of wagon and horses, and had the satisfaction of getting away, without exciting, as he hoped, the slightest suspicion as to his real character. His promise, however, did not prevent him from putting the animals to a sharp trot, that would probably have struck dismay into their owner's heart, as soon as he was well out of sight of the farm. Time, indeed, was precious. He had to reach the old fort, to tell his story, to persuade the ladies to follow his advice, itself likely, he fancied, to be a task of some difficulty, and to get back to Rome before sunrise the next day.

The sun was just setting when he reached the fort. Tying up the horses to a tree he approached the building, knocked, or to speak more accurately, kicked at the door, and asked for the old steward. The old man came to the door, expecting to be interviewed on some ordinary business, and of course failed to recognize his visitor, whom, indeed, he had seen once only in his natural semblance. Pudens intimated that his business was of a private kind, and on finding himself alone with the steward revealed his name, recalling to the old man's recollection the occasion on which they had met before. Nothing could exceed his astonishment. But when the soldier went on to unfold his errand, describing the imminent danger in which Pomponia and her young companion were placed, and the scheme by which he hoped to rescue them, the old man became cool and practical at once.

"Yes," he said, "there is a hope that you may succeed; but the first difficulty will be to persuade my lady. Her own inclination would be to stay here and face the danger, whatever it was."

"Shall I see her?"

"Not, I should say, before I have told her the story. The affair is enough to confound any one, much more a woman who has lived out of the world for many years, and it must be broken to her."

"Very good; arrange it as you think best. But remember that there is no time to be lost. I should be starting in an hour at the most, if I am to get to Rome before sunrise to-morrow, and I ought not to be later."

The old man hastened away at once to seek an interview with Pomponia. In about half an hour he returned.

"Come with me," he said. "My lady wishes to speak with you."

Pudens followed him to a room where the two ladies were sitting together. Ushered into their presence, he felt, and was ashamed of feeling, somewhat embarrassed by the consciousness of a ludicrous disguise, all the more when he perceived that Claudia, notwithstanding the gravity of the situation, could not resist a little smile.

"You have my thanks," began Pomponia, "for all the trouble that you have taken and the risk that you have run. But I must confess that I would sooner await here whatever God may please to send."

The steward broke in with the freedom of speech often accorded to, or at least assumed by, an old servant.

"Madam, if I may be permitted to say so much, there spoke the wife of a Roman Consular rather than the handmaid of Christ."

Pomponia flushed at the rebuke, but answered gently, "How so? I would not willingly forget my duty."

"Madam," went on the old man, "it seems to me that what God has sent, as far as we can see at present, is this young man. He comes with a well contrived scheme which he has taken much pains to carry out so far. But because it does not suit your dignity to fly from your enemies, or to put on a disguise, you refuse to avail yourself of it. Did the blessed Paul think it below his dignity to be let down in a basket out of a window in the wall of Damascus? Not so; he took the means of deliverance that God sent him, and did not wait for something else that might be more to his taste. And let me say again, madam, what I have said before. You may think it right for yourself to stop here and face the enemy; but you have no right to involve others, this dear young lady for instance, with you. She is young; she is new in the faith,—she will pardon an old man for speaking his mind,—and she may not have your strength when she is brought to the fiery trial. Nay, madam,"—he hesitated a moment before he uttered words that might imply possible doubt of his mistress' own courage and endurance,—"Nay, madam, who knows but what your own strength may fail, if you persist in trying it in a place to which you are not called."

The last two arguments affected Pomponia powerfully. What if this were a call? It would be a sin if she did not follow it, for herself and her young companion.

"Phlegon is right," she said after a short pause; "we will do as you think best."

It was arranged that the two female attendants who had accompanied the visitors should remain where they were. It was difficult, if not impossible, otherwise to dispose of them. Probably they would escape unmolested, passing as part of the small establishment which the owner of the house was accustomed to maintain. Phlegon would find shelter with friends in Rome, and would keep up, if possible, some communication with his mistress.

It is needless to describe the journey to Rome. It was affected without any difficulty; but one incident that occurred in the course of it proved how narrow an escape the fugitives had had. When about half the distance had been traversed, Pudens halted at a wayside inn to rest and bait the horses. At the very moment that he did so, a party of horse soldiers which was travelling the other way drew up before the door of the hostelry. It consisted of two troops, numbering together about sixty men, and was commanded by an officer of some rank, who was accompanied by a civilian. Pudens guessed their errand in a moment. They had come, he was sure, to arrest Pomponia, and it was quite possible that they might insist on searching the wagon. Boldness, he felt, was the only policy. Any attempt to escape would certainly be fatal. He came forward, made a clumsy salutation to the officer in command, and began to converse with some of the troopers. He ordered a flagon of the coarse wine of the country, and shared it with the newcomers. The liquor set the men's tongues wagging, and Pudens soon learnt that his suspicions were correct. They were bound, said one of the men, for an old country house to arrest some prisoners.

"Who are they? What have they done?" asked the supposed wagoner.

"By Bacchus!" cried the man; "I know nothing about it. I heard something about their being Christians, whatever that may mean. All that I can tell you is that it is some affair of Poppæa. You see that fat man by our chief's side? He has had a bad time of it, I fancy. He is not used to riding, I take it, and we have been pushing on at a good rate. Well, he is one of Poppæa's freedmen. That fellow there," he pointed as he spoke to a slave who was evidently in charge of a couple of troopers," is our guide. He knows, it seems, where the parties whom we want are, and was to have a turn on the 'little horse' if he didn't tell."

This, Pudens imagined, must be some poor wretch belonging to

Pomponia's household in Rome, who had been unlucky enough to overhear the name of the place where his mistress was to find shelter.

The easy bearing of Pudens had exactly the effect which he hoped from it, while the accident of the two parties meeting at the halting-place was all in favour of his escape. Probably, had the soldiers encountered him on the road, they would have challenged him, and overhauled the contents of his wagon. As matters turned out, the idea never occurred either to the officer in command or to any of his men. He acted his part so thoroughly well, that no notion of his being anything more than a countryman on his way to the Roman market with a load of produce, crossed any one's mind. Anxious to avoid the remotest cause of suspicion, he purposely prolonged his halt, though, it need not be said, intensely anxious to be off, till the soldiers had started again. It was with intense relief that he heard the officer in command give the order to mount. When the last of the troopers had disappeared in the darkness, he climbed to the driver's seat, tossed the hostler his fee,—which he was careful not to make the smallest fraction larger than usual,—and set his horses in motion. The two women, who had sat all this time under the covering of the wagon, hand clasped in hand, in a perfect agony of suspense, breathed a fervent thanksgiving when they felt themselves to be once more upon the way.

Nothing else happened to alarm the travellers during the rest of their journey; but the most critical time was yet to come. While they were still out of sight of the inn where the wagon and horses were to be put up, the two ladies alighted. Each was disguised beyond recognition, Pudens hoped, in the coarse cloaks usually worn by the market-women when they travelled by night, and each carried a large basket filled, or apparently filled, with goods that they were about to offer for sale. At the inn, of course, the wagon and the horses were well known, but Pudens, as a stranger, excited some curiosity.

"Well," he said, in answer to some question, "old Caius has a touch of fever,"—he had taken the precaution of ascertaining the name of the man whom the farmer usually employed,—"and I am taking his place. It is not to my liking at all," he went on; "I had sooner be in my bed, by a long way."

At the city gate the porter grumbled a little at being roused so early, but asked no questions. Catching a glimpse of Claudia's beautiful face, he paid the girl a rough compliment which made her shiver with fear and disgust. Pudens would have dearly liked to knock the fellow down, but, anxious above all things to avoid a scene, restrained himself.

"Hold your tongue," he growled to the man in the harshest country accent that he could put on, "and leave her alone. She is not your sort."

"Nor yours, either," retorted the man; "for a rougher bumpkin I never saw."

The "bumpkin," however, he perceived to be unusually tall and stout, and one who would be a formidable fellow to quarrel with. He returned into the gate- house, and the party passed on without further molestation. The streets were almost deserted, so early was the hour. Beyond one or two late revellers staggering home, and a few workmen engaged in some occupation that had to be begun betimes, no one met them. When they reached the temple servant's door where Statia was waiting to receive her new inmates, they had escaped, so Pudens had good reason to hope, all hostile observation.

14

THE PERSECUTION

THE streets were beginning to fill as Pudens made the best of his way from the temple servant's dwelling to his own house. Fortunately for him, as he naturally wished to escape notice, the attention of the passers-by was engrossed by the copies of the edict against the Christians, which the Imperial officers were now busy posting up in all the public places of the city. He was thus able to reach his home without attracting any observation. Once there, he hastened to put away his disguise in the safest hiding-place that he could find. The proceedings of the night he proposed to keep for as long as possible an absolute secret. The most honourable of men, he reflected, are less likely to divulge what they do not know than what they do.

A veritable reign of terror now began in Rome. In the course of a few days the prisons were crowded to overflowing. It was, indeed, a strange and medley multitude with which they were filled. The first victims were the more prominent members of the Christian congregations that were scattered throughout the city. Many of these were Jews who had separated themselves, or rather had been expelled, from the synagogues. Their names were naturally known to their unbelieving countrymen, who regarded them with a hatred that was peculiarly intense, and who eagerly seized the opportunity of wreaking their vengeance upon them. Accordingly, the officers charged with the execution of the decree were supplied by the rulers of the synagogues with lists of Jews, who, as they said, had abandoned the faith of their fathers to adopt a gloomy and odious superstition. These, then, were the first that were arrested under the terms of the Imperial decree. Next came a great number of persons who were more or less closely connected with the new faith. The Christian meetings had been conducted with as little ostentation as possible, but they had not passed unnoticed, and many were arrested because they had been known to attend them. Some of these had frequented the meetings from no other motive than curiosity, and these, finding themselves involved in what seemed to be a formidable danger, hastened to win the favour of the authorities by informing against others. So far the prisoners were either genuine Christians, or, at least, had been seen to consort with them. But mingled with these were others who had really nothing to do with the matter: persons who were suspected, in some cases, it may be, with reason, in many more, we may be certain, without any ground whatsoever, of having caused or spread the late fire, were seized and accused. In this way private grudges were often gratified. A creditor or a rival could be got rid of, and that with very little difficulty, if he happened to be unpopular, by a whisper dropped into the right place. Altogether it was a strange crowd that was thus swept as it were by a net into the prisons out of the streets of Rome.

Among the prisoners was the gladiator, or rather ex-gladiator, Fannius. He had made the acquaintance of Glaucon, a young man belonging to Pomponia's household, who, when that lady was obliged to leave Rome, had been given some employment by her nephew, Lateranus. Glaucon was a native of Cyprus, had been employed there by the Proconsul Sergius Paulus, and had witnessed the memorable scene in which the Apostle Paul had confounded the hostile sorcerer, and convinced the Proconsul of the truth of his message. When Paulus, on the expiration of his term of office, returned to Rome, he took Glaucon with him, and not long after recommended him to a situation of trust in the household of Pomponia. Glaucon was a fervent Christian, and he did not fail to use the opportunities of commending his faith to his new acquaintance. Fannius was just in the mood to listen with eagerness to his teaching. For some years past life had been a very serious affair to him, and all the more so because there was so much in his surroundings as an inmate of a "school" of gladiators that was hateful to him. His brutal comrades, whose sole virtue, it may be said, was courage, and who followed with a revolting simplicity the maxim of "Let us eat and drink, for to-morrow we die," set off by contrast this refined and pure-minded young Greek, who seemed moved by springs of action belonging to quite another world. Such an act of filial devotion as had brought Fannius into his present position, unfavourable to good-ness as this may have been in itself, could not fail to elevate his char-acter, while another purifying influence had been his faithful attachment to Epicharis. In the course of a few weeks, though not knowing enough to fit him for baptism, which indeed he could hardly have received while still a gladiator, Fannius was at heart a Christian.

And now occurred a difficulty of the most serious kind. The performance which Nero exhibited after the fire was the last in which Fannius would have to appear. Did he survive this, he would be enti-tled to his discharge. But could he consent to appear? Would the principles of his new faith permit him to exhibit his prowess in the arena? That he could not engage in combat with one of his fellow-men was perfectly plain. That would be a manifest breach of an elementary law of morals. The question was, could he take any part in the spectacle? Opinions were divided. Advisers of the severer sort declared against any participation; others were content with saying that he must do nothing that would endanger human life. This was the course which he followed. He went to the trainer, and declared, without giving his reasons, that he would not fight except against wild beasts. At first the man was furious. Fannius was, as has been said, a remarkably skilful swords-man, and his dexterity and force made him perhaps the most popular performer in the whole school;

all this would be thrown away if he were matched with a lion or a tiger.

"What!" cried the man; "you, my best fighter! I am not going to waste you in such a shameful way."

"There is no help for it," replied Fannius. "Set me to fight against a gladiator, and I shall simply drop my arms. Against a beast I will do my best."

And there was no help for it. The trainer had to make the best of it. He even consoled himself with the idea that he should be able to present a novelty to the spectators. Commonly it was a condemned criminal that had to combat with a wild beast, and it was very seldom that these wretched creatures made any real resistance. They were usually without skill in arms or physical strength; and they were terrified into helplessness. A practised gladiator of the very first class engaging in one of these desperate combats—and a struggle with a lion or tiger at close quarters was then, as it would be now without the help of fire- arms, well nigh desperate—might have a great success. At the same time, as Fannius' time of engagement was up, there was no risk. If he was killed there would be no loss; if he survived there would be the credit of having provided a novel and exciting entertainment.

So it was arranged. After a number of pairs of gladiators had fought without any particularly brilliant result, the herald came forward, and made the following announcement, permission having been first obtained from the presiding authorities. Fannius, it should be said, had nothing to do with the terms in which it was made.

"C. Fannius, having fought many times with men, and having as often secured victory, claims permission to fight with more formidable antagonists. He will, therefore, with the help of certain associates who have been allotted to him for this purpose, contend with a lion, a lioness, and a bear."

The "associates" were criminals who would in any case have had to undergo the ordeal.

The combat that followed proved to be a success, at least from the point of view of a Roman sight-seer. To us it would have seemed a peculiarly brutal exhibition. The result was that the lioness and the bear were killed, Fannius' companions perishing in the struggle. Fannius, in fact, dispatched both animals while they were mangling the dead. A fierce conflict with the lion ended in the victory of the gladiator; though sadly mangled by the claws and teeth of his savage antagonist, he escaped with his life, and, of course, received his discharge, together with a handsome present from the Emperor. He was taken down to the farm, and nursed with indefatigable patience and care by Epicharis and her aunt. The girl's heart was softened as she tended her suffering lover, and she consented to become formally betrothed to him, though only on the condition that before their marriage the vengeance for which she lived should have been first exacted.

It was in the midst of the joy and pride which he felt in securing an affection of which he had begun to despair, that Fannius imparted to Epicharis the secret of the conspiracy, the secret into which he had been himself initiated by Subrius. The matter had been left to his discretion by his superior, and he thought himself justified in what he did, by the belief, perfectly well founded, as we shall see, that he could not have secured a more zealous or more loyal associate. On her part the girl was almost frantic with delight. An object which had seemed almost unattainable was now within reach. It was not a weak woman; it was a powerful association of great nobles and great soldiers that had vowed vengeance against the tyrant. At the same time the love, for which hitherto there had scarcely been room in her heart by the side of the engrossing passion for vengeance, grew up and flourished apace. Before cold and distant, she now lavished upon her lover an affection which astonished as much as it delighted him.

Then the blow fell. To the trainer the conduct of Fannius in choosing to fight with beasts rather than men had been unintelligible. If he guessed at any motive he would have said that it was a desire for notoriety. But a rival gladiator, who conceived himself to be affronted by the terms of the proclamation, which indeed, though, as had been said, not through any fault of Fannius, had a certain arrogance about them—was more acute. He knew something about

Fannius, and was sure that he would not have committed himself to a desperate venture without some motive of solid worth. Fannius, he was sure, had every reason for wanting to live, and there must be some grave reason for his thus risking his life. What could it be but the same motive which prevented these gloomy sectaries, the Christians, from ever enjoying the spectacles of the Circus and the amphitheatre. On the strength of this conjecture he informed against Fannius as belonging to the forbidden sect of the Christians. The young man, who had now entirely recovered his health, came to Rome for the first time after his illness on the very day on which the edict was published, and was promptly arrested and thrown into prison.

Another of the prisoners was Phlegon, Pomponia's steward. He had been arrested at Subrius' country house. Whether the soldiers arrived before he expected them, or whether he deliberately lingered because he knew that they would not be satisfied without making some arrest, it is not easy to say. Two slaves belonging to the household were seized along with him. Both, it so happened, were heathen, and were therefore in no danger; and he had the satisfaction of knowing, on the other hand, that the two women servants, left behind by Pomponia and Claudia, contrived to escape the notice of the soldiers. To his own peril, now that it had come to him in the way of duty, he was wholly indifferent. He had long since counted the cost of his Christian profession, and had resolved to pay it.

The authorities were seriously perplexed by the abundance of prey which they secured. They did not know where to lodge their prisoners. It must be remembered that the Romans did not habitually use imprisonment, after conviction, as a punishment. Commonly the criminal, if he was not executed, was banished. Sometimes he was consigned to the safe keeping of some distinguished person, or was kept in his own house; but the long-continued imprisonment with which it is now customary to visit serious offences was unknown. Nero resolved to cut the knot of this difficulty in his own fashion. To the guilt or innocence of the prisoners he was absolutely indifferent. That they had nothing to do with the particular crime with which they were charged he had the best means of knowing; as to their offence in being Christians, he knew and cared nothing. What he did want was to shift upon them the notoriety which he wanted to divert from himself.

One means of doing this would be by the singularity of the punishment to be inflicted on them. To make a conspicuous example of some, and to permit the rest to escape, was the course which commended itself to him. How he succeeded will now have to be told.

During the two centuries and a half during which the Christian Church had to endure from time to time the hostility of the rulers of Rome, there were many persecutions that reached further, that lasted longer, that were in many ways more fatal; but there was not one that left on the minds of men so deep an impression of horror.

15

WHAT THE TEMPLE SERVANT SAW

IT was of course impossible that Pomponia and her young companion should remain in ignorance of what was going on in Rome. That something like a reign of terror prevailed, that multitudes of men, women, and even children were being daily arrested and imprisoned—no one exactly knew on what charge— they heard from their hostess, who, however, did her best to soften the story which she had to tell. But there came a time when they had to hear a tale which transcended in horror all that they could have imagined possible.

Commonly the temple servant's house was remarkably quiet. The old man was a peace-loving personage, who seldom entertained others, and still more seldom went out. The dwelling was so small that the apartment occupied by the ladies could hardly be said to be out of hearing of that where Statia and her husband sat in the evening. Commonly there was silence, the woman being busy with her needle, the old man sleeping in his chair. Now and then there would be heard a gentle murmur of conversation. Once or twice the ladies could distinguish a third voice, which they supposed to be that of an occasional visitor. One night, however, after they had been in their refuge about a month, they could not help overhearing what seemed to be a very loud and animated discussion. Fragments of talk even reached their ears, and though they did not attempt to piece them together, the words they heard left a general impression of uneasiness and even fear in their minds. The next morning their hostess was in an evident condition of agitation and excitement, divided between eagerness to tell her news, and a kind-hearted desire not to give pain to her guests.

"Oh, my lady!" she burst out, "there were terrible doings last night; such as were never heard of, they say, in Rome before, ever since it was a city."

The two women listened in silent dismay. That the storm which had been gathering would soon burst, they had clearly foreseen; in what terrible form its violence would break forth, with such a creature, permitted by God to plague the world for its sins, who could tell?

"I did not see them myself," Statia went on, "thanks be to the gods! But my husband did, and he was fairly sick and faint with the horribleness of the whole business when he came home. You see, he is not one that goes out much to sights. I haven't known him go to the Circus or the amphitheatre as much as once in the last ten years. You see, he would sooner stop at home quiet with me; and the best place, too, for an old man; aye! and for a young one, too, in my judgment. But last night a friend of his that serves the same temple would have him go and see some fine show, as he called it. The Emperor, my husband's friend said, was to throw open his gardens to the people, and there were to be such wonderful sights as had never been seen before. Well, my good man goes; and as I said, he comes home before it was over, quite sick with what he had seen. As soon as he was inside the gardens, he found a crowd of people hurrying to the theatre that there is in the gardens. Naturally he goes with them, and finds himself in a good place in front, where he could see all that was going on. In the arena were a number of animals,—bears, and lions, and tigers, and bisons, and other creatures that he did not know the names of,—at least, that was what he thought at first; but when he looked again he thought that there was something curious about them, they looked so awkward and clumsy. 'What ails the beasts?' he said to his next neighbour. The man laughed. 'They are not beasts at all!' he said; 'they are men!' 'Then what do they dress them up like that for?' asks my husband. 'Wait a moment,' says the other, 'and you will see.' And sure enough he did see. Some doors under the seats were opened, and a whole pack of dogs came leaping out—the biggest and fiercest looking dogs, my husband said, that he had ever seen. 'They've kept them hungry on purpose,' said the other man, 'giving them nothing to eat for two days, I am told.' 'But who are the poor creatures?' asked my husband, 'and what have they done?' 'Who are they?' answered the other, 'why, they are Christians, to be sure, whatever that may mean, for I don't rightly know myself; and 'tis said that it is they who set the city on fire.' "

"Hush!" cried Claudia, when Statia had reached this point in her story. "Tell us no more; it is more than my dear mother can bear."

And indeed Pomponia had grown paler and paler as the story went on.

"Nay," said Pomponia. "If our brethren actually endure these things, we may at least bear to hear them. Go on, my friend."

"Well, my lady," Statia resumed, "the poor creatures were not as much injured as one would have expected. Many of the dogs, when they found out that it was not real beasts that they were set to attack, left them alone; some were even quite friendly and gentle with them. 'They seemed to me,' says my husband, 'a great deal better than their masters;' and right he was, as you will say, when you hear what happened next. A herald came forward and cried, 'Fathers, knights, and citizens of Rome, the Emperor invites you to the Circus to witness a chariot-race, and hopes that you will regard with indulgence any deficiency of skill that you may perceive in the charioteers.' 'They say that he is going to drive one of the chariots himself, and Lateranus, who is to be Consul next year, the other,'—so my husband's neighbour, who seemed to know all about the show, told him. Of course it was very condescending of him to amuse the people in this way, but it does not seem to me quite the right thing for an Emperor.

"Well, by this time it was getting dark, and when my husband got outside the theatre, he found the gardens lighted up. All along the walks, on each of the lamp-posts, they had fastened a man,—yes, it is true as I am alive,—a man, dressed in a tunic steeped in pitch, and with an iron collar under the chin to keep the head up,—fastened them, and set them on fire. That was too much for my husband. He declared that he could stay no longer, and indeed, he was so poorly that his friend had to see him home, though he was sorry, he said, not to see the rest of the show. When they got back he and my husband had a great argument about it,—perhaps you may have heard them, my lady, for they talked very loud. My husband's friend would have it that it was only right. They were Christians, he said, which was only another name for atheists, and richly deserved all they got. But my husband does not hold with such doings, and told his friend so pretty plainly. 'After all, they're men,' he said, 'and you must not treat them as you would not treat a beast.' 'What! 'said the other,—and I will allow that this did shake me a bit,—'don't you know that if these people had their way, there would be no more offerings in the temples, aye, and no more temples, either, for the matter of that, and where would you and I be then?' But my good man stuck to his point for all that. 'I reckon that the gods can take care of themselves,' he said; 'and that anyhow, they won't thank us for helping them in this kind of way. It is not our Roman fashion to make show of men in this way. No, no! if a man has to be punished, there is the regular way of doing it; the cross for a slave, and the axe for the free man, with the scourge first, if he has done anything specially bad; but as for dressing men up like beasts, or turning them into torches, I don't hold with it. Our fathers did not do it, and what was enough for them should be enough for us.' That was what my good man said. I have never heard him make such a long speech ever since we were married, for he is not a man of many words. What do you think, my lady?"

The good woman had been quite carried away with her subject, for genuine as was her disgust at the Emperor's cruelties, she had a certain pleasure, not uncommon in her class, in the telling of horrors, and she had not noticed how her narrative had affected one of her hearers. Pomponia had quietly fainted.

"Ah! poor lady," cried Statia. "It has been too much for her. I am sure that she must feel for the poor things."

16

WHAT THE SOLDIERS THOUGHT

THE temple servant was not the only one among the spectators who had crowded the gardens of Nero, that had viewed the sight there presented to his gaze with disgust and horror. The Prætorians were particularly free and outspoken in the expressions of their feelings. Already they had begun to look upon themselves as the prop of the Imperial throne. It was to their camp that Nero had been carried almost before the breath had left the body of his predecessor Claudius; it was to them that the ambitious Agrippina had looked to give effect to the intrigue by which her son was preferred to the rightful heir; it was by their voices that Nero had been proclaimed Emperor, the vote of the Senate only following and confirming their previous determination.

On the morning after the exhibition described in my last chapter a wine shop, which stood just outside the Prætorian camp, and was a favourite resort of the men, was crowded with soldiers taking their morning meal.

"Well, Sisenna," cried a veteran, putting down his empty cup, after a hearty draught of his customary morning beverage of hot wine and water, sweetened with honey and flavoured with saxifrage, "what think you of last night's entertainment?"

The soldier appealed to was a young man who had just been drafted into the Prætorian force as a reward for some good service done on the Asiatic frontier. He did not answer at once, but looked round the room with the air of one who doubts whether he may safely express his thoughts.

"Ha! ha!" laughed the veteran, "you are cautious, I see. That's the way among the legions, I am told, and quite right, too; but it's all liberty here. Speak out, man; we are all friends here, and there is no one to call us to account for what we say. Cæsar knows too well what our voices are worth to him to hinder our using them."

"Well, Rufus," said Sisenna after a pause, "I will say frankly that it did not please me. It was not Roman, it was barbarian, though I must say that I never heard even of barbarians doing things quite so horrible."

"Who are these Christians?" asked a third speaker. "What have they done?"

"Didn't you read the Emperor's edict?" said a fourth soldier. "They set the city on fire, because they hate their fellow-creatures, and wish to do them as much damage as they can."

"Well," said Sisenna, "that, anyhow, is not my experience of them. They may hate their fellow-creatures in general, but they are certainly very kind to some of them in particular. Let me tell you what I know about them of my own knowledge. I was very bad with fever when I was campaigning on the Euphrates, and had to be invalided to Antioch. There I was treated by an old Jew physician, who was one of them—there are a good many of these Christians, you must understand, in the city, and many of them are Jews. Well, I was a long time getting well; these marsh fevers are obstinate things; come back again and again when one thinks that one is quit of them. So I got to know the old man very well, and we had a great deal of talk together. He used to tell me about his Master, as he called him; Christus was the name he gave him,—that's how these people came to be called Christians. Another of his names was Jesus; the old man told me what that meant, but I couldn't understand it altogether. But, anyhow, this Master seemed to have been a very good man."

"A good man!" interrupted one of his listeners. "Why, I have always heard that he was a turbulent Jew whom Claudius banished with a number of his countrymen from Rome."

"No, no," Sisenna went on, "you are mistaken; at least, if my friend the physician told me true; Christus was never in Rome, and he was crucified, if I remember right, eight years before Claudius came to the throne."

"Crucified, was he?" said one of the previous speakers. "Then he must have been a slave. Fancy a number of people calling themselves by the name of a slave!"

"No," answered Sisenna; "as far as I could understand, he was not a slave; but of course, he was not a citizen. He was a workman of some kind, a carpenter, I think the physician told me; but whatever he was, he was a wonderful man. He seems to have gone about healing sick people, and making blind men see, and lame men walk; aye, and dead men live again."

There was a general outcry at this. "No! no!" said one of the audience, expressing the common feeling; "that is too much to believe; the other things might be; but making the dead alive! you are laughing at us."

"I can only tell you," said Sisenna, "what the old man told me; he said that he had seen these things with his own eyes. One of the dead men was a friend of his own, aye, and had been his patient, too, in his last illness. 'I saw him die!' he said. I remember his very words, for I was as little disposed to believe the story as you are. 'I saw him die, for I had been with him all the time; I had done my very best to save him; and I saw him buried, too; then comes this Christus—he had been away, you must understand, when the man died—and makes them roll away the stone from the door of the tomb, and cries to the dead man, "Come forth!" I saw the dead man come out, just as he had been buried, with the grave clothes about him, and his chin tied up with a napkin, just as I had tied it with my own hands, when I knew beyond all doubt that he was dead.' These were the old physician's very words."

"He must have been mad," said one of the audience.

"Possibly," returned Sisenna; "but he wasn't in the least mad in other matters. He talked as sensibly as a man could, and a better physician I never hope to see."

"But tell me," said a soldier who had been listening attentively to Sisenna's word, "how did this strange man come to such a bad end? If he could do such wonderful things, couldn't he have prevented it somehow? And couldn't he have made himself alive again, if he made other people?"

A murmur of approval followed the speaker's words, as if he had succeeded in expressing the general feeling.

"Well," replied Sisenna, "that is just what I asked, and the old man did try to explain it to me, but I could not rightly understand what he said. Only I made out that he needn't have died if he had not been willing."

"No," cried the soldier; "that can't be true. A man choosing to die in such a way! It is past all belief."

"Well, so I thought," said Sisenna; "but as for what you said about his making himself alive again, that is just what the old man told me he did."

"Did he ever see him alive again?" some one asked.

"No, he did not. I particularly asked him, and he said he was not one of those who did. But he believed it. He knew scores of people, he said, who had seen him."

"This is all very strange," said the veteran who had begun the conversation, "and for my part, I can't make head or tail of it. But tell us, what sort of people are these Christians? do they do the horrible things that people charge them with?"

"I can't believe it," replied Sisenna. "I know nothing but what is good of them; and I never found any one who did know, though there are plenty who are ready to say it. My old physician spent all his time in visiting sick people, and I am sure not one in ten paid him anything. He wouldn't have taken anything from me, but that I told him I could afford it. They had a house, he told me, where they took in sick folks to care for them; not people that could pay, you must understand, but poor workmen and slaves and lepers, all the poor wretches that no one else took any heed of."

At this point in the conversation a newcomer entered the room. He was greeted with a cry of welcome. "Ha! Pansa," said one of the company, "you are just the man whom we want to see. Do you know anything about these folk that men call Christians?"

"Well, I ought to," replied the man. "Don't you know that the prisoner whom Celer and I had charge of up to the spring of this year was one of their chief men? He was a Jew, but a citizen. Paulus was his name. He got into trouble with his countrymen at Jerusalem, and was brought before the Governor; but thinking that he should not get a fair trial there he appealed to Cæsar; so the Governor sent him over here. For some reason or other it was a long time before his trial came on, and meanwhile he was allowed to live in a house of his own here in Rome. Well, as I said, Celer and I had charge of him all that time. I don't know whether there is any one here who has had a charge of a prisoner. If there is, he won't need to be told that you get in that way to know as much about a man as there is to be known. You can never get away from him, nor he from you; chained for twelve hours to me, and then twelve to Celer, that is how Paulus lived for two years. And if Celer were here—he got his discharge, you know, about three months ago—he would say what I say, that one couldn't have believed that there was such a good man in the world as our prisoner was. And I do maintain that if the other Christians are anything like him, they are a very admirable set of people. In the first place, his patience was quite inexhaustible. I needn't say that it is a trying thing to a man's temper to be chained to another man. If it was to his own brother, he would not much like it. Of course, it is part of our business, and it all comes in the day's work. But we don't like it. And I am ashamed to say that till I got to know what sort of man this Paulus was, I was often rough with him, and Celer was worse; you know Celer had a rough temper sometimes. But we neither of us ever heard so much as an angry word from him. But he had other things to try him besides us, and we, anyhow at first, were bad enough. He had but poor health; his eyes, I remember in particular, were sometimes very painful. Sometimes, too, he was very short of money. You see he had to live on what his friends sent him, and now and then their contributions fell short or were delayed on the way. Anyhow, he had sometimes scarcely enough for food and firing. But he never said a word of complaint. And whenever he had anything he was always ready to give it away. Prisoners, for the most part, I fancy, think very little of any one but themselves, but he was thinking day and night of people all over the world, I may say. There were letters always coming and going. He could not write himself—his eyes were too bad—though he would add commonly just a few big, sprawling letters with his own hand at the end of a letter. I don't pretend to understand what they were all about. They were in Greek in the first place, and I know very little Greek; and, indeed, however much I might have known, I should hardly have been much the wiser. But I could see this, that they gave him a vast amount of trouble and care. He was thinking about what was in them day and night. I could hear him talking to himself, and he would pray. I have seen him for an hour together, aye, a couple of hours, on his knees praying."

"Why, Pansa," cried one of the soldiers, "I do believe that you are more than half a Christian yourself."

"I might be something much worse, my man," said the soldier.

"Well, it is lucky for you that you are not one just now," retorted the other, "or we should have had you blazing away in a pitch tunic last night."

"Ah," said Pansa, "you may say what you like, but there is something in this business, you may be sure. You should have seen Paulus when the Emperor heard his cause. The boldest man in Rome would not have liked to stand as he did before the Emperor alone, with not a friend to back him up; Nero with a frown on his face as black as thunder, and Poppæa at Nero's side, whispering, as any one might have known, all kinds of mischief against him. You know she hates these Christians just as much as she loves the Jews. Well, I have been on guard pretty often at the hearing of a prisoner, but I never saw a man less disturbed."

"Well, what became of him?" inquired one of Pansa's audience.

"He was acquitted. At first, I could see plainly enough, Nero was dead against him. He would not let him speak a couple of sentences without interruption, and every now and then would burst out laughing. But he came round little by little. Even Poppæa was silenced. At last the Emperor said, 'Paulus, whether you are mad or not, only the gods know; if you are, your madness is better than most men's sound judgment. You seem to me not to have offended either against the majesty of the Roman people, or against the welfare of the human race. My sentence is that you are acquitted.' Then the smith, who was waiting outside, was sent for to strike off the prisoner's chain. While he was doing this the Emperor said, 'How long have you been bound with that chain?' Paulus answered, 'For five years, wanting a month; that is to say, for two years and four months at Cæsarea, and for two years and two months here in Rome, and the journeying hither was five months, seeing that I suffered shipwreck on the way.' Nero said, 'You have endured a wrong.' Then turning to Tigellinus, he said, 'See that he be paid two hundred gold pieces.' That evening Paulus sent for me to his house—the place where we had been in charge of him. When I got there, he said to me, 'Pansa, I fear that I have been a great trouble to you and your comrades these two years past. Pardon me, if I have offended you in aught. I have not been ashamed of my chain, but I know that it tries a man's patience sorely, and I may have erred in hastiness of speech.' I declared, as indeed I had every reason to do, that no one could have borne himself more admirably. He went on, 'I have given you no gifts in these years past, such as it is customary, I am told, for prisoners to give to them that keep them; I judged it not right to do aught that might savour of corruption, and indeed, I but seldom had the means out of which I might give. But now I am no longer bound with this constraint; will it therefore please you to take these twenty-five pieces out of Cæsar's liberality?' Twenty-five gold pieces, gentlemen, do not often come in a poor soldier's way; still I was loth to take them. 'Surely, sir,' I said, 'you need them for yourself.' 'Nay,' said he, 'I am otherwise provided for.' And I happen to know that he did not keep a single piece for himself. He gave to Celer the same sum that he gave to me; the rest he distributed among the poor.

After this he said to me, 'Pansa, it may and will be that you and I shall not meet again. Now I have never spoken to you at any time during these two years past of that which was nearest to my heart. I thought —my God knows whether wrongly or rightly—that I should not, because you would be constrained to listen, whether you would or not; my Master would have free servants only. But now it is permitted to me to speak.' After this he said many things which I cannot now repeat."

"But he did not persuade you?" said one of the listeners.

"Nay; he seemed to ask too much. On my faith, it seemed to me that to be a Christian was to be little better than being dead. Yet I have often wished it otherwise; and, if I see him again—but perhaps it is better to be silent."

"So you don't think there is any harm in these Christians?" said the soldier who had first questioned him.

"None at all, as I am a Roman," said Pansa.

"And you don't believe they set the city on fire?"

"Impossible! The Emperor has been deceived, and it is not difficult to see who deceived him."

After this there was a silence. Though the soldiers might boast of their freedom of speech, every one knew that there were limits to what might safely be said, and that now they were very near to dangerous ground.

Before long the silence was broken by the entrance of a newcomer. The man, who was evidently in a state of great excitement, looked hurriedly round the room, and caught sight of Sisenna.

"Sisenna," he cried, "you know Fannius, the gladiator?"

"I know him well," replied Sisenna. "I served with him in Armenia, and an excellent soldier he was. Well, what of him?"

"He is near his end, and has sent for you."

"Near his end!" cried Pansa in dismay. "Why, he had recovered from his wounds when I saw him a few days ago; and he told me that he was quite well. What ails him?"

"I will tell you as we go," said the messenger; "but make haste, for there is no time to lose."

17

IN THE PRISON

THE story which Pansa heard on his way was briefly this. Part of it we know already. An old comrade and antagonist had informed against him. The man had been vanquished by Fannius in the arena, and, what was a more deadly offence, had been detected by him in a fraudulent attempt to bring about a result that would have greatly profited some disreputable patrons. The arrest of Fannius had followed. But the malignant spite of his enemy had not been satisfied. He had induced the officer in charge of the business to thrust this particular prisoner into the most noisome dungeon in Rome.

Fannius had a great reputation for courage and skill in arms, and it was not difficult to make the officer believe, by dwelling on his lawless and violent temper, that he was a highly dangerous person. Accordingly, all other places of confinement being full, and even more than full, Fannius was thrust into the Tullianum, an underground cell, damp and fetid to a degree that made it almost intolerable. In fact, its original use had been as a place of execution rather than of confinement. In this King Jugurtha, after being led in triumph by his conqueror, had been left to starve. Here the profligate nobles who had conspired with Catiline against the Senate and people of

Rome had been strangled by the hands of the public executioner. In fact, whether the executioner was there or no, imprisonment in this frightful dungeon, at least if continued for more than a few hours, was a sentence of death. So Fannius had found it. Though he had apparently recovered from the wounds received in his conflict with his savage antagonist, loss of blood and long confinement to his bed had really weakened him. On the third day of his imprisonment a malarial fever, due to the loathsome condition of the place, declared itself, and before forty-eight hours had passed his condition was desperate.

Happily he was not suffered to die in this miserable dungeon. His jailer was an old soldier, who would probably have viewed with indifference the sufferings of a civilian prisoner, but who had a soft spot in his heart for any one who had served under the eagles. The man sent for a physician, and the physician peremptorily ordered removal. "He can hardly live," he told the jailer, when he had examined his patient; "but a dry chamber and wholesome air might give him a chance." The jailer had him forthwith taken to his own house. This was technically considered to be part of the prison, so that he might plead that he was only transferring his charge from one cell to another, and one practically as safe, considering that the sick man could not so much as put a foot to the ground, and indeed was more than half unconscious.

The change of air and the careful nursing of the jailer's wife brought about a temporary amendment. Fannius recovered sufficient strength to be able to speak. Summoning his host, as he may be called, to his bedside, he whispered to him the names of two persons whom he particularly desired to see. One of them was Sisenna, an old comrade in arms, whom he was anxious to make executor of his will; the other was Epicharis.

Sisenna was at hand, and, as we have seen, was fetched without delay.

"You are a true friend," said Fannius to him, as he entered the room; "you are not afraid of coming to see a prisoner; a prisoner, too, charged with the most odious of crimes."

"Afraid! No," said the soldier energetically. "And as for crime, whatever they may say, I know that you are altogether incapable of it. But tell me, how can I serve you?" "I wish you," replied Fannius, "to undertake the charge of distributing what little property I shall leave behind me. Subrius the Tribune has the charge of it. It is but a trifle, some two hundred thousand sesterces in all; but I should like some people to know that I have not forgotten them. I shall make my will by word of mouth, for there is no time now for writing. All will be left to you without the mention of any trust; but what I want you to do with the money is this. Half of the money is to go to the freedwoman Epicharis, lately in the service of the Empress Octavia. She is living with her aunt, Galla by name, at the Farm of the Two Fountains near Gabii. Of the other half I wish you to keep twenty thousand sesterces for yourself; as to the remainder, I have to give you a charge which may prove to be somewhat troublesome. Inquire whether I have any kinsfolk on the mother's side—such as I have on the father's side, are, I know, fairly well-off—who are both deserving and in need. Divide the money among such as you may find to be so, exactly as you think fit. If there are none, then distribute it among the poor at your discretion."

"Nay, my friend," said the soldier; "but it is a formidable thing to be trusted in this way. How do you know that I am fit for it?"

"How do I know?" replied Fannius with a smile. "Why, just in the same way that you knew I could not commit a crime. Do not refuse. You are a soldier, and, therefore, they are less likely to dispute the will, which, as made by a prisoner, is of doubtful force."

"Let it be, then, as you will," said Sisenna.

"That is well," said the sick man. "We shall need seven witnesses. There is the jailer and his wife and son; let them send for four others, for you, of course, cannot serve."

The witnesses were easily found. The seven were made up of the three inmates of the house, three soldiers belonging to Sisenna's own company, and the temple servant, in whose house Pomponia had taken refuge. It so happened that this man was an old friend of the jailer.

The form of making the verbal or nuncupatory will, as it was called, was of the simplest and briefest kind. The testator simply said:
—

"I, Caius Fannius, hereby nominate Marcus Sisenna, Centurion in the fourth Prætorian Cohort, as heir to my undivided property."

Immediately afterwards the will was reduced to writing and signed by the witnesses.

The whole of this business was finished about the seventh hour, or one o'clock in the afternoon. Just about sunset Epicharis arrived.

The physician had just paid his patient his evening visit, and was describing his condition to the jailer when Epicharis reached the house. She caught the sound of his voice through the door which happened to be ajar, and guessing from the first words that she heard who he was, and what was his errand in that house, stood in almost breathless suspense to listen. A rapid intuition told her that not to discover herself would be her best chance of knowing the whole truth. If he knew her relation to the sick man the physician would probably, after the fashion of his class, deceive her with some kindly meant misrepresentation of the truth.

"It is as I feared," said the old man. "The improvement of yesterday was a last flicker. They might as well strangle a man as throw him into that pit. Does he wish to see any one?"

The jailer told him that he made his will that morning, and that the woman to whom he was betrothed was coming. Would the excitement of seeing her harm him?

"Harm him!" cried the physician. "Nothing can harm him now. Let him have his will in everything. He can scarce live beyond sunrise to-morrow. I will see him again, though I can do no good. Now I have others to visit."

As he spoke the physician opened the door, and found himself face to face with the girl outside. What she had heard had equalled, even surpassed, her worst fears. That something was wrong, she had not doubted; else why should she have been sent for. Very likely there had been a relapse; he had been doing too much in Rome, and she would take him away again to country quiet and pure air, and nurse him back to health. And the girl, in the newly waked tenderness of her heart, remembered what a happy time the first nursing had been, the danger once over, and she took herself to task for a selfish wish that she might have the same delight again. And now to hear that the man she loved was within a few hours of his death. She stood, petrified with dismay, unable to speak or move.

The old physician at once guessed who she was. Assuming his set, professional smile, he said in as cheerful a tone as he could command, for, used as he was to suffering, his patient's case had touched him, "Ah, my dear girl, you have come, I suppose, to set our friend all right. You will find him a little low, and must be careful with him."

"Ah, sir," cried the girl, recovering her speech, "do not seek to deceive me. I heard all that you said, as I stood here."

The old man's manner changed at once to a grave kindliness. "You know it, then," he said. "You are a brave girl, I see; control yourself; you will have time for tears hereafter; now make his last hour as happy as you can. The gods comfort you!"

He pressed her hand with a friendly grasp, and hurried away, but it was long before he forgot the look of hopeless sorrow that was written on that beautiful face.

"I am Epicharis, whom you sent for," she said to the jailer's wife as she entered the room. "Stay," she went on, lifting up her hand as she spoke, "I know the whole truth. And now let me sit here a while and recover myself somewhat before I see him."

She sat down, and resolutely set herself to master the passion of grief that was struggling within for expression. A flood of tears would have been an inexpressible relief; but did she once give way to them, when could she recover her calm? Time was precious, and she must not risk losing it. By degrees she controlled herself, fighting down with success the dry, tearless sobs that for a time would rise in her breast. She consented, though loathing it in her heart, to drink the cup of wine which her hostess pressed upon her, and it certainly helped her in her struggle. In about half an hour's time she was calm enough to enter the sick man's chamber.

Fannius had fallen into a light sleep, but awoke as she came in. For a time, as will often happen in cases of weakness, he failed to collect his thoughts. He had been dreaming of past times, days in which Epicharis had been cold and disdainful, and the girl's real presence seemed only to carry on the visionary scene which sleep had conjured up before his eyes.

"Why does she come to torment me?" he said. "I had best forget her, if she cannot love me."

The girl's eyes filled with tears. It is hard to say which pained her more, the thought of the happiness which she might have had, had she been less set on her own purposes, or that of which she had had a brief glimpse, but could now see no more.

She threw herself on her knees by the bedside, and kissed the pale hand which rested on the coverlet.

The touch of her warm lips recalled the dying man to himself. His eyes lightened with a smile of inexpressible tenderness.

"You are come, darling," he said. "I knew that you would. You will stay with me now," he whispered after a pause. "It will not be for long."

After that he seemed content to be silent. Indeed, he was almost too weak to speak. But, to judge from the happy smile upon his face, it was bliss to feel her hand in his, and to keep his eyes fixed upon her face.

About an hour short of midnight he fell asleep. Epicharis sat on in the same posture, watching him as he slept with an intense earnestness. A little after dawn he woke.

"Give me," he said, "a cordial. I have something to say, and need a little strength."

The physician had left a cordial, some old Falernian wine with bettany root dissolved in it, in case the occasion for it should arise.

Epicharis raised the sick man's head from the pillow, and put the cup to his lips. He took a few sips and then spoke: "Tell Subrius the Prætorian that he is embarked on an ill business. It will not prosper. And you, too, beware of it. Put away these thoughts from you. It has been borne in upon me that these things will be your ruin. I have had a dreadful dream since I slept. I saw Nero sitting on his throne, and the ground round him was covered with dead bodies, as thickly as if there had been a battle. But I could not see their faces."

"But you told me yourself," said Epicharis, "of this undertaking, and seemed glad that it was set on foot."

"Ah! but things are changed since then with me. I did not know what I know now."

The fact was, that it was only a few days before his arrest that Fannius had discussed the subject with one of the Christian teachers. Probably there have always been two ways of thinking about the lawfulness of resistance to power, unrighteous in itself or unrighteously exercised. But among the early Christians there was certainly a greater weight of authority on the side of submission. "The powers that be are ordained of God" was the teaching of the great Apostle who had formed the views of the Church in Rome; and this view had been strongly enforced on Fannius by the teacher whom he consulted, one of those who had learnt all that they knew at the feet of St. Paul.

The mind of the soldier had been much agitated by conflicting emotions. The old loyalty to the Emperor, which was part of a soldier's training, was now reinforced by a religious sanction. On the other hand, he was deeply committed to comrades with whose desire to free Rome from the shame of its present degradation he strongly sympathized. And then there was Epicharis. She lived, he knew, to avenge a cruel wrong to one whom she loved. This aim was the thing nearest to her heart, nearer, he was aware, than her love for him. Could he endure to disappoint her?

Then came the arrest and imprisonment of the Christians. The tyrant who had given the order now seemed doubly hateful. Still it did not change the soldier's newly acquired views of duty. In one way it emphasized them. The more difficult submission appeared, the greater the obligation to it. "Not only to the good and gentle, but also to the froward," were words that rung in his ears. And in the near presence of his death this call of duty, as he conceived it, became louder and more imperative. To see Epicharis, and to implore her to abandon her scheme, became a pressing necessity.

"I implore you," he said, "as you love me, to give up your schemes. Leave the wrong-doer to be punished by God. His vengeance is stronger and surer than ours."

It was a critical moment. The girl indeed did not understand the reason which moved Fannius to speak in this way. She fancied that he was more concerned for her safety than for anything else. Still his entreaty weighed greatly with her. He was a dying man, and the last requests of the dying are hard to refuse; and she felt, too, that she owed him some redress. The words "I promise" were almost on her lips. Had she spoken them the fate of many persons with whom our story is concerned might have been different. But at the very moment she was about to speak there came a sudden interruption.

An official sent to inspect the prison had discovered the change which the keeper of the Tullianum had taken upon himself to make in the custody of Fannius. As he had been specially instructed to allow no relaxation in the severity of imprisonment, he at once directed that the man should be carried back to the dungeon from which he had been transferred. The jailer in vain represented that the prisoner was dying. "That makes no difference," was the answer. "I must obey my orders," and he pushed his way, followed by two attendants, into the chamber of death.

"There he is," he cried to the men; "carry him back, dead or alive."

At the sound of his voice, Epicharis rose from where she had been kneeling by the bedside, and confronted the two men.

"You shall not touch him," she cried.

The attendants fell back astonished, so majestic was she in the white heat of her wrath.

"Thrust her aside," cried their more hardened master, from where he stood in the background.

The men hesitated; she might have a weapon in her dress, and looked quite capable of dealing a mortal blow.

The inspector, infuriated at this delay, now himself made a forward movement.

At this moment a voice from behind changed the woman's mood.

"Epicharis!" said the dying man feebly.

She turned to him with a gesture of tenderness.

"Hinder them not," he whispered. "I can die as easily there as here. Kiss me, dearest. The Lord Christ bless and keep you, and bring us to meet again."

She stooped to kiss him.

Even the brutal official could not interrupt this parting. When it was over, his victim was out of the reach of his cruelty. Fannius was dead.

18

SURRENDER

POPPAEA and her advisers were not inclined, it may easily be supposed, to rest satisfied with their double defeat in the matter of Pomponia. That she had escaped from the illegal violence of the first attack was vexatious enough, but it was a thing that had to be endured. It was a different thing when she was found to have eluded a legal order for her arrest. The question was, how was the hiding-place of the fugitives to be discovered? Nothing was learnt by the strictest inquiries at Subrius' country house. The inmates, some of whom Tigellinus did not scruple to torture, evidently knew nothing about the matter. The two ladies had disappeared a few hours before the arrival of the arresting party; beyond that, nothing could be learnt. Supposed confessions, which were wrung out of one of the slaves, were found not to lead to any discoveries. It was soon seen that they were fictions, produced to obtain an immediate release from pain, as confessions obtained by pressure of torture frequently were. A more hopeful plan was to search through the multitude of arrested persons for some one who might really be willing and able to give such information as would lead to a discovery. Slaves who had been in Pomponia's household in Rome were found, but they could easily prove that they knew nothing more of her movements beyond her departure from the city. It was when she left Subrius' house that she seemed to have vanished into space. Poppæa, however, was not to be baffled. One person, she learnt, had accompanied Pomponia on her journey; this was the old steward. It was probable that he was in possession of the secret of her hiding-place. If he was arrested, it might be extorted from him. The detectives were immediately put upon his track, and it was not long before their search was successful. Sad to say, it was a fellow-believer, or, at least, one who professed himself to be such, that betrayed him. Even in days when nothing, it would seem, that could attract, was to be gained by the profession of Christian belief, there were some who made that profession without adequate conviction. The mere reckless desire of change, or a passing emotion that was mistaken for genuine faith, led them into a false position. Or they were of that class, who, as the Master had foreseen, would receive the word gladly, and in times of persecution fall away; and, it must be confessed, the trial was terrible. Under such pressure, strong natures might well have failed; much more this poor young slave, feeble in frame, and of a selfish, pleasure-loving temper, who gave the fatal information about Phlegon. The bribe of freedom, safety, and a sum of fifty thousand sesterces, that seemed to assure him of a future livelihood, were too much for his constancy and good faith. The information that he gave enabled the officers, before three days were over, to arrest the old man.

Even then Poppæa and her friends did not seem much nearer to the attainment of their object. Questioned as to whether he was acquainted with Pomponia's hiding- place, he did not affect to deny it. His sturdy principle forbade him to speak anything but the truth, however much it might be to his own injury. But at this acknowledgment he stopped. He could not, indeed, bring his lips to say the thing that was not; but beyond this he did not feel his obligation to go. Any information that might help the persecutors to secure their prey, he resolutely refused to give. Bribes were tried at first; they were contemptuously rejected. Threats were freely used, but seemed to make no impression. Torture was then employed. The old Roman rule that it was never to be applied to free persons had long since fallen into neglect. For some years past persons of much higher rank than the old steward had been exposed to it. When even Senators and knights had been stretched on the rack, and tortured with the heated plates of metal, it was not likely that an insignificant freedman would escape.

But even torture seemed little likely to be successful. Indeed, the limits of its possible application were very soon reached. Phlegon was old and feeble; a few minutes sufficed to throw him into a long faint from which it was no easy matter to recall him. The physician slave, who was in attendance, to guard against this very risk, warned the executioner that another application would very probably be fatal.

Yet, curiously enough, the very patience and courage of the sufferer helped to reveal the secret which he would gladly have given his life to keep. Phlegon had been confined in the Tullianum, though not in one of its lower dungeons; and the jailer, as being responsible for his prisoners, had been present when the torture was applied. Hardened as he was by more than twenty years of office, the events of the last few days had touched him. He had seen innocent men suffer before, but never men of quite the same stamp as Fannius and Phlegon. So full was he of the feelings thus raised, that as soon as he was released from his duties, he went to talk the subject over with his friends, the temple servant and his wife. And thus the tidings reached Claudia. From Pomponia herself all such things were carefully kept.

Statia had not heard from the jailer the name of the sufferer; but Claudia recognized in her description of him Pomponia's steward. And when she further heard that he was being tortured in order to compel him to reveal the hiding- place of a noble lady who was accused of being a Christian, any doubt that she may have had of his identity was removed.

It was with the greatest difficulty that the girl retained her self-control, while her hostess gossiped on, repeating, in her usual fashion, the description of the suffering and the fortitude of Phlegon, which the jailer had given her. Left at last to think over the matter, she was in sore perplexity. Should she keep what she had heard to herself, or should she communicate it to Pomponia? She could not, of course, entirely forget that her own life was at stake, and she grew sick and faint when she remembered the horrors of which she had been told. Still it was not this, it was her duty to Pomponia, that made her hesitate. Pomponia, beyond all doubt, would give herself up to save the old man's life. But would she save it? Would she not be only sacrificing her own? The old man was most certainly doomed. Why should another be uselessly involved in his fate? All this seemed reasonable enough. Still she could not persuade herself that it was right. What would Pomponia herself say? Supposing that she kept the matter from her now, would she ever be able to reveal it? Could she ever go to her and say, "I knew that your faithful servant was being tortured, and I kept it from you?" This thought in the end decided her. It must, she felt, be wrong so to act that there would be a lifelong secret between herself and her nearest friend.

Her resolution once arrived at, she lost no time in carrying it out. "Mother," she said to Pomponia, "the persecutors have laid hands on Phlegon, and have tortured him to wring out the secret of our hiding-place."

Pomponia's spirits had for some time been drooping and depressed. She knew that her fellow-believers were suffering. Why was she not among them? Why, when they were bravely confessing their Lord, was she in hiding? And yet she could not bring herself to feel that duty bade her deliver herself up, and still less that she ought to endanger her young companion. Her courage rose instantaneously to the occasion.

"Brave old man!" she cried. "And of course he has been silent. Nothing, I am sure, could wring from his lips a word that was false or base. But he must not suffer. They shall not have to ask him again. They shall hear what they want from me. But, my child, what shall we do with you? "

"Can you ask, mother? " cried the girl. "Whithersoever you go, I go also."

"Nay, my child," said Pomponia; "there is no need for that."

The girl stood up with flashing eyes, a true daughter of kings. "I hope you do not hold me unworthy of your company. Mother," she added in a softer tone, while she threw her arms round the elder woman's neck, "you will not bid me leave you?"

"Let us pray," said Pomponia.

The two women knelt together, hand clasped in hand. Such supplications, whether expressed in words, or only conceived in the heart, are too sacred to be written down. They rose comforted and strengthened, the path of duty plain before them. Whatever burden it might be the will of their Master to put upon them, they would bear it together.

"Bid our hostess send for a litter," said Pomponia. "We will go without delay to the palace."

An hour afterwards as Nero sat in council with Poppæa and Tigellinus a freedman announced that the Lady Pomponia, together with Claudia, daughter of Cogidumnus, King of the Regni in Britain, were below, and awaited the Emperor's pleasure.

Poppæa's eyes gleamed with a sinister joy.

On the other hand, neither Nero nor his Minister were particularly pleased. Tigellinus' spies and agents, of whom he had a vast number in Rome, had reported to him that popular sympathy was now turning in favour of the sufferers. Had they been the worst of criminals, the ferocity of the punishments inflicted on them would have roused a feeling of pity; and it was doubtful whether they were criminals at all. Of course the free-spoken comments of the Prætorians at what had happened were not unknown to him. If this had been the case in the case of obscure and insignificant persons, what would happen when the victim was a high-born and distinguished lady.

"How is it your pleasure to deal with them, Sire?" asked Tigellinus after a short pause.

"Let them be sent to the Tullianum," cried Poppæa, carried by her spite out of her usual prudence.

Nero turned upon them with an angry scowl.

"Peace, woman," he shouted in a voice of thunder. "You know not what you say. These ladies are ten times better born than you."

The Empress, furious as she was at the rebuff, choked down her rage, and murmured, "As you will, Sire."

"Let them be handed over to the keeping of Lateranus till it be convenient to hear their case," was the Emperor's decision.

"The Emperor remembers," said Tigellinus, "that Lateranus is the nephew of the Lady Pomponia."

"I know it," answered the Emperor. "It will serve well enough. She will be honourably kept and safely. That is enough. See that the necessary orders be given. Pardon me, my dearest," he went on, turning to Poppæa. "I would not willingly thwart you in anything, but there are reasons, which I am sure you will see, if you give yourself time to think. I will not ask you," he added with a bitter smile, "to be lenient to these prisoners because they are women. That, I have found out, is scarcely a passport to a woman's favour. But you must remember that Pomponia is the widow of a great general, whose name is still remembered among the soldiers, while her companion is the daughter of a King. You cannot deal with such as if they were the wife and daughter of a freedman."

"You know best, Sire," said the Empress in a voice from which she vainly endeavoured to banish all traces of sulkiness.

"Thanks, my Poppæa," replied Nero; "we shall doubtless agree. And now to more serious business. This is the first draft of what I propose to recite at the games."

Four years before Nero had instituted what was to be a Roman rival to the Olympian games. The second celebration was at hand, and he had been preparing a poem on the Deification of Romulus, which he proposed to recite in public. It was this that he now submitted to the criticism of his privy council.

19

EPICHARIS ACTS

THE conspirators had not been indifferent spectators of the events recorded in the preceding chapters. Everything combined to raise their hopes. The Emperor seemed to be madly rushing on to his own ruin. The monstrous freak, which common report more and more confidently attributed to him, of burning his own capital, the revolting cruelty with which he had sought to divert suspicion from himself to a set of poor creatures, who, at the worst, were harmless fanatics, the unseemly buffoonery by which he lowered his Imperial dignity, were all helping, they thought, to overthrow the throne. Every day appeared to be giving to their schemes a more certain prospect of success. As long as this was so, it naturally seemed a mistake to hurry on their execution. Give the wretch time enough, so they said to each other, and he will destroy himself; he will not have a single friend left among nobles, people, or army.

There were some, the Tribune Subrius among them, who chafed angrily at this delay. He never could rid himself of the idea that he had already missed a great chance, when he abandoned his plan of striking down Nero in his private theatre, and he strongly protested against losing more time. Conspiracies that are long in hatching were, he knew, infallibly betrayed either by treachery or by chance. "There are too many of us," he said to one of his military confederates; "we are too powerful; had we been only a few desperate fellows with nothing to lose, it would have been settled, and probably settled in the right way, long ago.

In this impatient mood Epichris found him a few days after that on which Fannius had breathed his last. In the morning he had been present at a meeting of the conspirators, and had again urged on them the necessity of speedy action. Pudens, who had been formally enrolled among the associates, as heartily supported him. He agreed with him in theory, and he found additional reason in the imminent danger of Claudia, of which he had by this time become aware. Their arguments were in vain; the majority overbore them.

The two friends, as they discussed the question in Subrius' quarters, became more and more convinced that in one way or another a crisis must be precipitated.

"These men," said Subrius to his companion, "are thinking of something else besides the one thing needful, which is to get rid of the tyrant. Laternus, for instance, is thinking about his own life; Piso is thinking about his own chances of the Empire. Now a man ought to care for nothing but how he may drive home his blow."

"Right!" cried Pudens. "Why should we not act for ourselves? Let us give them another seven days, and then cast lots who shall strike, you or I."

"Agreed!" said Subrius, stretching out his hand.

Just as he spoke, a soldier servant knocked at the door of the room, and, bidden to enter, announced that a young man wished to speak with the Tribune.

"Show him in," said the Prætorian, and the visitor was ushered into the room.

The newcomer wore the heavy hood which the Romans commonly used for purposes of disguise. Its depths hid the features of the face more effectually, as the wearer carefully took a place where the light fell from behind.

"Do I speak to Subrius the Prætorian?" said the visitor.

"That is my name," replied the soldier.

"And this?" the speaker went on, indicating Pudens with a slight wave of the hand.

"My friend, Marcus Annius Pudens, from whom I have no secrets."

"Then I may speak freely?"

"Certainly."

Throwing back the hood, the visitor revealed the features of Epicharis.

Pudens had never seen her before, but Subrius immediately remembered the features of the girl whom he had seen speaking to Fannius in the school of Thraso.

The name of the ex-gladiator, whom, indeed, he had missed for some days, without knowing anything of his fate, naturally rose to his lips.

"And Fannius?" he said. "How does he fare?"

"I have now another besides Octavia to avenge," answered the girl in a low voice.

"What?" cried the Prætorian. "Hath any evil overtaken him?"

Epicharis told him the story that we know. When she had finished she went on: "Fannius told me—it was when we were newly betrothed,"—the girl's voice broke for a moment as she uttered the word, but was firm again the next moment,—"that there were some who were minded not to suffer the wrongs which Rome has suffered to go unpunished any longer. He gave me no names; I asked him for none, though I think I can keep a secret. But ever since I first knew him he used to speak of you; and to you, accordingly, I have come. Let me speak plainly. If you have in your mind the purpose that I suppose you to have, let me help you. I have now only one thing to live for, to punish the monster who first killed my mistress, and then did to death my lover. If you have no such thoughts, if you think me a criminal for cherishing them, then give me up to Nero. I shall be content, for I have no more desire to live."

The situation in which Subrius found himself was perplexing in the extreme. That the woman was in earnest he did not doubt for a moment. He had heard, we know, her story from Fannius, and had been greatly impressed by it. And now her look, her words, carried with them an irresistible conviction of her earnestness; but he hesitated. The lives and fortunes of others besides himself were at stake. To confide in a woman was certainly a novel experiment, and at first sight at least dangerous. If failure was the result, how overpowering the shame and the disgrace of having made it. After a hurried review of the circumstances he resolved to temporize. Probably he was wrong. Everything did go wrong in this unlucky undertaking. But almost every one, viewing the circumstances as he viewed them, would have said that he was right.

"Lady," he began, "I will be as frank with you as you have been with me. If you have put your life in my hands, so will I put mine in yours. I do not deny that I and my friends have had the purposes of which you speak, yes, and have them still. But these things are not done in a hurry; we must watch our time, our opportunity; when that comes we shall not be wanting, nor shall we fail, if we need your help, to ask for it. Till then we must be patient and silent."

Epicharis was bitterly disappointed at this procrastinating answer. She was not in a mood to wait and be patient. Action, immediate action, was an imperative necessity. She rose to go, wrapping the hood again round her face.

"I am only a woman," she said, "and know less and can do less than you; yet I think that you are wrong. You say that these things cannot be done in a hurry; it seems to me that they must be so done, if they are to be done at all."

The next moment she was gone.

"By all the gods in heaven, she is right!" cried Subrius to Pudens when they found themselves alone. "I wish that I could have trusted her. But it was impossible. If any mishap were to come of it, what would not the others have said—'wheedled out of his senses by a woman,' and all the rest of it. It would be intolerable. And yet, I have a feeling that it would have been better."

Better it would certainly have been.

Epicharis, as has been said, was not content to wait. If Subrius would not help her, where, she asked herself, could she find some one who would? In a moment, for she was in that condition of exaltation and excitement when ideas have a rapid birth, a daring scheme presented itself to her mind. Nowhere was Nero more easily approached than when he was at one of his favourite seaside haunts. There he was accustomed to dispense with the etiquette and ceremony which surrounded him at Rome. His bodyguard, whom he always regarded more as a part of Imperial state than as a necessary protection, was often dismissed. He would spend many hours with not more than one or two companions, either wandering on the shore, or rowing in a boat, or fishing from the rocks. What could be easier, she thought, if only she could find an accomplice, to surprise him in one of those unguarded moments?

Resolving to seek such an accomplice herself, the first necessity that she perceived was of an effectual disguise. The man's dress which she had assumed in order to find her way to the quarters of Subrius had served its purpose well enough on that occasion. But it would not now suffice, and she accordingly resolved to assume the character of a singing-girl. This she could do with great ease; she had a particularly sweet voice, and could sing and play with more than usual skill. A further disguise was secured by wearing Syrian dress and ornaments, and by adding a deeper brown to her complexion. Another device, which she felt might be useful in carrying out her scheme, was to pretend ignorance of any language but Greek, except so far as the use of a few words of broken Latin might go.

Thus apparelled and equipped, she made her way down to Misenum, where a squadron of the fleet was stationed. She began by singing outside the wine shops to which the sailors were accustomed to resort, and speedily achieved a great success. Her reputation as an accomplished performer spread among the higher circles, and it was not long before she was engaged to perform at a banquet given by one of the captains to his colleagues. Other similar invitations followed. As the guests spoke freely before her, presuming on her supposed ignorance of Latin, while she always kept her ears open, and listened with an eager attention which suffered nothing to escape her, she soon learnt much about the characters and tempers of the officers in command.

One of these men, Proculus by name, she recognized as an old acquaintance. He had once been in command of the yacht which belonged to Agrippina, the Emperor's mother. It was one of the very few pleasures of Octavia's unhappy life to join her mother-in-law in occasional excursions round the Campanian coast. At these times Epicharis had often been in waiting, and Proculus had regarded her with much admiration. She gathered now from words that he let drop in her hearing, and from what was said by others, that he was in a dissatisfied frame of mind. He was accustomed to talk vaguely of great services which he had rendered to the Emperor, and which had received a very inadequate reward. This seemed to promise some sort of an opening, and she resolved, in default of anything better, to avail herself of it. It is true that she did not like or trust the man. In old times he had not been a favourite; his openly expressed admiration had, on the contrary, been extremely offensive to her. But she was almost in despair. She had not found in the fleet any of the explosive material, so to speak, which she had hoped to discover there. Nero seemed to be highly popular. He mixed freely with the sailors, treated them in a friendly fashion, and was liberal in his presents. Still, for her present purpose, one such adherent as Proculus would suffice. Carried out of herself by her eagerness for revenge, with her mind, in fact, thrown off its balance by this excitement, she resolved to make the trial.

One day, in the course of an entertainment, Proculus had paid her some compliment on her musical skill and gone on to express his admiration for her beauty. Crushing down disgust at his advances, for the man was personally odious to her, Epicharis gave an answer that encouraged further conversation, and induced him, with no little skill, to speak of himself, his disappointments, and his claims. Artfully expressing a sympathetic surprise that he had not reached a position more commensurate with his merits, of which he had indeed an unbounded opinion, she led him on to use language which certainly had an almost treasonable sound. As a matter of fact, this talk was mere bluster. He would not have used it to any one who would, he thought, have taken it seriously. But this was exactly what Epicharis did. When she judged that he had to a certain extent committed himself, she revealed her identity. The man, though somewhat confused with the wine which he had been drinking, at once perceived that there was something serious in the affair. Epicharis he had almost forgotten, but he was perfectly well aware that Octavia had left devoted friends behind her. He listened with attention when she began to hint at the scheme which was in her mind. She would tell him no names, but she gave him to understand that there were powerful people behind her, people who would be able and willing to remunerate him handsomely for any service that he might render. Only, she was careful to impress upon him, he must lose no time; he must not let any one else anticipate him.

For a time the man wavered. It might be worth his while, he thought, to make the venture. It might be possible to secure a position really worth having under a new order of things. He was ambitious, so far as a greedy, pleasure- loving temper could make him so, and for a few moments he seemed to see within his reach great power and wealth, and all the opportunities of pleasure which these two things command. And though he was a dull, brutal, utterly selfish creature, the enthusiasm of Epicharis, backed as it was by the charm of her beauty, touched his fancy if not his heart.

But when the magic of her presence was removed, he began to see impossibilities in the way which had not occurred to him before. In fact, the man's past was such that if Epicharis had but known it, he would have been the very last person in the world in whom she would have confided. The services which he had rendered to Nero, and for which he conceived himself to have been insufficiently paid, were such as to put an absolutely impassable gulf between him and the revolutionists. He had been Nero's tool in the perpetration of the very worst of his crimes, the murder of his mother. It was he who had been in command of the yacht in which she nearly met with her death. He was actually present and assisting when the hideous deed was finally accomplished. Nero might not be duly grateful for such services, but from any one else they would meet with no other reward than the halter or the axe. When Nero had received his due, then those who had helped to rid him of his mother and his wife would not be long in meeting with theirs. Epicharis' schemes, therefore, had, when he came to examine them, nothing attractive about them. Still, as he soon began to reflect, they might be made to yield a profit. Why not use them to put Nero under a second obligation? Why not give information of them, and pose as the saviour of the Emperor's life?

This last purpose was almost immediately carried out. Before the next day had dawned Proculus was at Antium, where Nero was then residing, and in the course of a few hours Tigellinus was in possession of all that he had to communicate. The Minister acted promptly. Epicharis, who had been eagerly waiting for some communication from Proculus, was arrested in her lodging by a Centurion, conveyed in a litter to the Emperor's villa at Antium, and almost immediately after confronted with her accuser.

She did not lose her self-possession and presence of mind for a moment. Proculus told his story, not, of course, without exaggeration, and the addition of details which made it more picturesque and effective. She met it with a flat denial. He had no witnesses to produce; and for the present, at least, her word was as good as his.

As for herself, she made no attempt at concealment. She had been a waiting woman of the Empress, and she had loved her mistress.

Questioned as to the reason why she had disguised herself as a singing- girl, she smiled and shrugged her shoulders. It was partly, she explained, a frolic, but chiefly because she was desperately poor. "My mistress," she explained with the utmost simplicity of manner, "left me a legacy, which would have put me beyond poverty; but it has not yet been paid to me."

The shaft struck home, as it had been intended to strike, though the intention was admirably concealed. Nero blushed and winced. He had had the meanness to refuse, or, rather, to postpone indefinitely, the payment of the few legacies which Octavia had left to her attendants.

Every inquiry she met with the same imperturbable composure. She missed no opportunity of planting a sting in the consciences of her questioners—if consciences they had; but no one could be sure that it was done with intention. In the end, she came out of the cross-examination, which was protracted and severe, without having made a single damaging admission.

When accuser and accused were removed from the presence, the Emperor summed up the case after this fashion. "Well, the woman has much more the look of telling the truth than the man. And he is, I know, a thorough scoundrel. However, where there is smoke there is pretty sure to be fire. See that she is kept in safe custody, Tigellinus, but don't let any harm come to her. We shall see what happens."

20

THE PLOT THICKENS

THE arrest and detention of Epicharis was soon known to the conspirators at Rome. At the result of the examination, they could only guess. However, as she was being kept in honourable custody, without having to suffer any indignity or hardship, it was safe to conjecture that nothing compromising had been discovered.

Still the incident was alarming, and made the necessity of immediate action more pressing than ever. A meeting of the conspirators, who now numbered more than fifty in all, itself a most dangerous circumstance, was held without delay. At this it was unanimously resolved, almost without discussion, that the attempt must be made at the very first convenient opportunity. The Tribune Subrius, who was generally recognized as one of the most daring of the associates, and who, if it had only been permitted, would have struck the blow long before, was invited to give his opinion as to the time, the place, and the manner of the deed, which, it must be understood, was nothing else than the assassination of Nero.

Subrius had thought out his plan, and had the details ready. "In my judgment," he said," we have already waited too long; but of that it is now useless to speak, except so far as to prove that we should wait no longer. We are in imminent danger. A woman, who knows at least the names of two of us, is in prison on this very charge; and though I know her to be brave and steadfast beyond the habit of her sex, the peril that lies in her knowledge is great. Let us anticipate it. To-night Nero goes to Baiæ, and takes up his abode in the villa of Caius Piso. There is no place where he lives in so little state; and state, with the multitudes of guards and attendants that it implies, is the same thing as safety. I propose that the deed be done to-morrow, and I offer myself as the doer of it. Suffer me to choose the hour, and also my companion, for more than one I shall not need."

A murmur of applause followed the speech. When it had subsided, all eyes were turned to Piso. His approval was necessary, not only as being the owner of the villa, but as being, so to speak, the heir presumptive to the throne. Piso rose immediately.

"It vexes me," he said, "to differ, as my conscience compels me, from the counsel of a most gallant and energetic gentleman. You have thought me worthy of succeeding to the dignity about to be left vacant by the most merited punishment of him who now unworthily occupies it. But I cannot consent to polluting the first auspices of my rule by an atrocious crime. It is not that I think the slaughter of an impious and bloodstained wretch to be anything but a worthy deed; it is that the vilest of mankind may gain pity, and even pardon, by the manner of his death. Nero, indeed, deserves to die; but that he should perish, a guest at the table of his host, while he is enjoying in security the entertainment which I offer to him, would be a thing equally odious to both gods and men. Power acquired by such a crime could not be exercised with benefit either to the Roman people or myself. Both as a private man, to whom the sanctity of his house is as precious as it is to all good citizens, or as the man about to be called by your suffrage to the Imperial power, I refuse my consent to the execution of this plan."

There was a general feeling of disappointment, and even dismay, when Piso sat down. It was generally felt that the reason which he had given for his dissent was both true and false: so far true that no one could dispute its validity; so far false that it did not express his whole mind. It was founded, not on a scruple, but a fear. Assure him of the succession, and he would have struck Nero as he sat at his table, with his own hand, all laws of hospitality notwithstanding. It was the obstacle that such a deed might be to this succession that he feared. He was not indispensable; to many he would not be the most eligible candidate for power. The scale might be thus finally turned against him. There might be a general agreement on some rival who would begin the new reign unstained by crime. Such a rival he had in his mind, a man of blameless morals and of race as noble as his own, with the added distinction of being a descendant of Augustus. Still, whatever his motives, his decision was final.

The next speaker was a Senator, Scævinus by name.

"Three days hence," he said, "the Feast of Ceres begins. The Emperor will certainly attend on the last day. Then will be our chance. When he comes down from his box, as he always does, will be the time."

"That," said Subrius, "puts it off for eleven days more, and no one knows what may happen in that time. Still, I shall be ready."

Scævinus stood up again. "The help of our friend Subrius will be welcome then as always; but I claim the chief part in the deed for myself; it is my hand that must strike the first blow."

A murmur of surprise ran through the meeting. No one had ever been able to guess why Scævinus had associated himself with the enterprise. He was a man of dissolute life, who had never shown any kind of energy except in the pursuit of pleasure. As for his present demand, it was nothing less than astonishing. However, it could not well be refused; the meeting had accepted the scheme, and its proposer must be allowed to take the chief share in it.

Subrius shrugged his shoulders. "What does the man mean?" he whispered to his next neighbour. "No one more unfit could have been found if we had searched Rome through from one end to the other. The man has neither strength nor nerve. If he ever had them, which I much doubt, for he comes of a bad stock, he has wasted them long ago."

The Tribune's feelings were shared by others, especially the soldiers; and there were manifest signs of dissent.

At this point Lateranus rose. "Suffer me to explain what we propose. I have a private request to make of the Emperor; as we are all friends here, I don't mind saying that it is a petition for a grant out of the privy purse in aid of the expenses of my Consulship. He has had notice that I am going to prefer it; he likes to make a parade of his liberality, and so he will not be surprised when I ask him this favour in public. I shall throw myself down on my knees before him, when he comes down from his box, and take care to do it in such a way as to upset him. When he is once down I shall not let him get up again. Then will be the time for all my friends who desire to have a hand in the affair to run up and do their best to rid the world of this monster. All that Scævinus demands is the glory of being allowed to strike the first blow!"

This explanation put a new and more satisfactory face on the matter. Lateranus was a man of huge stature and of great personal strength; of his courage and resolution there was no question.

"That sounds better," said the Prætorian to his friend. "Practically, Lateranus takes the first part; he is in every way fit for it, and besides, he has an unimpeachable reason for approaching the Emperor. Scævinus' privilege of striking the blow is only a concession to his trumpery vanity, which, I suppose, we need not grudge him. If he does not make haste about it, when his turn comes, I know that I for one shall not wait for him. And yet I can't help wishing that the silly fool had nothing to do with it. He may make a failure of it all yet."

A few more details remained to be arranged. It was obviously inexpedient that all the conspirators should take part in the assassination. Some would have to manage the not less important business of suggesting a successor. Accordingly a division of forces was made. Fifteen would be quite as many as were wanted to make sure of the Emperor's death. These were to find places as near as possible to the steps which led down from the Emperor's box into the arena. Others were to be scattered in prominent places about the building, and were to shout, as soon as the deed was done, "Hail, Caius Piso, Cæsar Augustus Imperator!"

For the rest of the conspirators a still more important function was reserved. The voices of the people were of little account without the consent and approval of the soldiers. Piso, it was arranged, was to be in waiting in the temple of Ceres. As soon as the deed was done, the remainder of the associates, including the most popular of the officers engaged in the conspiracy, and one or two Senators who had served in former years with distinction, and so were known to the soldiers, were to hurry the candidate for the Empire to the camp of the Prætorians. When the soldiers' voices were won by flatteries, promises, and bribes, all would be well. The Senate might be relied upon to register the decision of the men of war. Before nightfall, on the nineteenth of April, it was hoped that messengers would be on their way to the great camps on the frontiers, carrying the announcement that Caius Piso was now, by choice of the Senate and people of Rome, Cæsar Augustus, Imperator, Dictator, Tribune of the People, with perpetual authority.

During the intervening days nothing of importance occurred. Nero paid his proposed visit to Piso's villa at Baiæ. From thence he came to Rome, arriving in the city on the third day of the festival. He did not show himself at this or any of the five following days. But this excited no apprehension. It was not his custom to attend except on the last day. That he would be present then was practically certain, for it was advertised that the Emperor would contend with certain named competitors in a chariot-race.

Meanwhile the secret of the conspiracy was kept with a fidelity that, considering the number of the persons engaged, was in the last degree astonishing. On the eve of the appointed day everything was hope and confidence. Unfortunately there was one element of weakness, and that one was to have disastrous consequences.

21

BETRAYED

S CAEVINUS had been for some time repenting, if not of his share in the conspiracy, certainly of the impulse which had prompted him to demand the most prominent place in the execution of its purpose. It was now impossible to draw back; if pride had not forbidden—and with all his weakness he was still a Roman —his associates might suspect him of treachery, and summarily silence him. The only thing left for him was to fortify his courage as best he could.

His first step was to choose for the deed what he conceived to be a peculiarly lucky weapon. Though, like most of his contemporaries, he believed in little or nothing, he was curiously superstitious, a combination of apparent opposites which has never been uncommon, and which in the pleasure-loving society of Rome was peculiarly frequent. He happened to be the head of a family in which the care of a famous provincial temple, the shrine of Fortune at the little Latin town of Ferentinum, was hereditary. Among the most cherished treasures of this place was an ancient dagger with which a family legend was connected. In the days when the Gauls had captured Rome and were desolating Italy, a Scænvinus had struck down with this weapon the leader of a band of the barbarians which had cone to plunder the temple. His descendant now took it down from its place on the walls with much formality, and carried it about with him, not without throwing hints of some great achievement for which it was destined.

This, unfortunately, was only the beginning of follies. On the evening of the 18th of April he invited his freedmen to a sumptuous dinner, to which he carefully gave the character of a farewell entertainment. During the repast he was by turns obstreperously gay and depressed even to tears. After dinner he followed up the usual libation to the gods by drinking to the memories of the Elder and the Younger Brutus. This done he drew the sacred dagger from its sheath and handed it to the most trusted of his freedmen, Milichus by name, with the injunction to get it sharpened. "Mind," he said at the same time, "that you see to the point, that it be properly sharp, for it has a great work to do." When the weapon was brought back he had other instructions scarcely less significant to give.

"See, Milichus," he said to the freedman, "that you have plenty of bandages ready. One can never tell how soon they may be wanted."

The bandages duly provided, he proceeded to execute with the usual solemnities a new will. When this had been signed and sealed, he seemed still unsatisfied. "Why," he said to his guests, "should you wait for my death before you can enjoy my liberality, though indeed you will very likely not have to wait long."

Two favourite slaves were called up and set free. To others he gave presents of money. To the freedmen at his table he distributed keepsakes, rings, bracelets, writing-tablets, and valuables of all sorts. He might have been a father on his deathbed bidding farewell to his children with an appropriate remembrance of each. And this was the more remarkable because Scævinus, in ordinary life, was not a particularly generous person.

For some time Milichus had noticed a curious change in his patron's demeanour. Ordinarily, as has been said, Scævinus was not a man who took life seriously, and Milichus' sole employment had been to minister to his pleasures. For some months past all this had been changed. He had, to a certain extent, reformed his ways, and had assumed a more than proportionate gravity of demeanour. Not infrequently he had dropped hints of important business which he had in hand, and great functions in the State which he might be called upon to perform.

If these things had not aroused definite suspicions in Milichus they had certainly prepared him to entertain them when he witnessed the proceedings just related. That his patron had something on his mind, and that this something was approaching a critical time, he now felt convinced. When, shortly before midnight, Scævinus dismissed him with an unusually affectionate good- night, he resolved to take his wife into counsel.

The two discussed the matter for a long time. The woman was far more decided than her husband in her views, both of what was going on and of what he ought to do. "Depend upon it," she said, "this is a big thing, and means a chance for you and me such as we never had before, and are not likely to have again. My belief is that there is something on foot against people who are very high up indeed. Go to the palace at once,—that is my advice,—and tell the people there what you have seen."

The freedman hesitated. He had a feeling of kindness for his patron, stronger, perhaps, than he would have had for a better man. Scævinus had given him his liberty, had made him some handsome presents, and treated him generally with the kindness which commonly goes a long way further than money. It was always an odious thing for a freedman to turn against his patron; in his case it was particularly hateful. And then, if the whole business should turn out to have meant nothing at all! That would mean simple ruin and disgrace.

The wife took a more severely practical view of the situation. Of the personal feeling she made no account whatever. Naturally she did not share it herself, for Scævinus was almost a stranger to her. Anyhow she was sure that it must not stand in the way of business. Of the risk of being found to have made a groundless charge she made light. The circumstances were too suspicious. They must mean something. She wound up with the most cogent argument of all. "There were others present, you say, freedmen and slaves. Do you suppose that you were the only one who saw anything strange in the Senator's behaviour? If you don't go to the palace, you may depend upon it some one else will. And if anybody anticipates you, where will you be? It was you to whom he gave the dagger to sharpen; you who had to prepare the bandages; it is you, therefore, who are bound to speak. You won't save your patron by holding your tongue, you will only lose your own chance, and very likely involve yourself in his ruin."

This reasoning was too much for Milichus. "I will go," he said, "though I hate it."

"And at once," cried the wife. "There is not a moment to be lost."

The energetic woman seized him by the arm, and hurried him off. The day was just beginning to dawn, and it was only just light when the two reached the Pavilion gardens, where Nero was residing. At that untimely hour they had some difficulty in making themselves heard, and the porter, when roused, summarily bade them go about their business. Milichus would gladly have availed himself of the excuse, and postponed his odious task, but his wife was made of sterner stuff. She warned the doorkeeper that if he refused to admit them, he would do so at his own peril; they had come, she said, on urgent business, in fact, on a matter of life or death. Thus urged, the man gave way, and admitted the visitors, feeling that he would thus at least shift the responsibility from off his own shoulders. He sent the couple on to Epaphroditus, who may be described as the Emperor's Private Secretary.

Epaphroditus heard the outline of Milichus' story, and recognizing the gravity of the facts, determined that Nero himself should hear them without delay.

At first the Emperor was but little disposed to believe. He had a profound belief in his own inviolability, and the breaking down of the charge which Proculus had brought against Epicharis, had confirmed him in his incredulity. The sight of the dagger which Milichus, at his wife's suggestion, had brought with him, rather staggered him. It proved nothing, it is true. Still the sight of an actual weapon, which it was possible might be used against himself, seemed to make the whole thing closer and more real.

"Send for Scævinus," he said to his Secretary. "Let us confront him with this fellow, and hear what he has to say."

Scævinus, who had just risen from his bed, and was already disturbed by finding that Milichus had gone, no one knew whither, and had taken the dagger with him, was still further alarmed by the arrival of a quaternion of soldiers, bearing an order for his arrest. When, however, he was brought within the Emperor's presence, his courage rose to the occasion. The story of the dagger he ridiculed.

"It belongs to my family," he said, and briefly told the story connected with it. "I found that it was being devoured by rust, and took it down from the wall. I may have told this fellow to clean it, but certainly said nothing else. As for the bandages, that is a pure fiction, invented to back up the other story. As for the new will, I have often made wills, as any of my friends can testify; as for the presents that I made to my freedmen and slaves, what is there in that? It is my way to be liberal to them, perhaps beyond my means. Answer me, Milichus," he went on, turning to the informer, "have you not had money and valuables from me many times?"

The freedman acknowledged that this was so.

"And now, Cæsar," said Scævinus, "to be perfectly frank, as indeed the occasion demands, I have a special reason for being generous, if it is generous to give what is scarcely one's own. My affairs are not prosperous, and my creditors have begun to press me. Legacies would be of no use if there should be a balance on the wrong side when my estate is wound up; services have been rendered me which it was a matter of honour to repay, and I felt that I could do it only by gifts."

The accused spoke so calmly and coolly, and with such an appearance of frankness, that the Emperor was staggered.

"It is the Epicharis case over again," he said to Tigellinus, who had by this time been summoned. "People seem to be making a trade of these lying accusations. They shall find that they are not to my taste."

Scævinus saw his advantage, and pursued it. "I ask you, Cæsar, to protect me against the unfaithfulness and falsehood of this man, this villain, who owes to me all that he has, and now seeks to raise himself higher on the ruins of my fortune. About other things I care not so much, but it is terrible that he should seek to make a profit for himself out of the loss of my honour. Cæsar, I implore your protection against him."

"And you shall have it, Scævinus," said the Emperor. "As for you," he went on in a voice of thunder, turning to the freedman, "you have a patron who is far too good for you. Henceforth he will treat you, I hope, as you deserve. He has my leave to squeeze out of you again all that he has given you, to the uttermost drop. Assuredly it was the unhappiest hour of your life when you came to me with this cock-and-bull story of a dagger and bandages. And now, Tigellinus," he went on, "it is time to be getting ready for the Circus."

The freedman stood struck dumb with disappointment and dismay. But his wife did not lose her courage and presence of mind.

"Ask him," she whispered, "whether he has not lately had many conferences with Natalis, and whether he is not an intimate friend of Caius Piso's."

The freedman caught eagerly at the suggestion. "Cæsar," said he, "ask Scævinus what dealings he has lately had with Natalis and Caius Piso."

Scævinus could not repress a start when he heard the names of two of the most prominent conspirators thus openly joined with his own, and the start did not escape the watchful eye of Tigellinus.

"There may be more in this, Sire, than you think," he whispered in Nero's ear. "Natalis is a notorious busy-body, and Piso is the most dangerous man in Rome."

"What do you advise, then?" asked the Emperor, impressed by his Minister's earnestness.

"Send for Natalis," replied Tigellinus, "and question him; but don't question him in the presence of the accused. Ask them separately what they have been interesting themselves in; if there is anything that they don't want to have known, they will certainly contradict each other."

The suggestion was immediately carried out. Natalis, arrested just as he was setting out for the Circus, and having a dagger actually concealed upon his person, lost his presence of mind. Interrogated by Tigellinus as to the business discussed at recent interviews with Scævinus, with a scribe sitting close by to take down his words, he hesitated and stammered. His invention seemed to fail him as well as his courage. At last he managed to blunder out a few words to the effect that Scævinus had been consulting him about the best way of investing some sums of money which would shortly be coming in to him from the paying off of sundry mortgages and loans. This was a peculiarly unlucky venture in the face of Scævinus' recent confession of poverty. Tigellinus smiled an evil smile as he listened. Natalis caught the look, and stammered worse than ever, for he knew that he had blundered.

"Thank you, my friend," said the Minister in the blandest of voices. "I am sure that the Senator Scævinus is a lucky man to have so admirable an adviser. Still you will pardon me for saying that you are a trifle obscure in your description. It will be instructive to call in the Senator himself, and hear his account of the matter."

Scævinus accordingly was brought in. The look of terror which came over his face as soon as he caught sight of Natalis was as good as a confession. Tigellinus, who hated him, as he hated every man better born and better bred than himself, smiled again.

"The Emperor," he began, in his soft, unctuous voice, "who feels a paternal interest in the affairs of his subjects, is anxious to know what was the subject of discussion when you were closeted yesterday so long with our friend Natalis."

Scævinus, who had by this time recovered his self-possession, answered without hesitation. His course was, it need hardly be said, clear before him. Indeed, he congratulated himself on the happy thought of having pleaded his poverty to the Emperor.

"I was consulting my friend about raising a loan on more

moderate interest than what I am now paying." The Emperor laughed outright.

"Scribe," said Tigellinus to the slave who had been taking down the depositions in shorthand—for shorthand was an art well known to the Romans by that time,—"scribe, read aloud the answer of Antonius Natalis."

"One of you has certainly lied," said Tigellinus, "and probably both; but there are means of making you speak the truth."

He made a sign to a guard who stood at the door of the apartment. In a few minutes half-a-dozen slaves appeared, bringing with them a rack and other instruments of torture.

Scævinus started at the sight. "Cæsar," he cried, "is this with your permission? Torture to a Senator of Rome!"

"Silence, villain!" said the Minister. "You know that when the life of the Emperor is concerned—and what else meant you by the dagger?—all means of discovering the truth are permitted by the law."

The slaves began to prepare the rack for use. Natalis lost all his fortitude at the ghastly sound of the creaking beams, as the executioners worked the hideous thing backwards and forwards to see that it was in order.

"Spare me, Caesar," he cried, falling on his knees, "and I will confess all that I know."

Scævinus was not so lost to shame. He hesitated. He was even ready, if his companion had backed him up, to brave it out. But the cowardice of the other was contagious. If Natalis was to save himself by confession, why not he? His friends were lost anyhow; they would not fare one whit the worse for anything that he might say.

"Caesar," he said, still striving to keep up some show of dignity, "if you will deign to listen, I have something to say."

Tigellinus gloated with malignant pleasure over the man's useless humiliation. A Senator, offering to betray his friends and refused! What could be more welcome hearing to a parvenu!

"Nay, sir," he said; "we must observe due precedence. Every man according to his rank. In honourable things the Senator before the knight; in dishonourable the knight before the Senator. Is not that so, Sire?"

"Yes," said Nero; "speak on, Antonius Natalis. Meanwhile let our honourable Senator be removed. It has already been very interesting to observe how his account of things differed from his confederate's, and it may be interesting again."

22

VACILLATION

SCAEVINUS — for we must do the poor cowardly wretch such justice as he deserves — had made an effort to save his friends, and, one ought perhaps to add, himself. While Natalis was being interrogated, he entered into conversation with the slave who had been told off to attend on him. The slave was a young man of mixed Greek and Asiatic race, with an extremely intelligent countenance, but sickly and lame. It was impossible for any one with the least insight into character to look at him and to hear him speak without perceiving that there was something out of the common about him. In after years he was to become one of the most notable exponents of the Stoic philosophy, for this Phrygian cripple was no less a person than the philosopher Epictetus. At the time of which I am writing he was only a feeble lad with, however, a certain air of ability and courage which greatly impressed an intelligent observer. Scævinus, feeling that his situation was practically desperate, resolved to make a last effort. If it failed he could hardly be in a worse position than the present; if it succeeded it was just possible that the fortunes of the conspiracy might yet be retrieved.

"Can you take a message for me to a friend?" he said in Greek to Epictetus.

The soldiers who were guarding the door of the apartment heard without understanding.

"Certainly," said the slave, "if any good is to be achieved."

"You shall have ten gold pieces for your trouble."

"Nay, this is a thing which I would sooner do without payment. That is not only more honourable, but also more safe."

"I cannot write it, indeed, there is no need; all that is needed can be said in a few words. Go to Caius Piso, and say to him, 'All is discovered; act.' And mind—not a word of this to any one else. Let not wild horses wring it out of you. That would be fatal to both you and me."

The slave smiled. "They might as well try to wring words out of a stump or a stone. For, indeed, what else is a slave? When my old master kicked me and broke my leg—" and he held out as he spoke the maimed limb—"I said, 'Why do you damage your own property?' So I should say to them. If they choose to kill me, that is their own lookout; all that concerns me, for a slave has something of a man about him after all, as Aristotle says, is that I don't dishonour myself."

When Scævinus was recalled into the Emperor's audience-chamber, Epictetus lost no time in making his way to Piso's house. Some of the prominent persons connected with the conspiracy were assembled, and were busy making their final arrangements for the proceedings of the day.

Epictetus, as soon as he was safe within the doors, wrote down on a tablet the following words: "The bearer of a message from Scævinus asks for admission." He was brought up without loss of time into an ante-chamber, where Piso saw him alone. He delivered his message, and immediately departed.

Piso rejoined his assembled friends, and told them what had happened. Subrius, with characteristic promptitude, rose to the occasion.

"Piso," he said, "the task before us is different from that which we had planned,—different and possibly more difficult, but certainly not hopeless. We shall not proclaim you Emperor after Nero is dead; we shall have to proclaim you while he is yet alive. And I must own that the affair is now more to my taste than it was. I was ready, as you know, to play the assassin, when it was a question of delivering the human race from a tyrant; but I would sooner play the soldier, and meet him in the field. That, Piso, is what we must do. Let us go to the Forum, and appeal to the people, or, as I would rather advise, to the camp, and appeal to the soldiers. In both places, among both audiences, we shall have friends. They will shout their applause, and others, who at present know nothing of the matter, will join in. That is a line of action for which, depend upon it, Nero is not prepared. Even brave men are sometimes confounded by so sudden an attack; how will a stage-playing Emperor and his miserable minion encounter it? Don't think for a moment that we can escape; there are too many in the secret. Some one will be sure to sell his honour for money, or find his courage ooze away in the presence of the rack. Indeed, we know that the treachery has begun. Let us act, and at once, for even while I am urging you on, opportunities are passing away."

These spirited words made no impression on Piso's somewhat sluggish and inactive nature. He was one of those men who are slow to move from their course, and have an inexhaustible supply of passive endurance. He shrugged his shoulders.

"The Empire," he said, "does not approve itself to me if it is to be won in a street broil."

"I understand," said the soldier. "It would be more seemly, I acknowledge, if the Senate, headed by the Magistrates, and the Prefects, and Tribunes of the Prætorians, with the Vestal Virgins in the front of the whole procession, were to come and salute you as Emperor. But that is not the question. The question is this: You have two alternatives; think which suits your dignity, your name, your ancestors, the better. One is to put your fortune to the trial, if things go well, to be the successor of Augustus; if the fates will otherwise, to die, sword in hand. The other is to wait here till Nero's myrmidons come to chain you, to drag you off to the place of execution; or, if the tyrant strains his prerogative of mercy to the utmost, to suffer you to fall on your own sword, or open your own veins."

Piso heard unmoved. His courage was of the passive kind. He

could meet death when it came with an undaunted face, but he could not go, so to speak, to seek it.

"The gods have declared against us, and I shall not resist their will. I thank you for your good-will and your counsel; but you must permit a Piso to judge for himself what best suits his own dignity and the glory of his ancestors. I am determined to await my fate."

The bold spirit of the Tribune was not crushed, nor his resources exhausted by this failure. There was still a possible claimant to the throne in Lateranus. He had not, it is true, the pretensions of Piso, neither his personal popularity nor his noble birth. Still, he had courage, favour with some classes of the people, and a commanding presence. Here another disappointment awaited him. Lateranus had been arrested. Apparently, Nero had had the same thought that had occurred to the Prætorian, that the Consul- elect was among the dangerous characters of Rome. The house was in the utmost confusion; indeed, the soldiers had only just left it. Subrius' inquiries were answered by the Chamberlain. He, poor man, came wringing his hands and weeping, overwhelmed, it was evident, by terror and grief. "Ah! my poor master," he said; "we shall never see him again. They hurried him off without a moment's notice."

"Who?" asked the soldier.

"Statius the Tribune," replied the Chamberlain, "who had some twenty men with him. He would not give him time even to say good by to his children. And when my poor master said, 'If I must die, let me die by my own hand,' even that was refused him. 'We allow nothing to traitors,' the brute answered. They bound him hand and foot and dragged him off."

"We allow nothing to traitors, indeed," murmured Subrius to himself. "What, I wonder, does Statius call himself? I hope that he, anyhow, will get his deserts."

Statius, it should be said, had been one of the most active promoters of the conspiracy.

Again the Tribune's hopes were dashed to the ground. Still he refused to think that all was lost. A last chance remained. The conspiracy had spread widely among his brother officers of the

Prætorians; and they, at least, he hoped, would make a struggle for their lives. Civilians might be content to fold their arms and bare their necks to the sword of the executioner, but soldiers would die, if die they must, with arms in their hands. And then, if they wanted a great name to catch the popular ear, was there not Seneca? I don't think much of philosophers," Subrius thought to himself, "but perhaps I may be wrong. Anyhow, the men of the world have failed us. They are as weak as water. Perhaps there may be sterner stuff in the man of books."

Obviously there was no time to be lost. He must hurry to the Prætorian camp at once, and urge Fænius Rufus, who was one of the joint Prefects, and, as we know, was involved in the conspiracy, to act.

Calling to the driver of a car which was plying for hire, he proceeded at the utmost speed to which the horse could be put, to the camp. Just outside the gate he met the officer of whom he was in search.

Rufus, who was on horseback, and was followed by an escort of ten troopers, signed to his brother officer to halt. "Well met, Subrius!" he cried. "I am on my way to the palace, and I want you to come with me. Give the Tribune your horse," he went on, turning to the orderly who was riding behind him; "go back and get a fresh mount for your-self, and come on after us."

The man dismounted and held the horse while the Tribune jumped into the saddle.

"Not a word," whispered the Prefect to his companion, as they rode along; "not a word; we must brave it out, and all may yet be well. But leave it to me.

The Tribune had no choice but to obey. His superior officer's conduct was unintelligible, even astounding. Still he could do noth-ing. It would have been sheer madness for him, a simple Tribune, to stand up in the camp and bid the Prætorians abandon the Emperor. If such a movement was to begin at all it must begin with the Prefect. Meanwhile, he could only obey orders and possess his soul in patience.

Rufus, anxious, it would seem, not to give his subordinate a chance of any further speech, beckoned to the Centurion who was in command of the escort, and kept him in conversation till they reached the palace gates.

The two Prætorians were ushered into the chamber where Nero had just taken his seat, and was preparing to examine some of the prisoners who had been named by the informers. The Emperor was evidently in a state of great agitation and alarm, and Subrius observed that the detachment of the body-guard in attendance was exclusively composed of Germans. He hardly knew whether the circumstance was encouraging or not. For the present, indeed, it would make any attempt very difficult, if not impossible, but it was an ominous thing for Nero if he had begun to find that only barbarians could be trusted.

The Emperor signed to Rufus to take a seat immediately on his left hand, the chair on the right being occupied by Tigellinus. Subrius himself sat immediately below his superior officer, and within a few feet of the Emperor.

The prisoner under examination at the moment was the poet Lucan. The Emperor and Tigellinus had been questioning him for some time, but hitherto with little or no result. He had denied all knowledge of the conspiracy. Still the keen eyes of his judges had not failed to perceive signs of waning courage. Nero whispered to Tigellinus, and the Minister beckoned to an attendant. The man drew aside a curtain and revealed the rack.

"Marcus Annacus Lucanus," said Tigellinus, using almost the same words that he had addressed to Scævinus, "when the life of the Emperor is at stake, the law permits and even enjoins all means of discovering the truth."

The wretched man turned pale. Still he made an effort to brave it out. "You are more likely to wring out falsehood than truth by such means," he said in a faint voice.

"Of that you must leave us to judge," answered Tigellinus with a sneer.

The executioner advanced and laid his hand on the prisoner's shoulder. He started at the touch, and grew ghastly pale.

"Cæsar," he cried, appealing as a last chance to the feelings of the Emperor, "Cæsar, we were once friends, and worshipped the Muses together. Will you suffer this?"

Nero only smiled. He had long ago steeled his heart against pity. Lucan he hated with that especially bitter hatred which wounded vanity sometimes inspires. He aspired to be a poet, as he aspired to be an actor, a singer, a charioteer, and he could not conceal from himself that the author of the Pharsalia far surpassed him.

Then the unhappy man's courage broke down. "Stop!" he cried, "I will confess. I am guilty of conspiring against the Emperor."

"That we know," said Tigellinus. "What we want to hear from you is the names of your confederates."

"Must I speak, Cæsar?" moaned the wretched man. "Is it not enough that I have confessed the crime myself?"

"You have confessed nothing," said Nero. "Your guilt I knew already. And you I could afford to despise, for you can only strike with your pen, but doubtless you know others who know how to use their swords."

Lucan then gave two or three names, all of them, as it happened, already known.

"Still we have learnt nothing new from you," said Tigellinus. "If you wish to merit the Emperor's clemency, you must tell us something that we have not heard before."

In a voice half stifled with shame the accused said: "My mother knew of the affair almost as soon as I did."

A thrill of disgust went through the audience as these humiliating words were uttered. Even to these men, hardened as they were, the son who could betray his own mother seemed a monster.

"That is enough," cried the Emperor, making a sign to a Centurion; "remove him!"

A shameful scene of baseness and cowardice followed. One after another the accused were brought before the tribunal; one after another they failed in the hour of trial. Men of noble birth, men who had served their country in high offices, and who had distinguished themselves in the field, could not summon up courage enough to endure this ordeal. Some volunteered confession, and neither force, nor even the threat of force, was needed to make them betray their comrades. Others stood firm at first, but failed when they were confronted with the engines of torture. Subrius sat filled with a disgust and a shame which hardly left him time to think of his own danger, as friend after friend, men of courage and honour as he had always believed them to be, proved themselves to be traitors and cowards.

As for the behaviour of Rufus, he watched it with ever increasing astonishment. The Prefect took an active part in the examination. Not even Tigellinus was more truculent, more savage, more brutal. He cross-examined the prisoners, he plied them with threats, and still by a strange agreement in silence, his name was not mentioned by one of them.

"What is his plan?" thought Subrius to himself. "Can he hope that he will escape altogether, that no one out of these scores of accomplices will name him, or is he biding his time?"

"Tigellinus," said Nero to his Minister, after some six or seven confessions had been taken, "do you remember that Greek freedwoman whom Proculus accused? Let her be brought before us again. Perhaps she may have a different story to tell. Meanwhile, while she is being fetched, we will adjourn for a brief space. A cup of Falernian will not be ungrateful after this morning's work."

He rose from his seat, and left the Court, leaning on the arm of Tigellinus. The Prefect of the Prætorians followed immediately behind, and the Tribune, again, was close to his commanding officer. Behind these again were some dozen German body-guards.

"Is this the chance that he has been waiting for?" said Subrius to himself.

"Shall I strike?" he whispered to the Prefect, laying his hand on the hilt of his sword.

Rufus hesitated for a moment. That there was an opportunity such as never might occur again, he saw; the chances were ten to one that if Subrius were to strike, he would not strike in vain. But then, could he hope to escape himself if the deed was done? The German body-guards were devoted to their master, and would infallibly avenge his death on his assassin, and, it could hardly be doubted, on himself.

"Hush!" he whispered to his subordinate. "It is not the time; we shall have a better opportunity than this."

Subrius muttered a curse under his breath, but the habit of obedience was strong in him, and he held his hand.

23

A LAST CHANCE

SUBRIUS was on duty that afternoon in the camp, and his place in the Court, where the Prefect was still in attendance, was filled by another Tribune. No one who saw him going, with an imperturbable calm, through the numberless little details which had to be looked after by the Tribune on duty, would have imagined how much he had at stake. The fact was that he had hardened his heart to any fortune, while he was both by temper of mind and by deliberate conviction a Stoic and a fatalist. Still he could not help feeling what may be described rather as a vivid curiosity than an anxiety as to what the day might bring forth. The Greek freedwoman who was being examined that afternoon, whatever she knew of the conspiracy, whether it was little or much, anyhow knew his name. Would she keep the secret? It was scarcely likely. He had seen men, who had every motive of honour and affection to keep them silent, quailing under the threats of pain, and sacrificing everything in their desperate clinging to life; would this weak woman, who had no honourable traditions of birth and training to which she would be bound, show herself braver and more faithful than soldiers and nobles? Who could imagine it? And yet when he thought of that strong, resolute face he thought it not impossible.

And he was right. He was making his way to his quarters when he encountered the officer who had been occupying his place in the Court during the afternoon.

"Subrius," said his friend, "you have missed the strangest sight that ever man saw. Ah! and I wish that I had missed it too, for it was almost past bearing. A Greek freedwoman was brought before the Court—Epicharis was her name. It seems that she had been accused of conspiring against the Emperor some time ago, but that nothing could be proved against her then; now that all this has come out, she was to be examined again. One of the Secretaries read over the confessions of the prisoners who had been before the Court in the morning, and then Tigellinus said: 'You hear this. What have you to say?' 'Nothing,' she answered. Well, he went on asking questions. 'Had she ever heard anything about the affair? How could she account for all these confessions? She had declared that Proculus had invented his story; was it likely that all these witnesses, knights, Senators, and soldiers, had also invented theirs?' She went on answering, 'I know nothing about it,' or was silent. Before long, Tigellinus broke out, 'You have lost your memory, woman, it seems; well, we have charms for bringing it back.' At the same time he made a sign to a slave that stood by and the man uncovered the instruments of torture. I assure you that the girl—she was only a girl—did not so much as flinch or start. Well, they put her on the rack, and the executioner gave it a turn. I assure you it makes me almost sick when I think of it. At the second turn the woman said, 'I have something to say.' 'Ah, madam!' cried Tigellinus, 'I thought we should find your tongue for you. Loose her!' The men took her off the rack, and set her in a chair; she was quite unable to stand. 'Cæsar,' she said, 'since you are resolved to force the truth from me, you shall have it. I have conspired against your life, and had I been a man, and had had the opportunities which others have had, I had done more; I would not only have plotted, but would have struck. Would you know why? Because you are a murderer. You slew your wife Octavia because she was ten thousand times too good for you. It is she whom I would have avenged. The gods have willed it otherwise; they have assigned the task to other hands. You may kill me as you will. I do not care to live. But do not flatter yourself that the Furies of your mother, your brother, your wife, will suffer you to rest. They will find some sword to reach your heart, though this has been broken.' By Mars! Subrius, the woman looked like a Fury herself as she said this. She had started up from her chair, though how she could stand I cannot imagine, and poured out her words as if she were inspired. The Emperor seemed struck dumb, but Tigellinus cried, 'Gag her; cut out her tongue!' Before they could touch her, she said again, 'Would you know my associates?' Tigellinus made a sign that they were to leave her alone. She was so frantic, he thought, that she might let out something almost without knowing it. 'I will tell you; my associates are all brave soldiers, all good citizens, all who love their country. To-morrow, Cæsar, if not to-day, these will be on my side, and they will be too strong for you, for all your legions. Mark my words: before five years are past, you will desire and yet be afraid to die, and will hardly find a friend to press home the last blow!'"

"Brave woman!" said Subrius, "and what then?"

"After that," replied the other, "she said nothing more. Not a single word could they wring out of her lips, though they tortured her in a way that, as I said, made me sick to see. At last the physician told them that unless they stopped they would kill her. So she was carried off, to be brought back again to-morrow, I understood."

"Great Jupiter! how she shames us all," said Subrius to himself, when he had parted from his brother officer. "To think of the shameful exhibition that those freeborn men made yesterday, and then see what this woman has done! And what of myself? Would she —had she been in my place—hold her hand? And yet I was bound to obey orders. The gods grant I may find Rufus in a bolder mood at last!"

This bolder mood unhappily was what not even the necessity of his desperate position could create in the Prefect. Subrius found him still unwilling to act, clinging frantically to the hope that his share in the conspiracy might yet pass undiscovered. In vain did Subrius ply him with arguments and remonstrances.

"It is sheer madness," he said, after going again and again over the familiar ground; "nothing but madness, to hope that you will not be named by some one of the condemned. It is a marvel that it has not been done already. But if you think that they will all endure to see you sitting as their judge, cross- examining, threatening, when by a word they might bring you down to stand at their side, you are simply fooling yourself. Why should they spare you?"

"If any one does name me, I can deny it," said Rufus.

"Deny it!" cried the Tribune; "what good will that do you? Nero is so panic- stricken that to be named to him is to be condemned. And what of Tigellinus? Don't you know that he has a protegé of his own for whom he covets your place?"

"It is my only chance," murmured the Prefect. "It is too late for anything else."

"Possibly," returned Subrius gloomily; "we have lost too many chances, and this is a fault which Fortune never forgives. But it is not too late to die; that is the only thing, I take it, that our folly has left us free to do. Let us cast lots who shall play the executioner. We shall do it at least in a more seemly fashion than Nero's hangsman."

At this moment there was a tap at the door. The Prefect turned pale; any moment, he knew in his heart of hearts, might bring with it his arrest. Subrius put his hand upon his sword-hilt, ready to sell his life as clearly as he could.

The newcomer was another Tribune of the Prætorians, Silvanus by name.

"Well, Silvanus, what news?" asked Rufus.

"I will tell you," replied the other, "and you must judge what is to be done. Yesterday Cæsar sent for me, after he had finished his examination of the prisoners. Tigellinus was with him, and Poppæa; Antonius Natalis was there, with handcuffs on his hands, and a soldier on each side of him. 'Repeat, Natalis,' said Cæsar, 'what you have told us about Seneca.' At that Natalis said: 'I went lately to see Seneca when he was sick. Piso sent me. I was to complain of Seneca's having always denied himself to him of late. They were old friends; he had much to say to Seneca; it would be greatly to their mutual profit if he were

allowed an opportunity of saying it. I took this message to Seneca,'
Natalis went on. 'His answer was that he did not agree with Piso, but
thought, on the contrary, that it would not be to the interest of either
of them that they should have much talk. He quite saw, however, that
he and Piso must stand and fall together.' When Natalis had finished,
Cæsar said to me, 'You hear, Silvanus, the evidence of Natalis.' 'Yes,
Sire,' I said, 'I hear.' 'It shows plainly that there was an understanding
between them,' the Emperor went on. 'Is it not so?' 'Doubtless, Sire,' I
said, for one does not contradict an Emperor, you know. 'Well,' he
went on, 'go to Seneca, repeat that evidence to him,—to make sure
that you have it right, you had better put it into writing,—and ask
him how he can explain it. Of course you will take a guard with you!'
Well, I went. Seneca, who had just come back from Baiæ, was at his
house, between the Anio and the Mons Sacer, and when I got there
was at dinner with his wife and two friends. I read Natalis' evidence
to him. He said: 'It is quite true that Natalis came to me from Piso
with a complaint that I denied myself to him. I said that I really was
not well enough to see any but a very few friends; indeed, the physicians prescribe absolute rest; of course, if the Emperor wants me, I
must come, but I cannot be expected to sacrifice my life for any one
else. As to what I am reported to have said about Piso and myself
standing and falling together, I don't understand it. I may have given
the common message, "If Piso is well, I am well," but I never went
beyond it. That is all I have to say,' he went on, 'and if Cæsar does not
know by this time that I am in the habit of speaking the truth,
nothing that I can say will persuade him.' Well, I went back; when I
reached the palace, Nero was at dinner with Tigellinus and Poppæa. I
repeated Seneca's words exactly. I had taken the precaution, I should
say, of writing them down. The Emperor said, 'Did the old man say
anything about killing himself?' 'Nothing,' I said. We heard him
mutter to himself, 'The old dotard is very slow to take a hint. What
could be plainer? You are sure,' he said, turning to me again, 'you saw
no signs of anything of the kind?' 'Nothing,' I answered; 'he was as
calm and quiet as ever I saw a man in my life.' 'Well,' said Cæsar, 'then

we must speak more plainly. Go back and tell him that he has three hours to live, and no more.' "

"What then?" said the Prefect. "What did you do?"

"Instead of going back, I came to you," replied Silvanus.

"And why?" asked the Prefect.

"Do you ask me why?" cried Silvanus. "Surely you must know. Am I to go or am I not to go? Say the word. I am ready to obey."

At this point Subrius broke in. "Silvanus is right. He sees that this is our last chance. Piso is dead, Lateranus is dead. Seneca is the only man left whom we can put up with any hope against the tyrant. For Heaven's sake, away with this frantic folly of thinking that you can escape! Speak the word, Fænius Rufus, and I will go with Silvanus here to Seneca's house. We will take him, whether he will or not—for he is more likely to refuse than to consent—and bring him into the camp, and salute him as Emperor."

"No! No!" cried the Prefect, wringing his hands in an agony of perplexity. "It is hopeless. It must fail!"

"Anyhow," retorted the Tribune, "it is not so absolutely hopeless as your plan. We have lost better chances than this; but this has, at least, the merit of being our last."

"I cannot do it," said Rufus after a pause. "Carry out your orders, Silvanus; there is nothing else to do."

"So be it, then," said Subrius. "you have sealed our fate and your own. I will go with you, Silvanus. I would fain see how a philosopher can die; it will not be long before we shall need the lesson."

24

THE DEATH OF A PHILOSOPHER

S CARCELY a word passed between the two Tribunes as they traversed the distance, some four miles or so, that lay between the camp and Seneca's villa. Silvanus was heartily ashamed of his errand, and Subrius, who bitterly felt his own helplessness, could only pity him, and would not say a word that might sound like a reproach. Under these circumstances to be silent was the only course. Arrived at the villa, Silvanus called a Centurion, took him apart, and gave him his instructions.

"I shall not go in," he said to his companion. "It would be past all bearing."

"You will not hinder my entering?" asked Subrius.

"Certainly not, if it pleases you to go."

Silvanus gave the necessary orders to the Centurion, and the two were ushered by a slave into the apartment where Seneca was sitting with his wife and his friends.

The Centurion stepped forward and saluted. "Lucius Annacus Seneca," he said, "Cæsar, having come to the conclusion that it is not to the interests of the State that you should live any longer, graciously, of his clemency, permits you to choose for yourself the manner of your death."

The unhappy wife of the doomed man uttered a loud shriek, and fell back half fainting in her chair; his two guests started up from their seats with pale and terror-stricken faces. Seneca remained absolutely calm and unmoved.

"This," he said with a smile, "is not the usual fee that a pupil pays to his teacher, but it may not be the less acceptable, for that. Sir," he went on, turning with a courteous gesture to the Tribune, "is our friend, if I may call him so, who has just brought me this gift, under your command?"

"The gods forbid!" cried Subrius eagerly. "I had never come on such an errand. Yet I knew that it was to be executed. Forgive me if I intrude unseasonably."

"You need scarcely ask my pardon," replied the philosopher. "Condemned men are seldom troubled by a too great abundance of visitors and friends. How much time do you allow me, friend?" he asked, turning to the Centurion.

The man hesitated. "Would two hours suffice?" he asked. "I would fain return to Cæsar before he sleeps."

"Jupiter forbid," said Seneca, "that I should keep Cæsar from his needful rest! That would be ill-done of his old tutor. And surely two hours will suffice to rid an old man of what little life remains to him. But the time is not long, and I must not waste it. Let me see then what has to be done. First, then, my will."

The Centurion interposed. "It is not permitted to any one so circumstanced to change his will."

"Why so?"

"Cæsar grants validity to the wills of those whom he suffers thus to execute justice on themselves, but his clemency must not be abused, possibly to his own injury, or the injury of loyal persons."

"You mean that I might strike out a legacy that I had left to Cæsar himself, or to Tigellinus. Nay, I was but thinking to make my friends here a little present in remembrance of to-day. And to you, sir," he added, addressing the Centurion, "I would gladly have offered some little token of my regard. The bringers of good news should not miss their reward. But if it is otherwise ordered, we must obey. After all, the best thing that I have to leave to my friends is the picture of my life. Is it permitted to me to spend the time that remains in the company of my wife and friends? You can easily make sure of my not escaping."

The Centurion intimated that there would be no objection to this, saluted, and withdrew.

"You will stay with me, sir?" he said to Subrius; "though indeed it is presumption in a civilian to pretend to show a soldier how to die. Nay," he added, for the Prætorian, inexpressibly touched by the cheerful composure with which the old man met his fate, could hardly keep down his emotion, "Nay, but we look to you, who have faced death so often, to help us to be calm."

He turned to his two friends, who were weeping unrestrainedly. "Surely I have been the dullest of masters if I have not taught you better than this. By all the gods! if you would not disgrace me, command yourselves better. Philosophers forsooth! and the moment your philosophy is wanted, it breaks down. Life is brief, and death is sure. These are the very commonplaces of wisdom, and yet one would think that you had never heard them. And what is there that surprises you? That an old man should die, and an old man whom Nero hates? The only marvel is that I have been suffered to live so long. He has murdered his brother, his mother, his wife; it was only fitting that he should murder his tutor. All that I taught him has perished; it is time for the teacher to follow the way of his precepts."

The philosopher then turned to his wife Paulina. He changed his tone to one of tenderness.

"Dearest," he said, as he clasped her in his arms, "we must part. That is a sorrow which all husbands and wives must face; and, after all, the tyrant has not anticipated fate by many years. I will not ask you not to grieve for me; that would be against nature; but it is also against nature to grieve without ceasing. The years that have been given us have not, I trust, been ill-spent; to recollect them is a solace of which no one can rob you."

"Nay," cried Paulina, "I shall need no solace, for there shall be no parting. Nero bids you die, but he does not forbid me to die with you."

"Well said," answered Seneca. "That is worthy of my own true wife. It was only right to show you that there might yet be happiness in life for you, but if you prefer the glory of death I must not hinder you. And yet," he added with a smile, "of any one but you I should be inclined to be jealous. You put me into the shade. I have no choice between living and dying. I do but prefer one death to another; but you prefer it to life."

To open the artery in one of the arms was reckoned the easiest and least painful way of inflicting death. Husband and wife held out their arms together, and the former administered the stroke. For some reason it failed of its effect. Possibly in the case of the wife the old man's strength did not suffice to make the wound sufficiently deep. Anyhow she survived. It was to the interest of some of those who surrounded her that she should live. Accordingly the Centurion who was in waiting outside was informed of what had happened, and despatched a mounted messenger to Nero with an account of what had been done and a request for instructions. The man returned in a very short time with strict injunctions that the wife must not be permitted to die. The wound was bound up, and she survived, though as long as she lived the bloodless pallor of her face showed how near she had been to death.

With Seneca himself the process of dying was long and painful. He could not bleed to death, it seems, for, what with the weakness of old age, and the excessive spareness of his diet, there was but little blood in his body. To no purpose did he sever the veins in his legs. Painful convulsions followed, but death still seemed remote.

His fortitude remained unshaken. "If I cannot die," he said to his friends, "at least let me make use of life. Send me my secretaries."

The secretaries came, and he dictated to them, in a voice that was surprisingly firm and distinct, his last thoughts about life and death. Never had his eloquence been more clear and forcible.

He had just finished when a newcomer was announced. This was the physician Annæus Statius, a long-tried and faithful friend, who had been Seneca's medical attendant for many years. The philosopher's chamberlain had sent for him as soon as he was aware of the errand on which the soldiers had come.

"You are come in good time, Statius," said Seneca. "Your art has so fortified me against death that when I want to depart I cannot. Have you the draught ready?"

"Yes, it is ready," replied the physician. "I brought the hemlock ready pounded, and Stilicho has mixed it."

He clapped his hands, and a slave brought in the cup.

"Ah!" said the old man with a smile, as he took and drained it, "I am after all to have the crowning honour of a philosopher's life, and die as Socrates died."

But even this was not to be. The poison, which would have sent a fatal chill through a frame warm with vigorous life, seemed powerless to affect one so cold and feeble.

"How is this, my friend?" said Seneca after a while. "My time is more than past, and our good friend the Centurion will be wanting to finish the work himself. What say you?"

"I half feared it," replied the physician. "There is no life in you for the poison to lay hold of."

"What do you advise then?"

"A hot bath might hasten matters," replied the man of science. The hot bath was tried, but the old man grew cheerful and even playful.

"The feast is ended, and though some of the dishes have been tasteless and ill- cooked, it has not been ill-furnished on the whole. Now it is time for the libation. To Jupiter!—not the 'Preserver'; that he is for those only who seek to live,—let me rather say ' Liberator,' for he is indeed about to set me free." As he spoke he scooped up some of the water in the hollow of his hand, and threw it on the slaves that were in attendance. A few minutes later he spoke again.

"There must be an end of this. Take me into the hot chamber. That will finish it. Is it not so, Statius?" he said, looking to the physician.

"Doubtless," replied Statius; "but it will be a painful process."

"Well," said the philosopher, "that is only to be expected. For what says Cicero? 'The departure of the soul from the body does not happen without pain.' "

A few minutes afterwards he had ceased to live.

25

THE FATE OF SUBRIUS

T HE physician, whose house was in the immediate neighbourhood, offered Subrius hospitality for the night. The Tribune, unwilling to compromise any one by his presence, declined it.

"There are reasons," he said, "why I should not come under your roof; don't ask me what they are, for it is better that you should not know. Besides, it is necessary for me to get back to Rome as soon as may be."

Subrius had given up all hope for himself. Resistance and escape were equally out of the question. Nor could he hope to do anything for his confederates. Most of them were already in the hands of the authorities; the others would be infallibly named by one or other of the informers. The only one whom he saw a chance of saving was Pudens. Pudens was unknown to most of the conspirators,—a simple soldier on leave who might, it was possible, be sheltered by his obscurity. The Tribune was inclined to reproach himself for having involved the young man, whose frank and engaging character had greatly attracted him, in an undertaking which he now saw had been doomed to failure from the first.

It was just possible that the mischief might be undone. It still wanted some three or four hours of midnight. Whatever was to be done must be done before morning, for beyond that time the final blow could hardly be delayed. If Pudens could be found that night, he might possibly escape.

The Tribune accordingly proceeded straight to the place where the young officer was still employed in the superintendence of public works before described. Late as it was when he arrived, Pudens was still busy. It was, in fact, the last day of his engagement, and he was busy completing his final report and making up his accounts, for he had latterly been intrusted with the payment of the workmen. He was not alone, for the Christian freedman, whom for some time he had employed as his assistant, was with him, and was helping him to wind up the affairs of his office. Curiously enough, no tidings of the exciting events which had been going on in Rome had reached him.

As briefly as possible Subrius put his young friend in possession of the state of the case. "All is lost!" he said. "By whose fault this has come about it does not profit to inquire. For the present the fact is enough. All but a few of our friends are already in prison; the rest will soon be there. But there is a chance for you. You were a stranger to most of those who were concerned in the affair. Neither Scævinus nor Natalis, who are the principal informers, knew you by name. It is the greatest good luck that your engagement here has come to an end. As it is, your going away need excite no suspicion. My advice to you is this: Go to-morrow morning with your report and your accounts to your chief; but mind, don't go a moment before the usual time. Keep as cool as you can. If he says anything of what has happened, you, of course, will know nothing about it. Afterwards bid good by to any acquaintance that you may have. Mind, whatever you do, be leisurely and calm. Let there be nothing like hurry, for hurry is suspicious. After that I must leave everything to your own judgment and ingenuity. You have, I fancy from what you told me, a certain talent for disguising yourself. You will want it. Make your way, I should say, to the armies in the East. The particular spot that will be safest you must judge hereafter. The gods preserve you!"

"And you!" cried the young man. "Will not you come with me?"

"Nay, my friend," replied Subrius, "I should spoil it all, destroy your chance, and not profit myself."

"But Pomponia and Claudia!" said Pudens, after a pause. "How can I leave them when I might be of some help?"

"You can do nothing," answered Subrius. "If they are to be helped it cannot be by you. I don't even know where they are. Lateranus, as I told you, was arrested and executed. They were in his house. I did not hear of their being taken at the same time. Anyhow it will not profit them for you to thrust your head into the lion's mouth."

At this point the freedman interrupted the conversation.

"I think, sir," he said, "that I may be of some use, both to the noble ladies, if they are not already removed from Lateranus' house, and to my friend here, if I may be permitted so to speak of him. As for him, I do not think that it would be advisable for him to put the plan which you suggest into execution at once. That he should make his way some time to the army in the East, I agree; but, I should say, not now. Now, it is certain, all the roads, all the ports, are watched. A little time hence this vigilance will be relaxed; then the attempt can be made with more chance of success."

"What then do you suggest?" asked Subrius.

"We of the faith," answered the freedman, "have a hiding-place, where we keep our most precious things,—our books, our sacred vessels, and, in case of need, the persons of those whom we desire to conceal from the rage of our enemies. More I am not at liberty to say, for I am bound to secrecy; but there is a hope, I assure you, and I will certainly do my best to fulfil it."

"What say you, Pudens?" said the Tribune, turning to the young man.

It will readily be believed that Pudens did not hesitate for a moment. The idea of making his own escape, and leaving the two women to their fate, had been extremely distasteful to him. Though he had been compelled to confess to himself that he could give them little or no help, he still felt a desire, perhaps an unreasonable desire, to be near them, even, if it was so to be, to share their fate. He caught eagerly at the freedman's proposal.

"I will stay," he said, "and take my chance here."

"Then," cried Subrius, "if that is settled, I will go." He took an affectionate farewell of his friend, and departed.

Some time had been occupied in the discussion, more than would be supposed from the brief summary that has here been given of it. It was now nearly dawn, and broad daylight before the camp was reached.

Here, somewhat, perhaps, to his surprise, the Tribune found everything quiet. The sentinel at the gate saluted as usual. His soldier servant, who had been waiting for him, showed him all the customary respect, and roused him, after two or three hours of slumber, with the message that the Prefect wished to have his attendance at the Emperor's Court.

He obeyed the summons, impressed with the profound conviction that that day was to see the end of the desperate game which the Prefect had been playing.

The first intelligence that he received on reaching the Court was that Epicharis was beyond the reach of her enemies. While on her way to the Court, where she was to be again subjected to the torture, she had contrived to put an end to her life.

"Thank the gods for that!" muttered the Tribune to himself. "She, at all events, is at peace. And now for our turn!"

The turn came soon enough. The Prefect had been bearing himself all the morning, as prisoner after prisoner was being examined, with more than his usual confidence. At last Scævinus, who was again being questioned, when taunted with keeping back much of what he knew, turned upon his persecutor.

"No one knows more of these things," he said with a meaning smile, "than yourself, Fænius Rufus. You are very jealous for your Emperor; don't you think that you can show your gratitude to him by making a confession of your own?"

One would think that the man must have foreseen that, sooner or later, one of the accused would thus attack him. Yet he seemed as utterly unprepared for it as if such a contingency had never occurred to him. He might have flatly denied it; he might have passed over it with a pretence of silent contempt. He did neither. He hesitated, stammered, corrected and contradicted himself, in so manifest a condition of panic that his very appearance was equivalent to a confession.

The example once set, Scævinus did not want for followers. Prisoner after prisoner stood up, and gave details so numerous, so minute, so consistent, as to put the fact of the Prefect's complicity beyond a doubt.

"Seize him," cried Nero. "To think that this villain has been sitting unsuspected by my side for days!"

A soldier, Cassius by name, a man of gigantic frame and vast strength, stepped forward, seized and bound him.

"And then," cried one of the prisoners, "Cæsar, there is another conspirator among your guards. I charge Subrius Flavius, Tribune of the Prætorians, with treason."

Nero started up in terror from his chair. His emotion was not mere terror. He knew the Tribune, knew him as a man of singular courage, and as he had always believed one who had always entertained a strong affection for himself.

"Say, Subrius, I implore you," he cried, "say that this is not true. I cannot believe that you, too, are among the traitors."

"Is it likely, Cæsar," replied the Tribune, "that I should league myself with cowards and traitors such as these?"

The defence may have been serious; more probably it was ironical. Anyhow it was soon thrown aside. The witnesses heaped up evidence on evidence, and the Tribune, standing calmly and contemptuously silent, tacitly admitted its truth.

"Tell me, Subrius," said the Emperor, and there was even a touch of pathos in his voice, "tell me why you have forgotten your oath. You swore to be faithful to me. How is it, brave soldier as you are, that you have leagued yourself with traitors?"

"Listen, Cæsar," cried the Tribune, "and hear the truth if for once only in your life. I conspired against you because I hated you. You had not a more faithful soldier while you deserved to be loved. But when you murdered your mother and your wife, when you became a charioteer, an actor, and an incendiary, then I began to hate you."

These bold words struck the tyrant like a blow. He grew pale and shook with terror, and could not have been more utterly panic-stricken had the speaker been standing over him with a dagger.

"Away with him!" he cried, when he had recovered his voice; and he was immediately pinioned and dragged away.

His daring had at least one result that a brave man would have desired. Possibly he had calculated upon it. He was not kept in suspense about his fate. A fellow-tribune was ordered to lead him off to instant execution. A pit was dug in the field where he was to suffer. Subrius looked on with unmoved countenance while the work was being done. When the Centurion in charge saluted and reported it as finished Subrius looked at it with a critical eye.

"Too narrow, too shallow!" he said. "You can't even dig a grave according to regulations."

"Hold out your head, and don't flinch," said the Tribune, who had been charged to administer the fatal blow with his own hand.

"Flinch you as little when you strike," said Subrius, eying with scorn his pale face and trembling hand.

And indeed it needed a second blow before the head was severed from the body.

"Ah, the villain felt that he was dying!" said Nero, when the Tribune reported and even made a boast of what had happened.

It would be tedious to tell in detail the story of how Nero, his rage redoubled by his fear, pursued the conspirators with an unrelenting severity. Scarcely one escaped, and, strangely enough, some whom by some capricious indulgence he either acquitted or pardoned, put an end to their own lives, unable it would seem, to endure existence under such a master.

26

A PLACE OF REFUGE

T HE freedman Linus had lost no time in making his way to the mansion of Lateranus. He found everything there in a state of the wildest confusion. The wife and children of the dead man had fled for refuge to the house of a relative, taking with them nothing but what they could carry, and leaving everything else at the mercy of the slaves. These had thoroughly ransacked the house; they had broken into the cellars, where some of the plunderers lay at that moment in a state of hopeless intoxication. Others, of a more prudent type, had carried off whatever valuables they could lay their hands on. All the money and plate, in fact, every scrap of the precious metals that could be discovered, had disappeared. The chambers had been stripped of coverlets, curtains, and hangings. The handles of the doors had been removed, and even some of the best designs in the tessellated pavements had been pulled up. A more deplorable scene of ruin than that presented by the house when the freedman entered it could hardly be imagined.

He found, however, to his great relief, that Pomponia and Claudia had not been molested. The soldiers sent to arrest Lateranus had received no mandate about the two women, and had accordingly left them alone. One faithful slave had remained, and had been doing his best to minister to their wants. For these, indeed, there still remained in the house a sufficient supply, though much had been wasted by the pillagers. But the outlook before the two women was gloomy in the extreme. They had no friend or kinsman to whom they could look for help. They could not even hope to remain long forgotten. At present the thoughts of all were engrossed by the examination and discovery of the conspirators. But it could hardly be long before Poppæa would bethink herself of her victims. All the Christian fortitude of Pomponia was wanted to keep up her own courage and to administer comfort to her young companion.

It may be imagined then that the coming of the freedman was welcome in the extreme. He had not been able to reach the house in time to do anything that day. Even after nightfall, as long as the streets were full, it would not be safe to make a move. It was necessary for the party to wait with as much patience as they could exercise, till the quietest period of the twenty-four hours, the time between midnight and dawn.

The place in which Linus hoped to find a refuge for his patroness and her young companion was a spot which was then known only to a few, but which has since attained a world-wide fame, the Catacombs of Rome. The greater part of the vast subterranean region now known by that name did not then exist. But a beginning of the excavations had been made. Already there were chambers which could be used for temporary dwellings, others in which worship could be celebrated, and others, again, in which the remains of the dead could find a final resting-place.

The entrance to the excavations was by a sand-pit which had been long since disused. Happily for the secrecy which it was so essential to maintain, the place had an evil reputation. More than one murder had been committed there in former times, and every one, therefore, was careful to avoid it.

Linus succeeded in removing the two ladies to their new shelter without attracting any attention. About thirty persons were already assembled there. The bishop or chief presbyter of Rome was not there; he had been called away, it happened, on Church business

some time before, but one of his principal colleagues was acting in
his stead, and had charge of the little community. He gave the
newcomers a hearty welcome, and committed the two women to the
special charge of a deaconess, who conducted them to the chamber
which was assigned to them, and did her best with the very scanty
means at her command to provide for their comfort.

A few hours of rest were exceedingly grateful; but both insisted
on attending the service which was held shortly after sunrise in a
little chamber set apart for purposes of worship.

It was the first day of the week, and the minister celebrated,
according to custom, the rite of the Holy Eucharist. It was the first
time that Claudia was admitted to partake of the Elements. It had
been arranged some months before, immediately, in fact, after her
arrival at Rome, that she should present herself at the Communion,
but no opportunity had occurred for her to carry out her intention.
The delay, though it had troubled her much, was not without its use.
Her feelings had been deepened and strengthened in no common
degree by all that she had gone through. As she knelt by the side of
her adopted mother to receive the bread and wine from the hands of
the minister, she felt raised to a spiritual height which it is seldom
granted to human nature to attain.

To one who watched the rite from without—for he was not privi-
leged to enter the sacred precincts—Claudia seemed to wear a look
of more than human sanctity. This observer was Pudens. He had
carried out the instructions of Subrius to the letter, had parted with
his chief on the friendliest terms, and, after concealing himself
during the day, had managed, but not without meeting with one or
two dangerous adventures, to reach the spot indicated by the freedman. Here the password, communicated to him by Linus, had
secured his admission from the guardians of the entrance. He had
arrived in time to witness the solemn scene just described, and to
listen to the address, partly of thanksgiving, for the deliverance
vouchsafed in the past, partly of exhortation to courage and faithful-
ness in the future, which the minister addressed to his little congregation at the close of the holy rite.

The days which followed, were full, for the young man, of curiously mingled emotions.

It was a delight to be near the woman whom he loved, and yet how remote she seemed from him! The follies of his youth, even the scheme in which he had been lately engaged, with its self-seeking and the pettiness of its motives and aims, as he now looked upon them, seemed to separate her hopelessly from him. The girl herself, on the few occasions which he had of seeing her, was friendly; she was more than friendly, she was profoundly grateful. But her looks, her demeanour, everything about her showed plainly enough that he was not in her thoughts in the way in which he wished to be.

Happily for him this painful ordeal—for such he felt it to be—did not last very long. About a week after his arrival there came tidings from the upper world, if so it may be called, which materially altered the prospects of the refugees. The intelligence was brought by a slave from the palace, one of the sympathizers whose presence at headquarters was, as we have already seen, often useful to the Christian community.

The main fact which the newcomer had to communicate to his friends was the death of Poppæa. Every one felt that the worst enemy of the Church was removed.

"When did she die?" asked one of the Elders.

"Yesterday," said the messenger.

"And how?"

"Cæsar struck her a violent blow with his foot. He had been driving his chariot, and came into the room where she was sitting, in his charioteer's dress. She was sick and suffering. Something, too, had happened to cross her temper. She taunted him. 'A pretty dress for Cæsar!' she said. 'I shall dress as I please,' he answered. 'At least you should do such things well,' she went on. That touched him to the quick, you may be sure. To be a charioteer does not trouble him, but to be a bad charioteer—that is intolerable. He fell into a furious rage, and kicked her. Three hours afterwards she died. The physicians could do nothing for her. I believe that she never spoke again. Indeed, she was not conscious. Cæsar, when his rage was over, was fairly mad with grief. He could not endure to be present at the Conclamatio, which was made last night."

"Poor creature!" said one of the audience. "May God show her more mercy than she showed to others!"

"She is to be embalmed and buried in the Mausoleum of Augustus, but there is to be a great burning all the same. Orders have been given for an image of the deceased to be made, and this to be burnt on the pyre. And Cæsar is to pronounce her funeral oration himself."

"Will this affect us?" asked the Elder who had first spoken.

"Greatly," replied the slave. "I have with me a copy of an edict which will be published in the course of a few days."

The edict was produced and read.

"Seeing that the people called Christians have already suffered sufficiently for their misdeeds, Cæsar decrees that they shall henceforth be permitted to live in peace, provided that they do not again offend against the safety of the Roman people."

As soon as the edict was posted up in the city—and this was done on the day of the funeral oration—the refugees returned to their homes. Pudens took the same opportunity of making his escape from Rome.

His original intention was, as has been said, to return to the army of Corbulo; but this plan, fortunately for him, was not carried out.

The causes that prevented it, however, very nearly cost him his life. He arrived at Antioch, on his way eastward, just at the beginning of the summer heats. Malarial fever, following the subsidence of the spring floods, was rife in the city, and Pudens, predisposed to infection by the fatigue of a very rapid journey, as well as by anxiety and distress, was soon prostrated by it. Happily a travelling companion, whom he had joined at Corinth, and who had found out that they possessed many mutual acquaintances, had hospitably invited him to take up his quarters at his house. Pudens, who could hardly have survived the neglect that would probably have been his lot at the public inn, was carefully nursed. Even then he had a hard fight for his life, and summer was passing into early autumn before he could be said to be on a fair way to recovery.

One day, about the middle of September, he was taking a walk in the garden, when he was joined by his host, a Roman knight, it may be said in passing, who managed some extensive affairs connected with the public revenue of the province of Syria.

"I must be thinking of going on," said Pudens, after the usual inquiries about health had been duly answered.

"That is exactly what I wanted to talk to you about," returned his host. "Of course you know that the longer you stay with me as my guest the better pleased I shall be. But you have your own plans, and naturally want to carry them on. Now let me be frank, and tell you exactly what I know, and what I think you ought to do. It would not surprise you to hear that you have been delirious?"

Pudens nodded assent. There were blank spaces in his memory, and other spaces all but blank, but haunted with a dim sense of disturbance and trouble. Without any remembrance of actual pain he could easily believe that he had been in the condition which his host described.

"No, indeed," said our hero. "It is no surprise to me; I must have given you a world of trouble."

"Not a word of that; but hark!" and the speaker dropped his voice to a whisper, "you said things which made me take care that no one should watch you but myself and my wife."

Pudens could not help starting.

"Yes!" went on the other, "high matters of State which would touch a man's life. Now I do not ask for your confidence, but if there is anything in which I can help you, I am at your service."

Pudens saw at once that absolute frankness was his best policy, and related the story of the conspiracy.

"That is exactly what I supposed," returned his host, "and you thought of taking up again your service with Corbulo."

"That was my idea," said Pudens.

"And not a bad idea either, in some cases. There are camps where you would be safe, even though you were known to have had a hand in the conspiracy, supposing, I mean of course, the general-in-command wished it to be so. You would be safe with Verginius on the

Rhine, or with Galba in Spain. They are too big men for the Emperor
to disturb, and if they don't choose to give a fugitive up, he has to be
content. Corbulo is big enough in one way, but he has no idea of
disputing the Emperor's will. It is more than fidelity with him. It is
subservience, except that he does not think of getting anything by it.
If Nero sends a Centurion for Corbulo's head, he will put out his
neck, mark my words, without a murmur. And they are after you; that
I know. While you were lying insensible, a Centurion passed through
here with a warrant for the arrest of a conspirator, whose name I
happened to hear,—indeed, I was applied to for my help,—and the
name was Caius Pudens. No! you must not go back to Corbulo; it
would be putting your head into the lion's mouth."

"It is a disappointment," said Pudens. "I had counted upon
Corbulo. But what do you suggest?"

"That is exactly what I have been thinking of. It would be a risk to
go westward again; though once in Spain or Germany you might be
safe. No; I should advise you to stay here, or hereabouts. I have an
idea," he resumed, after a few minutes' silence. "You must tell me
what you think about it. Briefly, it is this; enlist under another name
in the local force which our King here keeps up. It is a somewhat
audacious plan, but none the worse for that. You can wear the beard
which you have grown during your three months' illness. It is not
uncommon in the force. That will be something of a disguise."

The suggestion was carried out, and with success. No one thought
of looking for a conspirator in hiding among the troops of King Anti-
ochus, and so no one found him. The events of the years that
followed may be told in a few words. Two years after his enlistment
Pudens heard of the fate of Corbulo, a fate which singularly justified
his friend's conception of his character. Not long after he had the
relief of hearing that Nero was dead. In the year of civil strife that
followed this event, the year which saw three Emperors fall in rapid
succession, he was, happily for himself, better employed than in
supporting one pretender or another. Vespasian, appointed to
command the legions of Syria in the year of Corbulo's death, had a
keen eye for a good soldier; he saw the capacity of Pudens, and

offered him a place on his personal staff, during the earlier operations of the Jewish war. Vespasian, going to Rome in the autumn of 69 to take possession of the Imperial throne, handed over his aide-de-camp to Titus. A brilliant period of service followed. The most famous siege in history, the siege of Jerusalem, was going on, and Pudens had a share in all its perils and glories.

27

MEETING AGAIN

JERUSALEM fell on September 2nd. About six weeks after, Pudens was once more in Rome, the bearer of a despatch from Titus to his father, the Emperor, announcing his success, and giving the details of the final assault and of the events which followed it.

He had reached Rome late at night, too late to present himself at the palace. He snatched a few hours of sleep at an inn which was conveniently near, and proceeded to discharge his duty at the earliest possible hour next morning. The day had scarcely dawned, but the Emperor's ante-chamber was already open, and already contained two or three occupants. Vespasian was a very early riser, and Pudens, who announced himself to the usher in waiting as the bearer of despatches from the army of the East, was not kept waiting more than two or three minutes. Admitted to the Imperial presence, he met with a very warm greeting from his old chief; the despatches were read, and the information they contained had, of course, to be supplemented by a number of details which Pudens was able to supply. The interview was naturally protracted to a very great length, and when Pudens was at last dismissed, not without a hearty assurance of future favour from the Emperor, he found the ante-chamber crowded with applicants who had been vainly waiting for an audience. Their hopes were summarily dashed, at least for the day, by an announce-ment from the usher that the Emperor was too much occupied by a sudden pressure of business to see any other visitor that morning.

A groan of disappointment went up from the little crowd.

"You have done us all an ill turn, sir," said a young man with a remarkably clever face and brilliant eyes, shabbily dressed, but evidently a gentleman. "But doubtless your business with the Emperor was much more important than all of ours put together. You are a soldier, I see, and if I guess rightly, from the East. Is your news a secret, may I ask?"

"Not at all," answered Pudens. "All Rome may, and probably will, know it in the course of a few hours. Briefly, Jerusalem is taken."

"Ah!" said the other, "there have been rumours of the kind about for the last two or three days. And so it has actually happened. No wonder that the Emperor could think of nothing else."

"I hope, sir," said our hero, "that the business which I unwittingly interrupted or postponed was not very pressing?"

His new acquaintance, whom I may introduce to my readers by his full name of M. Valerius Martialis, smiled. "Certainly not, it was a trifle. I have a little poem in my pocket, which I should be glad if you would do me the favour of hearing at your leisure, and I wanted to get an order for some more of the same kind from the Emperor. To tell you the truth, he does not care much for poets and their verses, and his ideas of remuneration are of the most moderate kind. A very frugal person, sir, is Cæsar. Perhaps it is as well, for another Nero would certainly have made the Empire hopelessly bankrupt; but still there's a limit, and when it comes to paying ten sesterces a line for really tolerable verses,—if I may say so much of my own work,—one may say that the virtue is a little in excess."

"I hope," remarked Pudens, "that private patrons are more liberal, and that there are those who buy."

"As for private patrons," returned the poet, "there are good and bad, and as I said of my own epigrams, a few good and more bad. As for the public that buy, very little of their money comes to us. The publishers send us in large bills, and what with copying, price of parchment, ink, vermilion, pumice-stone, polishing, and I know not what else, there is very little left. And then, if a book does sell, there are rascals who copy it, and give us nothing at all. But I am running on, and tiring you with things that don't interest you. Will you dine with me to-day? Mind, there will be simple poet's fare—a few oysters, a roast kid, and a jar of Alban wine. If you want flowers or perfume or Falernian, you must even bring them yourself."

Pudens, who had very few friends in Rome, gladly accepted.

"Remember, then," said the poet, "at the eleventh hour. I have some work to do, and I cannot afford to be fashionable and early."

"You must see the great beauty about whom all the golden youth of Rome is raving," said Martial, in the course of their after-dinner talk. "That is to say, if you can contrive it, for it is no easy matter to catch a glimpse of her. She is never at the theatre or the Circus. Her mother—mother by adoption, you will understand—is a very strange person, follows some curious superstition, I am told, the chief part of which, it seems, is to take all the pleasure out of life. But the girl is a great beauty, not in our Roman style at all, but dazzlingly fair, a British princess they say she is, whatever that may mean."

Pudens, of course, recognized Claudia in this description. He did not care to betray his acquaintance with her, nor indeed to encourage his host in talking about her. Martial's way of speaking about women, was, to be candid, not very edifying, and though he had nothing but good to say about this northern beauty, Pudens did not care to hear her name upon his lips.

The years which the young soldier had spent between his departure from the capital and his return to it had been a time in which he had learnt and thought much. In particular, the knowledge of Christianity which he had begun to acquire under the instruction of Linus had been greatly deepened and broadened. The new faith had been commended to him by the purity, the courage, the self- devotion of its professors. He now began to realize what a power it already was, to what vast proportions it was likely to grow. In the East, while he was living in Antioch, and afterwards, while he was in camp before the walls of Jerusalem, he had many opportunities of hearing the marvellous history of its origin and its growth. Scarcely a single generation had passed since it had been founded by an obscure Galilean peasant, and already there was not a city or town, scarcely a village, in which it did not possess a company, often a very numerous company, of devoted followers. The young man had never heard or read of anything like it. That, he felt, could be no mere superstition, which, without any attraction of pomp or power, offering to its followers nothing but a life of self-denial, made burdensome by the hatred and contempt of society, had yet found disciples wherever it had come. Here was something which, before long, would match, and more than match, the world-wide influence of the great Roman Empire itself. The impression thus made had been deepened by his intercourse with men, of whom he met not a few both at Antioch and in Judæa, who had had personal knowledge both of the Founder and of his first followers. The story which they had to tell of wonders which they had witnessed, and of which, in some cases, they had been themselves the subjects, interested him profoundly. He was even more touched by the picture they drew of a sanctity, a purity, a burning zeal for the good of mankind, which was more marvellous than the healing of the sick, the restoring of sight to the blind, even the bringing back of the dead to life.

And with this influence in the young man's life there had always mingled his recollection of Claudia. She embodied to him the noblest ideal of womanhood, an ideal, too, inseparably linked with the faith of which he had been learning so much. For these years he had heard nothing of her, and of course did not escape the fancies and fears with which lovers are wont to torment themselves. She might be dead, or, a thought even yet harder to endure, she might be lost to him.

It was therefore with no common emotion that he had now heard from his new acquaintance that she was in Rome, that she was well, that, possibly, she was still free.

As early as possible the next morning he presented himself at Pomponia's house. His reception was all that he could have desired. The elder lady had a grateful recollection of his kindness and zeal, and Claudia had no more forgotten him than he had forgotten her. The two women listened with an untiring interest to the story of adventure which the young soldier had to tell. When the great siege in which he had been taking part came to be discussed, the conversation inevitably turned on the subject of Christianity. Pudens was led on to speak of the thoughts which had been occupying his mind, and Pomponia particularly inquired whether he had made a regular profession of the faith which had so greatly impressed him. Pudens answered that he had not. Circumstances had hindered him from submitting himself to a regular course of instruction, but his mind had been made up; he had only been waiting for an opportunity of giving expression to convictions which he had long since formed.

"You will come with us to-morrow," said Pomponia to her visitor, when, after some hours of conversation, he rose to take his leave. "We have a duty to perform which it will interest you, I am sure, to witness, if you cannot actually take a part in it. We leave the house early, before daybreak, indeed, if that is not too soon for you."

Pudens did not fail to present himself at the appointed hour. A carriage was waiting at the gate of Pomponia's mansion, and the ladies were already seated in it. He joined them, and became so engrossed in the conversation that followed that he did not notice the direction in which they proceeded. It was with no little surprise and emotion that when the carriage stopped he found himself at the entrance to the Catacombs.

"We commemorate to-day," said Pomponia, "those who had the privilege five years ago of witnessing their faith and love by their deaths. You will watch the rite from without; another year, I hope, you will be one of us."

Thus did Pudens, standing with the catechumens, of whom he

was reckoned to be virtually one, witness again the solemn act of worship on which he had looked, under very different circumstances, five years before. This ended, came the commemoration itself. The presiding Elder read the list of saints and martyrs who had sealed their testimony with their blood. Foremost on the list came the two Apostles, Peter and Paul, who had suffered two years before, the first the death of a slave, the second by the headsman's axe on the Ostian Road. Then followed a list of names, unknown and yet known, long since forgotten upon earth, but remembered by Him Who is faithful to keep all that is committed unto Him.

There is little more for me to tell. Pudens lost no time in putting himself under instruction. The Elder who undertook to examine and teach him found him so well prepared that there was no need to delay the rite. Pudens was received into the Church at the festival of Christmas, and a week afterwards became the husband of Claudia.

Many old friends were gathered at the wedding, among them Phlegon, still vigorous in spite of his fourscore years, and Linus, who, as Pudens did not fail to remember, had been the first to show him what Christian belief and practice really were. Nor did he forget his debt to another, without whose courage and devotion he had scarcely lived to see that happiest hour of his life, the Tribune Subrius. As he knelt with his bride in silent prayer after receiving the minister's final blessing, he put up a fervent supplication that some rays of the light which had fallen upon him might reach, he knew not where or how, the brave, true-hearted man to whom he owed life and happiness.

A few days after their marriage the young couple held a reception of their friends and acquaintances. Among them was the poet Martial, who brought with him not the least acceptable of the wedding gifts which they had received, an epigram written in praise of the bride. It ran thus:—

"Our Claudia see, true Roman, though she springs
From a long line of Britain's painted kings;
Italia's self might claim so fair a face,
And Athens envy her her matchless grace."

The author, though he spoke of his offering as a gift, was not displeased when the bridegroom pressed into his hand a roll of ten gold pieces. He whispered to a friend, "There is a real lover of the Muses! He would have made an admirable Emperor, at least from my point of view; but he is certainly happier as he is."

THE END

Made in the USA
Middletown, DE
09 June 2024

55512300R00130